"A" IS FOR ACTRESS

A MALIBU MYSTERY

REBECCA CANTRELL

SEAN BLACK

MMP

Copyright Information

For Caitlin and Max

ABOUT THE BOOK

After a decade spent in the glare of the Hollywood spotlight as the star of kids' TV show Half Pint Detective, Sofia Salgado has had enough. Desperate to build a life outside showbiz, she quits acting to do something that everyone around her– including her family – thinks is plain nuts. Get a real job.

They think she's even crazier when she announces that she's going to become a real detective, instead of playing one on TV. She's convinced the technical consultant from her TV show, Brendan Maloney, to take her on in his detective agency, but can accident-prone Sofia hack it?

∾

Want news about the latest Malibu Mystery books plus exclusive free content?

Then sign up here to join our mailing list.

Your email will be kept confidential. You will not be spammed. You can unsubscribe at any time.

You can also follow us on Facebook here:

https://www.facebook.com/malibumysteries/

Sofia Salgado's third grade teacher back in Indiana had been right. Every day really was a school day. There were always new things to learn. In fact, life was pretty much one big educational experience. Today's lessons for Sofia seemed to be:

1. No matter how much you loved the peach ice tea at the Marmalade Cafe, it was *not* a good idea to take the waiter's offer of a third refill if you planned on spending the entire afternoon sitting in your car on a stakeout.

2. If there was even the remotest possibility that you might lose control of your bladder while sitting in your car, any meal involving asparagus was *not* a good lunch choice.

3. Like so much in life, you never really appreciate toilets until you need one.

Of course Miss Kanouse had also dropped some pretty heavy hints to Sofia's mom before they left Indiana for Los

Angeles, saying things would never work out for the girls' acting careers in California and they should just stay in Indiana and learn typing, so she wasn't entirely infallible. But when it came to viewing life as one big learning experience, she'd been dead on. None of which solved Sofia's immediate problem. She desperately needed to go pee without ruining what, at least up until now, had been her first perfectly executed covert surveillance operation.

Without permission, she couldn't abandon her post, a quiet side street with a clear view of the main entrance to the somewhat unfortunately named Big Rock Rehab Clinic. Or to give the place its full title: The Big Rock Rehabilitation and Spiritual Renewal Clinic.

She had already spent the best part of the last hour scouting the immediate area for a bush she could duck behind. But the area was sadly devoid of bushes. In fact, the only large cover was provided by a stand of three large saguaro cacti. Looking at their two-inch-long spines made her shiver. The idea of losing her balance and falling naked-ass backward into a six-foot-tall cactus was even more off putting than the prospect of trying to explain why the interior reeked of asparagus-scented urine to the guys who valeted her car in Santa Monica.

That left her the third option, which was potentially more embarrassing than needles in the butt or pee on the upholstery: she'd have to confess her predicament to the other half of her surveillance team. She hated to do it, but it was an emergency.

She scooted down a little farther, reached over, and grabbed the phone lying on the passenger seat. She made the call, but waited a second before speaking. "Aidan?"

There was a long silence before he finally answered.

"How many times? You don't use real names on a stakeout. I'm Nighthawk, and you're Little Sparrow."

She rolled her eyes. "This isn't a Jason Bourne movie."

They were sitting outside the rehab clinic on behalf of a movie studio that wanted to make sure the star of their latest action movie franchise completed his twenty-eight days without sneaking out to score some Bolivian marching powder, thus driving the insurance premium on the next movie in the series sky high. This was not a life or death situation. Code names weren't required.

"There's still a procedure," he said.

She was starting to wonder if there really *was* a procedure, or if he'd just invented one to drive her crazy. She squirmed in her seat, trying to find a position that might relieve the pressure on her bladder. "Okay, Nighthawk, here's the deal. I really need to take a comfort break. Can you cover my position for ten minutes?"

Moving had been a bad idea. She needed to go even worse than she had a moment ago. She tensed, trying to hold on, and already planning her next move. There was a deserted lot about four hundred yards down the hill on Big Rock Drive. She was pretty sure the lot wasn't overlooked. She could pull in, dive out, use her car to shield her from any passing traffic, go, and be back at her post in no time.

"Why?" Aidan said.

"What do you mean 'why?'"

"I mean, why do you need a break? We've only been here a couple hours."

He must be deliberately playing dumb to drive her crazy. He thought that just because he'd done a few years in the LAPD and his dad ran the detective agency that he was her boss. Fine, she'd tell him the truth.

"I had too much iced tea at Marmalade, and now I have to pee. Okay? Happy?"

She threw the phone back down on the passenger seat and hit the button to start the engine. Sweet relief was only a short drive away.

"Request denied," said Aidan.

"What do you mean 'request denied?'"

"Hold your position."

"If I wait any longer, my position is going to be under water." She took a deep breath, doing her best to stay calm. The more irritated she sounded, the more he'd screw with her. It was pretty much how their relationship had been from the first day they'd met all those years ago on the set of *Half Pint Detective* when Aidan's dad, the show's technical advisor, had brought his then twelve-year-old son onto the set in Burbank to meet Sofia, the eleven-year-old movie star.

He made a weird snorting sound into the phone that she was pretty sure was a laugh.

"Didn't you hear what I just said?" She sounded far from calm. "I have to pee. In fact, scratch that, I don't have to. I'm going to. Any minute now. And I don't want to do it sitting in my car."

"Go find a bush." Aidan was, as usual, completely unsympathetic to her plight.

"There aren't any bushes." He knew that. He'd driven by the artistic landscape of rocks and cactus to get to his position in the back of the clinic. There probably were bushes back there. He'd probably gone pee twice already.

"Look," said Aidan, "if I cover the front for you, that means no one will be covering the back. You're going to have to wait."

"I'm not kidding. I can't wait. Believe me, if waiting was a possibility, I wouldn't have asked." Now each passing second was fresh agony. She wondered if the CIA had ever contemplated using denial of peeing rights as part of their enhanced interrogation tactics. She figured they had, but it had probably fallen into the 'cruel and unusual' category and been ruled unconstitutional.

"Sorry, but we have to have eyes on at all times. We can't lose a key data point like five minutes of visual contact on the rear entry."

"I know just what I'd like to do with your key data point," she told him. "It involves rear entry where no visual contact can be made, and not in a way that you'd want to retrieve the data."

"We need that data." He was laughing so hard she could barely understand him.

"Improvise." She moved the car into drive.

"Hold up!" said Aidan. "Give it ten more minutes. Surely you can hold it for that long?"

"Ten minutes? Then I can go pee?"

"Promise."

She really wasn't sure she could make it for another minute, never mind another ten. And she didn't exactly trust him to hold to his word. But she didn't want to show weakness, either. When his dad had agreed to take her on as a trainee investigator, Aidan had been less than happy. If she made him too mad, he might run back to his father and tell him she couldn't do something as simple as a routine surveillance operation.

"Okay, ten minutes. But not a second more," she said.

If she sat perfectly still and focused all her energy on the job, she could do it. Sheer willpower would carry her through. She had done things way harder than not pee her pants. Right now she couldn't think what those things were exactly, but she was sure she had. She started doing a breathing exercise she'd learned from an acting coach. It was supposed to help you focus.

"Little Sparrow?"

This better be good. As in their target had better be vaulting the wall and jumping into a drug dealer's car with a bunch of hookers.

"Yes," she said, teeth gritted.

"Do you know what I'm looking forward to most when we finish here?" Aidan asked. "A nice, long shower. All that water cascading down from the showerhead. Just torrents of water, gushing down like a big waterfall."

She leaned forward carefully to get the phone. She didn't dare lean too far, though, and the phone had slid to the far side of the seat.

"Speaking of waterfalls," he continued, "you should check out the pool they have back here. Think it has a waterfall feature. Here, if I hold my phone up you might be able to hear it running..."

She reached the phone and ended the call. She slammed the car back into drive, but it was too late to actually go anywhere. She couldn't hold on any longer. Instead, she put the car back in park and turned it off.

She looked around. Apart from a couple of parked cars and a van that had been here when they'd arrived, the parking lot was empty. There wasn't a person in sight, and the only house that had a direct view of her was the rehab facility itself, and that was mostly obscured by a long wall. She could shield herself a little with the car door, and nobody would see her. She just had to act fast and hope for the best.

She pushed the car door open, got out, pulled down her jeans and underwear, and squatted next to the side of the

Tesla. As soon as the fresh air hit her, she peed. She reached her hand up against the car to steady herself.

Within seconds, a raging torrent ran to the edge of the sidewalk and into the gutter. It ran down the street in a stream. She smelled the asparagus, but she didn't care. The relief was almost orgasmic.

A scruffy-looking young guy sporting a goatee, an over-sized Lakers shirt, and a backward-turned baseball cap appeared from nowhere. He was pointing a handheld video camera right at her. The light was blinking red.

So much for hoping for the best.

2

_____

"**S**ofia Salgado," said the videographer triumphantly. "Man, I knew it was you. Recognized the car. Not that many red Tesla Roadsters around. Not even in the 'Bu."

Sofia desperately tried to cut off the torrent. It was no use. She couldn't stop the flood. The dam had well and truly burst, and no amount of willpower or clenching would halt the flow. She was just going to have to tough this out.

The videographer's face contorted. "Oh, man, did you have asparagus for lunch? Jeez, dude, that reeks."

Great, that was on film, too. As if the whole situation wasn't embarrassing enough.

Her phone in the car, she couldn't even summon help. All she could do was finish what she doing, pull her pants back up, and deal with the inevitable fallout. She dropped her head and let her hair fall across her face. It wasn't nearly enough, but she didn't have any better ideas right this second.

Still holding the camera so he didn't miss a second of her humiliation, the videographer half turned toward the van parked a hundred yards away. Another man had climbed out of the back with a camera sporting a huge zoom lens. He was busy taking pictures as he advanced on them. Video and still photos. It just kept getting worse.

"Hey, Raul," the videographer shouted to his paparazzi companion, who was still busy snapping pictures. "That's five bucks you owe me. Told you it was her."

Raul nodded without missing a shot.

"You checking in here or what?" The videographer tapped a finger to the side of his head. "Smart move. Rehab's a no-brainer if you want to relaunch an acting career. This town loves a good comeback."

Her panties were caught in bunch at the top of her jeans. She yanked them free, pushing her left hand out to block the video camera lens as she straightened up. Finally, she yanked her jeans up and zipped them closed.

"I'm not here for rehab! I'm here on a..." She couldn't go public with her new job. It would attract way too much attention. Attention that might get her fired. Brendan had already taken a risk by hiring her. She couldn't do that to him.

Raul the photographer joined the cameraman. They kept taking pictures and shooting video, but at least she had her pants on.

"No, I'm not going into rehab." She tried to sound calm and casual, the exact opposite of how she felt. "I was visiting a friend, but they were out. I had too much ice tea, and I couldn't find a bathroom."

Judging by their expressions, both men didn't believe a word she was saying. She didn't blame them. Being caught, quite literally with your pants around your ankles on a public street in the middle of the day, was hard to talk your way out of.

The photographer nodded back in the direction of his van. "Feel your pain. I installed a chemical potty in the back of my van. If you'd asked me, I would have let you use it."

"Thanks." Sofia was cursing her stupidity. She hadn't even thought that someone else might have been conducting surveillance outside the rehab center. But she knew that Malibu's many rehabs were a magnet for the paparazzi. There was almost always some kind of a celebrity (it was a pretty elastic term these days) in any of the bigger rehabs. Of course, there had been someone else there.

"Do you think you could do me a favor and give me that footage?" she asked in her nicest voice.

Both men laughed.

Goatee man kept the camera running. "Do you have any idea what this is worth? It'll pay for my kid's braces. He has teeth like a beaver."

At least her suffering would help out a buck-toothed kid somewhere, even if it would give her mom a heart attack.

Behind them the screech of tires sounded as a black Escalade raced toward the entrance to the rehab facility. The two paparazzi spun round and ran toward it. It was their lucky day.

She was fairly sure she caught a glimpse of the action star she was supposed to be watching for in the Escalade's back seat, but couldn't be certain. It was already too late to go check. The gates closed after it, and the Escalade disappeared behind the high walls.

Sofia had held her position for the rest of the day watching the cactus shadows creep along the parking lot until Aidan called to tell her that she could go home. She hadn't mentioned the peeing incident. It was none of his damn business.

As Sofia made the turn from Big Rock Drive onto PCH (Pacific Coast Highway), her iPhone lit up with a call. The caller ID read 'Aidan.' He might have been the last person she wanted to speak to right now, but it could be work related, and she had already screwed up once today, got herself filmed, and maybe missed his big data point. She couldn't afford to ignore him.

She tapped a button on the Tesla's touch screen to answer. "What's up?" she said, doing her best to sound upbeat.

"Not your pants?"

"Hilarious. I haven't heard a joke that funny since at least, oohh, let me think, first grade."

"That's strange. I haven't seen someone pee their pants since first grade," said Aidan.

The woman driving in the next lane stared at her while they crawled north on PCH. Sofia grabbed a pair of oversized sunglasses and put them on.

"So what did you want, Nighthawk?" she asked.

"You seen TMZ?" said Aidan.

TMZ was the go-to website for celebrity gossip. The initials stood for 'Thirty Mile Zone,' an obscure Hollywood insider term that referred to the thirty-mile zone around the Hollywood studios used by union film projects to determine per diem rates and driving distances for crew members. Basically, if a celebrity of any description did something noteworthy in the greater LA area or beyond, TMZ was usually the first to have the incriminating photographs or video footage.

It was no great surprise that TMZ would have been the first people to get ahold of the evidence of her peeing outside a rehab in Malibu. She'd known as soon as she saw the camera that she'd be making an unscheduled appearance all over social media and the Internet.

Sofia sighed. "No, and I don't intend to go look."

"You made a pretty big splash." Aidan chuckled.

"Thanks for letting me know." She reached over to kill the call.

"Hey, Sofia?"

"Yes?" Her finger hovered over the red end call icon.

"I know you're probably a little peed off right now, but you have to be in the office at nine o'clock sharp tomorrow so no *mooning* around feeling sorry for yourself. And no staying up into the wee, small hours."

She hit the end call button, cutting him off.

It was more than a little ironic that even though she had quit acting and the whole showbiz world that went with it in order to escape the limelight and do a real job, she was now going to be an object of public ridicule. On the plus side, at least her car didn't stink of asparagus pee. She had that going for her.

The traffic inched forward. Up ahead the sign for Moonshadows restaurant beckoned. She often had dreams that bordered on the erotic about their spicy Hawaiian ahi tuna tartare. She thought about stopping, but right now, she wanted to go home. The woman in the next lane nudged her companion and nodded toward Sofia. Sofia ignored her, hoping she would go away.

Sofia looked across to see the woman in the next lane frantically waving for her to lower her window.

Ugh. Just because she'd been on TV, people could completely forget their manners. She was public property. And if she got on with trying to live her life and ignored them, she would be considered stuck-up or ungrateful. She had always, always been polite and respectful, going out of her way to answer every letter she could, and sign every autograph or pose for every photograph but all she wanted now was to be left alone. Which wasn't going to happen.

With a sigh, Sofia lowered the Tesla's window. The woman was grinning at her.

"Sorry," the woman began, a verbal opener that clearly indicated to Sofia that she was from out of town. No one in LA would apologize for yelling at a stranger in traffic. "I just wanted to ask. It's really you, isn't it?"

For a fleeting moment she wondered if this was a deep, existential question such as 'if you're not really you, then who are you?' Or, 'if a person on PCH asks you if you're really you, then are you really you?' Or maybe 'how do you know if you're you?'

"Uh," said Sofia, "that kind of depends on who you think I am."

The woman glanced back to her passenger. Sofia assumed it was her husband or boyfriend. He leaned over the woman. "I knew it was you. I said to Michelle here, 'It's definitely her.'"

Sofia smiled and nodded. "Right."

She was happy they were happy. At least someone was happy today. All she wanted to do was get home, feed Fred, take a long soak in the tub, have a glass of wine, make dinner, go to bed, and try to forget that today ever happened. At least back home at the Cove, she'd be left alone. If she could ever get there.

Michelle shot her male companion an irritated look. "I knew it was her. You didn't need to tell me anything, Brian."

Based on that tone, Michelle and Brian were clearly either married, or at least in a long-term relationship. Sofia smiled. "Well, you were right."

Michelle turned back to Brian and with more than a hint of triumphalism said, "See!"

Both the cars in front of them inched forward. Sofia was wondering about the etiquette if her lane started moving faster. Did she scoot forward, thus terminating the conversation? Or did she let the gap open? In the land of the car gun it was probably better to be mildly rude to some out-of-towners than to mildly inconvenience and thereby enrage some hardened road warrior trying to get home to the valley after a day slogging their guts out on the Westside.

Michelle leaned farther out of her car. "I hope you don't think I'm rude, but I am so relieved you're not seeing that Bieber boy anymore."

Sofia tried to remember if she'd ever met Justin Bieber, never mind dated him. Maybe, if the supermarket tabloids were to be believed, the experience was so horrendous that she had completely suppressed it to save herself from further psychological torment.

"Me, too," said Sofia.

It was Brian's turn to lean in. "That kid is heading for a hard landing. Little punk."

Michelle shoved Brian back into his seat. "Don't call him that. Selena here might still have feelings for him."

"Selena?" Sofia said.

"You're Selena Gomez, right?"

4

Sofia's home, Nirvana Cove in northern Malibu, was arguably the world's most up-market trailer park. Sofia pulled her Tesla into the main resident's parking lot. Apart from golf buggies and service vehicles, cars were prohibited from using the narrow access roads in the Cove. Anyone with a car had to leave it in the lot and either walk or take a golf buggy to their trailer. It was one of the quirks of living there that Sofia enjoyed most. She usually walked. It gave her time to decompress from whatever she'd been doing that day. Today she had a lot to decompress from. She could probably walk to San Francisco, and it wouldn't be far enough.

Stretched out below her was Nirvana Cove Beach. Beyond the beach, the Pacific Ocean danced and shone in the sun. On a clear day like today, she saw all the way across to Catalina Island. It was a view that she never tired of, and she spent a second staring at it.

An older lady in running gear scooted up. "Beautiful evening."

"Evening, Tex!"

Tex, one of Sofia's near neighbors, flew past in a blur of neon pink Lycra. One of the features of the Cove was that most of the older residents had more get-up-and-go than pretty much anyone. They were a force to be reckoned with if things didn't happen as they wanted.

If she was even vaguely aware of Sofia's new notoriety as the phantom urinator of Big Rock, Tex never let on. Not that anyone living in the Cove would. It was a pretty tight-knit community of a lot of people who had worked or still did work in the entertainment industry. More than a few A-list movie stars had homes there. They bought a place at the Cove because it was one of the few places in the greater Los Angeles area where they knew they would be left alone.

Sofia had bought her double-wide, two-bedroom home a little under four years ago, a few days after her eighteenth birthday, when she was finally allowed access to the earnings from her acting career. The price tag had been just north of half a million dollars. For that she got an eggshell-blue trailer with a living room cum kitchen/dinette, two bedrooms, a master bathroom with a shower over tub, and a front porch. She had stayed living with her mom and stepfather for the first few months while she remodeled it. She'd had the outside repainted, put in a new kitchen range, and had a tiny claw foot bathtub installed.

While the little blue trailer took a big bite out of her savings, she figured that as long as she could make the service fees, she would always have a roof over her head. If things got rough, she could always sell it. And, it sure as hell beat paying rent. At least those were reasons she had given her mom, sister, manager, and accountant. The truth was that she had been visiting a friend at the Cove, seen the little blue trailer for sale, and fallen hopelessly, madly in love with it. It was home, and she didn't want to live anywhere else.

As she walked farther down the path, she took off her shoes and socks. She took a left into her lane and walked barefoot along the path to her little blue trailer. A loud cawing sounded from overhead, and a seagull swooped by. She scoped out the black ring around his left leg as he hopped from the path up onto her front porch railing. The seagull was a regular visitor. Her niece and nephew had named him Fred Segal, after the upmarket clothing store and the name had stuck.

"Heya, Fred!" she called.

She didn't have the free time she needed to have a regular pet, so Fred had become her surrogate pet. He showed up every morning to be fed and was there as soon as she came home in the evening. As pets went, Fred the seagull was pretty low maintenance. His only character flaw was that he was overly possessive. Not only would he chase away any other seagull interlopers, but he also targeted dogs, cats, and even other humans. Anyone who came too close was subjected to repeated dive bombing until they got the message that this was really Fred's place. Sofia suspected that if she stopped feeding him, she'd be added to Fred's hit list.

"Just a second," she told him.

Walking past Fred, she took out her key, unlocked the front door, put down her shoes and socks and purse, and walked into the kitchen. She opened the fridge, took out a half full bottle of wine, poured herself a glass, pulled a slice of bologna out of the fridge and walked back out to the porch. She took a sip of wine and laid out the lunchmeat on the railing for Fred to peck at. He squawked something she chose to interpret as 'thank you.' She closed her eyes and let the crisp white wine settle on her tongue. She was finally home safe.

Bliss.

"Three words. *Celebrity Second Chances!*" said a voice far too close to her ear.

Her eyes popped open. A deeply tanned man in his early fifties wearing nothing but a pair of red board shorts and a dazzlingly white grin stood on the path directly in front of her porch.

"Before you say anything, I already spoke to Steve Kazalian at Fox, and he is totally prepared to put serious money down to get you on board with this."

Sofia closed her eyes. Maybe if she kept them closed long enough, when she opened them again, her former agent would have disappeared. She started to count down slowly from one thousand. She had reached seven hundred and eighty-nine when she heard:

"High six-figure fee for one week's filming. Maybe even seven if I push him hard enough, and you're prepared to do Dr. Phil."

She opened her eyes. "One week's filming? Rehab is twenty-eight days long."

"Yeah, but this is TV. Shooting for seven days is a lot cheaper than twenty-eight. I mean, duh! Plus the story beats for that show are all there already." Her former agent narrowed his eyes. "You don't actually *really* need to go to rehab, do you?"

She stared at him, not prepared to dignify that question with an answer.

"Please tell me you don't," he said. "Because if you do, that puts the completion bond insurance sky high, and your fee will have to take a hit."

"No, Jeffrey, I don't need to go to rehab. I was on a stakeout, and I needed to pee really bad, and I couldn't find a bathroom, so..."

Jeffrey Weiner looked skyward. From his position on the railing, Fred was eyeing her ex-agent suspiciously. He was lucky the gull was busy eating.

"No one needs to know that. Plus, I'll be honest here. I could really use the ten percent. I mean this job you have," he said, air-quoting the word *job*. "It's like Joaquin Phoenix wanting to become a rapper, or Rick Moranis wanting to spend more time with his family, right?"

Fred must have sensed her rising temper because he stopped pecking at his food and cocked his head. "Rick Moranis's wife died, and he wanted to take care of his grieving kids! That's real, and it's more important than acting. Your kind of attitude is exactly why I quit the business."

Jeffrey cocked his head, mirroring Fred's head tilt. Both of them doing it was making Sofia dizzy.

"How was I to know you were serious? I mean, you're an actress." He stopped, obviously sensing that she really was angry. "A fantastic actress. One of the finest of your generation. I'm just trying to look out for you here."

"The finest of my generation, huh?" said Sofia. "I was in a show called *Half Pint Detective*, and then I did a couple of movies."

Jeffrey raised himself up on his tiptoes to his full five feet four inches. "Do not run yourself down. I will not stand for it. You were all set to be the next J-Law, if you hadn't got this crazy notion into your head about getting a real job, encouraged no doubt by that crazy ex-cop."

Sofia could feel her eyebrows threatening to leave her head. "Jeffrey, why don't you go for a swim? Find some sharks to play with."

He gave her his best agent's smile. "Sharks wouldn't go near me. Professional courtesy."

She stared at him and didn't speak. Fred had finished his food. He flapped his wings and squawked menacingly in Jeffrey's direction.

"Good bird," she said.

"Think about it, okay? A million bucks for seven days work plus press. Is this the greatest country in the world, or what?" said Jeffrey before turning around and disappearing into the twilight toward his home on the upper bluff.

Sofia looked at Fred. "Go poop on his head, and I'll double your rations."

WHILE SHE MADE HERSELF DINNER, Sofia couldn't help but think about Jeffrey's offer. Not that she would ever do that particular show, but maybe she was fooling herself with this real job thing. Her career had been in a good place when she'd quit. Most young actresses would have killed to have had her career trajectory. The three movies she'd done, one for a studio and two small indie films, had gathered great reviews. She had been touted as the actress most likely to become the next Jennifer Lawrence. The problem was that she didn't want to be the next Jennifer Lawrence. She was fairly sure that there were days when Jennifer Lawrence didn't want to be Jennifer Lawrence. Sofia didn't blame her.

The difficulty was that because so many people wanted to be famous, they regarded anyone who gave up fame as suspect. Or ungrateful. To be given something so many people wanted and then to turn your back on it seemed like a betrayal.

But Sofia had never wanted fame. She hadn't even wanted to be an actress. That had been her sister's dream.

But fate had conspired to give the big break to her rather than Emily.

It wasn't that she hadn't enjoyed her acting career. It had meant she didn't have to go to school and instead worked with a series of increasingly mellow tutors. She had made money for herself and her family, money her mother had really needed at the beginning. And being on a long-running TV show was like having a huge extended family. Until she had gotten into her teens, the media had pretty much left her alone. It wasn't so bad.

Eventually though, things had changed. Or, more accurately, she had changed. Jeffrey might have sneered at people who did real jobs, but Sofia didn't think like that. It had always mystified her that people like police officers and plumbers and nurses and engineers, people who actually made a real difference to the world, were somehow deemed inferior to people who pranced around a stage or appeared on some dumb TV show. It was like the world was stuck on opposite day.

As she drizzled Ranch dressing over her salad and checked on the chicken breast in the oven, her cell rang. It was her mom. No doubt she'd got news of today's events. Sofia let it go to voicemail. She should call her back after dinner.

She took another sip of wine and a bite of salad. Her cell rang. This time it was her sister's number. Sofia grabbed her phone and wrote a text. "I'm fine. Will call you tomorrow. Love you. S x."

She switched her cell off. She'd had enough drama for one day.

5

Sofia pushed open the office door and headed straight for her desk. In the corner, Aidan was already at his desk, staring at not one, not two, but three huge computer screens. A flat screen TV mounted on the far wall ran shaky handheld footage of Sofia with her pants around her ankles. The footage ran for forty or so seconds then looped back to the beginning. At least it was from the front, and her bare butt wasn't in the shot. Sofia walked over to small waiting area with its seats and coffee table, grabbed the remote, and switched off the TV screen.

"Hey, I was watching that," Aidan protested.

"Why are you such an ass ... ?" Her rhetorical question was interrupted by the inner office door opening and Brendan Maloney's head appearing.

"Sofia? My office. Five minutes. We have a couple of things to discuss."

The first time she had been introduced to Brendan when she was eleven-years-old, he was the most intimidating person she had ever met. She had literally stood to attention when he shook her hand. With his salt-and-pepper hair, broad Irish features, and intimidating former prize fighter's physique, he looked exactly like a homicide detective should look. As she had gotten to know him over the years, she discovered that in some ways, he didn't fit the stereotype. He didn't drink. He didn't smoke (apart, she had recently learned to her complete shock, from an occasional spliff — "Dumbest thing we ever did as a nation was making booze legal and cannabis illegal. Stoners commit way less crime than drunks."). He hated sports, but had a serious opera addiction. And he did not tolerate swearing because he claimed "it betrayed a poverty of language." Sofia had not only never heard him curse, but Aidan had told her he had fired people if they swore while they were working. She wondered if Aidan had made that up just to mess with her, but today wasn't a good day to test that theory.

If peeing in public hadn't already gotten her fired from Maloney Investigations, Brendan hearing her use the word "asshole" might have.

"Sorry, what am I?" said Aidan.

Sofia stared at Brendan's now-closed office door. "I said you're an asshat."

From behind his screens, Aidan laughed. "An asshat, huh? At least I'm an asshat with bladder control."

She put down her bag on top of her desk, which was strewn with papers and files, and marched over to Aidan. "Why exactly were you watching me pee on a loop?"

Aidan swiveled round his chair. Minus the gray hair, he did look pretty much like his father, and too cute for his own good. "I wasn't watching you."

On two of his screens was the same footage that had been looping on the TV when she came in. Sofia jabbed a finger at the screens. "What's that then?"

Aidan clicked the mouse on his desk. The footage froze.

He clicked again and highlighted the upper left hand corner of the still image. He clicked again, and it filled both screens. "Look."

Sofia peered at the screen. "What am I looking for?"

Aidan jabbed a finger at the screen where a black SUV turned into the street. He clicked the mouse again. The footage jumped forward. He clicked one more time, pausing the video.

"In the back of the SUV," said Aidan. "That's our boy in the rear passenger seat."

She looked again. He was right. The actor they'd been tasked with performing surveillance on was sitting in the back of the SUV with the window down, staring at Sofia while she went pee. There was no mistaking his high cheekbones and ice-blue eyes. His being driven into the rehab was significant because when he had been admitted three days before, he was ordered not to leave the facility under any circumstances.

"It gets better." Aidan pulled the footage back a half-dozen frames.

In the driver's seat was a big guy in a leather jacket. He had slicked-back black hair and was wearing giant round shades. But even with shades, Sofia recognized him as a Ronnie Wilson, well-known drug dealer to the stars.

"Boom!" said Aidan. "Rehab my ass."

In contrast to Aidan's elation, Sofia felt oddly deflated. She'd been hoping that they wouldn't find any dirt on the young actor. This incident didn't mean his career was over, but it would make it a lot more difficult for him to book jobs. Movies and big-budget TV shows cost tens of thousands of dollars a day to shoot, and an actor with a drug problem made insuring the production much more costly, if not impossible.

"You know," said Aidan, "if you hadn't been taking a leak, the guy would probably have kept his window closed, and we wouldn't have been able to see him through the tinted glass."

"Terrific," Sofia said with no enthusiasm whatsoever. Her need to pee had ruined two people's day.

"Every cloud, huh?" Aidan grinned.

Brendan's door opened. His head appeared. "Come on in, Sofia."

The door closed. Sofia took a deep breath. Aidan pulled up another window on his computer. On the left hand side of his Twitter account #sofiasprays was trending worldwide.

She let that breath out in a sigh and went into Brendan's office.

6

Brendan settled himself down into his leather office chair and motioned for Sofia to sit opposite. She had already decided she wasn't going to make any excuses for what had happened. She hated people who messed up and then didn't accept responsibility for their own actions.

"Brendan, I just want to say that if you don't think I'm cut out for this, I would totally understand. I screwed up. You gave me a chance, and I blew it."

Brendan put down the papers he'd been looking at. He eased back in his chair, and put his hands behind his head. "Holy smokes, Sofia, I hope you're never arrested for anything. You'd be every copper's dream come true. I haven't even said anything, and you're already singing like a canary."

Brendan got up and walked to the window. "I ever tell you about the time me and Charlie were on this stakeout in Shootin' Newton?"

Sofia shook her head. Charlie had been Brendan's partner when he started out in uniform years before. As described in Brendan's many stories as a chain-smoking, hard drinking, old school cop, Sofia had been surprised to be introduced to a petite blond lady with a mouth like a sailor suffering from Tourette's syndrome.

"So we'd been outside this apartment for like six hours solid. Guy we were looking for was an OG Crip we had in the frame for a double homicide. Long story short, Charlie had the same problem you had yesterday. She sneaks out of the car, drops her drawers, and answers the call of nature. Halfway through this guy appears, and he was carrying. He makes me straight away, pulls his piece. I'm still trying to get my gun out of the holster and get my door open when BLAM, Charlie drops him. Two shots in his chest. Dead center. She finishes up, pulls her drawers back up, and we call it in. Didn't miss a beat."

All Sofia could do was stare at Brendan. She was searching for a parallel between the two incidents. But apart from a woman peeing in public, she couldn't see one. Brendan seemed to sense her confusion.

"The point is this, Sofia. Charlie had to put it in the report to explain why she was outside our unit and with a perfect angle to shoot this perp. You can imagine the kind of stuff she had to put up with from the other cops. It was pretty embarrassing, but she toughed it out." Brendan let his hands fall back onto his lap. "Things happen in this kind of business. Hell, in any business. You have setbacks. That's life. You pull up your pants, and you get back to work."

"Umm...ok." She was relieved that she wasn't being fired.

Brendan reached down and grabbed a manila folder from a pile on his desk. He tossed it over the desk at Sofia. "Here."

She opened it slowly. Despite Brendan's pep talk, there was a part of her expecting to see a piece of paper that read

'Termination of Employment.' Instead, she was confronted by a not altogether unattractive man in his late-forties with graying hair in a well-tailored suit. She thought she recognized him from some TV show but couldn't be sure— half of the population of West LA looked like they could be on TV and about five percent of them probably had been, or were actively auditioning.

"That's Nigel Fairbroad. He's an English reality TV producer. He allegedly has an eye for the ladies. Mrs. Fairbroad is looking for a divorce, and her attorney thinks she'd get a better deal if she had all her ducks in a row before she pulls the trigger and files."

"Okay." Sofia wasn't entirely sure what to do with this information.

"You're one of the ducks," said Brendan. "Or rather you will be. Go home, get dolled up, and be at Frank's Grotto in Malibu at seven o'clock tonight. According to Melissa Fairbroad, her husband is usually there most weeknights around that time. If he's not there, that will provide us with another line of enquiry."

"Is this my punishment for messing up on the stakeout? I have to sleep with a reality TV producer?"

Brendan laughed. "I'm not that cruel. No, it's a straight-up honey-trap. You proposition him and see if he bites. In fact, I would advise against sleeping with the guy. It would kind of complicate matters if you were subpoenaed."

Sofia had heard of honey-traps. They were a mainstay of a lot of private detective businesses. Some PIs pretty much did only honey-trap and related surveillance investigations. It was fairly easy, and the money was good, kind of like actual prostitution but without the icky part.

She took another look at the picture. He wasn't her type.

But for a man his age, he had a certain something. There was one problem. The location.

Jose, the barman at Frank's Grotto, was a friend of hers. Well, slightly more than a friend. More of a friends with benefits-type of friend. The main benefits being he was tall, dark, and drop dead gorgeous. He had a twelve-pack stomach, gorgeous brown eyes, spoke little English outside what was required for his job, and would happily head over to the Cove any time she was in need of company. Relationships for Sofia had always been fraught. With her hectic schedule and fishbowl life, she and Jose, the hot Latin lover, kind of worked. She didn't want to mess that up, but this was her job, without air quotes, and she wanted to do it right.

"I just have to make a pass at him and see if he says yes?" she said.

"You'll have to wear a body cam so we have evidence in case her attorney needs it. That's the other reason I wanted to take this gig. The attorney recommended us, and he throws a ton of business our way. So, even though it's not our regular type of gig, we want to stay onside with this guy if we can."

Hell, it has to beat sitting outside a rehab clinic all day. If she needed to use the restroom, there would be one right there. She was sure she could explain to Jose what the deal was afterward. In terms of what Brendan was asking her to do, it should be as straightforward as it got. She was an actress— she could do this.

"Uh, Brendan," she said.

He had already gone back to sorting through the papers on his desk. He looked up, almost surprised that she was still sitting in his office. "Yup?"

"Isn't there kind of a snag with all of this?" Sofia said.

"What's that?" Brendan asked.

"He works in the industry. He's bound to recognize me. I mean, even if I put a wig on or color my hair."

Brendan shrugged. "I already thought about that. It kind of works in our favor."

She didn't follow. How would someone recognizing her help? "How does it work in our favor?"

Brendan let out a long sigh, like he didn't want to have to actually say what he was about to. "Sofia, you were just papped taking a leak on the street outside a rehab clinic in Malibu. Half the town probably thinks you have a drug problem, and the other half is probably thinking you've lost your marbles. Chances are our boy Nigel will assume you're desperate and hooking."

The deadening realization that Brendan was right hit her. "He'll think I'm a prostitute who needs the money for drugs?"

Brendan looked at her. "It's the perfect cover, right? We couldn't have done a better job setting it up if we'd planned the whole thing."

"But what if I don't want people thinking I'm a prostitute?"

Brendan set down the papers he was reading over. "Sofia, let me give you a little hard-won advice. One of the most powerful abilities a person can have is not to care what other people think about them. As long as you're doing the right thing, it doesn't matter a fig what people think."

Brendan was right. That was real logic, not Hollywood logic. "Seven o' clock at Frank's Grotto?"

"You got it. Aidan will help you out with the surveillance equipment."

Sofia walked back out into the main office where Aidan was hunched behind his screens. She walked past him to her desk. There was a package on her seat. She picked it up. A large pack of adult diapers.

"Very funny," she said to Aidan.

Aidan's head popped up from behind the screens. "Just looking out for you."

Sofia moved the diapers under her desk, resisting the temptation to launch them at Aidan's stupid Irish head.

7

Sofia arrived at Frank's Grotto to discover, much to her relief, that Jose wasn't working. Once she was done here, she might give him a call to see if he wanted to come over and give her a back rub. Jose's back rubs were pretty amazing, though he tended to move a little too quickly from her back to other parts of her anatomy. She had never quite understood men who moved so fast when they knew they were going to get lucky. It was probably like dogs who wolfed their food down in seconds. Even though they knew their bowl probably wasn't about to be taken from then, they must figure, why take the risk?

Sofia handed her key fob off to the valet and walked inside. For tonight's operation, she had gone for a look which a casting director would describe as Business Slutty —a short black skirt, white shirt unbuttoned a little too far, matching lacy white underwear, and black high heels. She took a seat near the end of the bar and ordered a glass of dry white wine. As the bartender poured her drink, she reached down her blouse, found the tiny button that activated her hidden camera, and clicked it. The camera was linked by

Bluetooth to her smartphone. From now on everything in front of her would be recorded, and later, Aidan could download the footage from her phone. She hoped nothing too embarrassing would happen. She trusted him not to leak the footage to TMZ, but she didn't trust him not to play it over and over again in the office.

The bartender put her drink down on the bar. She took a pencil from her handbag and started to scribble onto a cocktail napkin a list of all the things that she figured might be required to get the average middle-aged, married American male to make a pass at a woman who was not his wife. Three small sips of wine later, she had come up with:

1. Two arms.
2. Two legs.
3. A winning smile.
4. A vagina.
5. Breasts.
6. A heartbeat.

She chewed the end of the pencil, thought about it a little more deeply, and put a line through the first three items on her list. At a pinch, and in her experience, a full set of limbs and a come-hither look were optional. A man walked in through the entrance and headed for the bar. He had dark hair, designer stubble, and was wearing penny loafers, dark blue pants, and a white dress shirt. He looked to be about the same height as her intended target.

It was only when he got closer that she realized the man wasn't Nigel Fairbroad. It was an Australian movie star named Bruce Brunt. Even by movie star standards, he was a piece of work, best known for making a pass at every woman who crossed his path. She looked back at the list and put a line through number six.

Her heart sank as Brunt took a seat a couple of bar stools away. She could feel his eyes on her. From the corner of her eye, she saw him linger first on her legs and then on her breasts. She resisted the urge to button up her blouse. He flagged down the bartender.

"The usual," he said in his trademark Australian accent.

"Soda water with a dash of lime usual? Or double Scotch on the rocks with a water back usual?" said the bartender.

"Funny guy. Make it a treble," said Brunt.

"Yes, sir," said the bartender.

Brunt swiveled round on his bar stool, arms folded and legs apart. "It's Sofia, right?"

Sofia wondered how she should play this. Of all the people who could have set up camp next to her at the bar, this guy was the worst. Ignoring Brunt wasn't going to work. Nigel could walk in at any minute, and then an already difficult situation would become next to impossible.

She had to find a way of letting Brunt know she wanted to be left alone without making a scene. But what if Nigel walked into the bar in the middle of her giving Brunt the cold shoulder? How could she then come on to him without it appearing extra weird? How would Brunt react if she did?

The male ego was a fragile thing. A regular male actor's ego was even worse. A male movie star's ego was off the scale. They weren't used to hearing the word 'no,' not ever. Once they reached a certain level, they were surrounded by agents, managers, and personal assistants who catered to their every whim. Unfortunately, Brunt was at that level.

She turned round to face him. Yup, it was definitely Brunt. "I'm really sorry, but I'm meeting a friend."

Brunt shot her a gleaming smile that no doubt worked

on most women. He held up his hands in a gesture of mock surrender. "I don't mean to intrude. It was just that I couldn't help but notice that you've been in the news recently." He hopped off his stool and climbed up onto the one next to her as the bartender put his treble Scotch down on the bar. "I was going to offer my commiserations as a fellow victim of the media. I've had a few embarrassing public moments myself."

"Right. I appreciate the support. I really do," said Sofia.

Sofia was well aware, along with the rest of the country, of Bruce Brunt's "embarrassing public moments." They included numerous bar brawls, DUIs, and on one occasion, telling a female LA County sheriff's department patrol officer to suck on his "didgeridoo, Sheila" while taking down his pants and waggling little Bruce in her general direction as cars shot past on PCH near Cross Creek. The last incident was caught by the officer's dash cam and earned him a thirty-day stay in LA County jail.

"I'd love to chat," continued Sofia. "But I'm meeting a friend."

Brunt raised his glass and reached it over to clink it against Sofia's wine glass. "Cheers. So is this a girlfriend or a boyfriend you're meeting?"

Sofia smiled politely. What was it with guys in public places who couldn't take a hint? "A friend."

"I just got divorced." Brunt eyed Sofia over the top of his glass as he took a sip.

"No kidding." She couldn't imagine what would drive any woman to leave such a charming specimen.

If Brunt had picked up on her sarcastic tone, he wasn't letting on. "Straight up. Always room at the top," he said with a wink.

Sofia's mouth opened. She struggled with what to say to that. She had nothing. She took a slug of wine.

"You were in that kids show? *Tiny Detective*?"

"*Half Pint Detective*," she corrected him.

"Isn't that what I said?"

"Listen, it's been nice talking to you, but I..." said Sofia as he reached over and grabbed the napkin she'd been writing on.

He peered at it. "What's this all about?"

Over his shoulder, Sofia spotted a middle-aged man entering the bar. She didn't need to look at the photo Aidan had put on her iPhone to know it was Nigel. He took a stool at the opposite end of the bar.

Brunt meanwhile looked up from the napkin. "Vagina? Why are you writing things like that down, eh? Desperate for it?" He had moved past over-friendly bonhomie into creepy, leering territory. It hadn't taken long.

Sofia snatched the napkin, picked up her glass of wine, and scooted past Brunt as fast as she could. "That's my friend. It's been nice talking to you."

Brunt kept talking behind her. "That guy?" he said, obviously stunned that any woman could resist his Aussie, movie star charms.

Sofia took a seat next to Nigel. He didn't even glance at her. He was busy fidgeting with his phone. She leaned over to him.

"Excuse me?" she said.

He finally looked up. He was actually fairly good looking for a guy his age. If he had been playing away from home, she imagined it wouldn't have been that difficult for him to find partners.

"Yes?" His accent was like something out of Downton Abbey.

"I don't mean to bother you, but that guy down there was hassling me," said Sofia.

Nigel looked past her to Brunt. With her back to him, Sofia didn't see Brunt's reaction, but she definitely heard it.

"What are you looking at, mate?" Brunt shouted from the other end of the bar.

Nigel looked back to his cell phone. "Right."

Sofia smiled sweetly. "Would you mind pretending that you're meeting me? I think he might leave me alone if he thinks I'm with someone." She reached over and touched the sleeve of his jacket. "I'd really appreciate it."

Most men couldn't resist the chance to play the knight in shining armor with a young woman. She was hoping Nigel would be no exception.

He swallowed. "Is that Bruce Brunt?"

"Yeah, I think so."

"Jesus." Nigel's pasty face went paler. "He seems even more obnoxious in real life. Not to mention bigger. I've heard he's a bit of a brawler. Doesn't like producers much, either. Dangled one off a balcony in Singapore once."

"It's all talk. Probably," said Sofia. "Hey, are you a producer? You look kind of familiar."

She was already cringing inside. Even as an actress, she couldn't imagine how women did this kind of thing for a living. Yuck. It was bad enough pretending to hit on some guy at a bar for surveillance.

Nigel looked back to his cell phone and then back at her. "Sorry, what were you asking me?"

"Just if you could pretend we're together." She shot him another sweet smile that set her teeth on edge. This was just another role, she reminded herself. Slutty Businesswoman Looking for a Good Time. She could do that.

"Oh, yes, of course," said Nigel, most of his attention on his cell phone.

"Tell you what, seeing as you're doing me a favor, can I get you a drink?" she asked Nigel. She wondered if she was coming on too strong. So far he hadn't shown any interest in her whatsoever. Not that it was necessarily a bad thing. Her job was merely to gather evidence that Maloney Investigations would filter back to his wife. Maybe he was a straight arrow.

Nigel finally smiled. "Sure. What's that you're drinking?"

She held up her glass. "This is a 2012 La Fiera Pinot Grigio."

"You know your wine," said Nigel.

"I just asked for a Pinot and then read the label as the bartender was pouring it." She adjusted her position so that her skirt rode up a little.

He looked at the wineglass.

She reached out her hand. "I'm Sofia." Her first name was usually enough to bring at least a glimmer of recognition.

Nigel looked blank as he shook her hand. "Nigel."

"Sofia Salgado," she said, hoping that would do the trick.

"Oh, yes," said Nigel. "You were just filmed having a wee outside a rehab clinic down the road."

Sofia died a little inside. Nine years of TV and three years of movies and now she had become 'the girl who got caught peeing in public.' That had to say something about the nature of modern celebrity. She wasn't sure what it said, but she was sure it was pretty depressing.

"So, Nigel," she said, hoping to move the conversation along. "Would you like to invite me to join you for dinner? If you're not busy."

Nigel's cell chimed with the noise of an incoming text.

He snatched the phone up from the bar. "Sofia, I'm awfully sorry, but I have to dash."

"Now?"

Nigel had already stood up. His drink arrived, and he pushed it over the bar to her. "I know I must seem terribly rude, and I'm sorry to leave you to Bruce Brunt's tender mercies, but I really do have to leave."

With that, he was gone. She glanced over her shoulder to see Brunt leering at her. "Hey, love, you fancy going back to my place and seeing my didgeridoo now?"

Sofia tried to think of something she'd like to see less and came up blank. She slapped a twenty down on the bar and headed for the door. Outside, in the early evening sunshine, she handed her ticket to the parking attendant. She was just in time to see Nigel pull out onto PCH in a brand new Mercedes SLK and head south toward Pacific Palisades. Whatever he had on his mind, at least she could reassure his wife that it wasn't chasing younger women.

Unfortunately, the same couldn't be said for her booty call, Jose. As Nigel disappeared into the distance, Sofia saw Jose get out of his beat-up Ford pickup with a girl who looked barely out of high school. She had long, bleached-blond hair, gravity-defying boobs, and was dressed in cut-off denim Daisy Dukes. Jose at least had the decency to look mildly embarrassed when he saw Sofia.

As Jose escorted his date to the entrance, Sofia heard her say, "So you, like, own this place? Like no way. That's like, amazing?" Each sentence was delivered, Valley girl style, like a question.

Sofia walked straight past them and got into her car, tipping the valet as Jose disappeared inside with his date. Without looking back, she pulled the red Tesla Roadster out onto PCH.

She stamped down on the accelerator and drove fast. She was the worst kind of mad. Mad for no reason. She and Jose were strictly friends with benefits. They had agreed early on that they were free to see other people. It wasn't as if she would have had a serious relationship with Jose if he'd offered. She would have laughed at the idea. She wasn't ready for a serious relationship with anybody.

So, why was she so mad?

Her cell pinged with an incoming text. She reached over and tapped the screen. It was from Brendan.

Brendan's texts weren't noted for being long. This one was no different. It simply read "Great job, Sofia!"

For the first time in a few days, Sofia actually managed a smile. Maybe she had a shot at this private detective gig after all. Her cell pinged again.

This text read "Footage all good AND you didn't pee yourself. BTW, who's the blonde with your boyfriend? She's kinda cute. Nighthawk."

Sofia flipped her cell the bird. The red Roadster punched its way through the warm Malibu evening, heading north and back home to Nirvana Cove.

8

Sweat pouring down her face, Sofia slammed three quick left jabs into the heavy bag. She moved round, keeping her guard up, and imagined Aidan Maloney's stupid Irish potato head as she pivoted round to hit the bag with a solid right. The bag moved a fraction of an inch. She moved back, conjuring a vision of Aidan spilling back on his heels, his hands up to defend himself.

She shifted her feet, moving round before stepping in and launching a fresh flurry of blows. Keeping her head down, she got close and pummeled him with body shots. With every punch, the tension of the last few days fell away. She stopped, reached down, and grabbed her towel—a tricky operation when wearing boxing gloves—and dabbed sweat from her face.

Jack's Gym in Venice had been a haven for her for the past four years. Jack's Gym was owned not by Jack, long since retired, but by Luis Cordabre, a former Hispanic prize fighter turned boxing trainer. Sofia had met Luis when he'd been hired to train her for a small studio movie about a young woman, abandoned by her boxer father, who steps into the ring to try to win back his love. It had been a pretty good script with a hot, young British director, but the financing had fallen through a week before the start of principal photography, and the project was condemned to Hollywood purgatory, also known as 'turnaround.'

Luis ruled the four-thousand-square-foot gym with an iron glove. But he was also a devoted family man with three sons and a daughter as well as being one of the kindest, most generous people Sofia had ever met. There was a calm about him that seemed to fill the gym, which was why it had become a kind of refuge for Sofia over the past few years. Anyone who stepped out of line, or disrespected Luis or anyone else who used the place, was unceremoniously banished. Depending upon how bad the person messed up, and how well he knew them, he might only be allowed one strike. Second chances were rare.

The door into the gym opened, and Luis walked in. He was deep in conversation with a young fighter he'd been training the past few months. Luis had told Sofia the kid had huge raw talent, but he was worried he might lack the discipline to turn what he had into a successful career. She felt just the opposite—she could bring discipline to this detective career, but she didn't know if she had any talent for it.

The kid broke off to go warm up with the jump rope. Luis headed over to Sofia. He greeted her in his usual manner by giving her a hug. Hugs were the other side of Luis. Everyone got hugged like a long-lost brother. Luis took a step back and looked at her. "How you holding up, little sister?"

"Good," she said. "I'm good."

"If you want, I can find those paparazzi who took those pictures and lay down some pain on them."

What may have been mere bravado from many people came off as completely sincere from Luis. That was why she had to decline, politely. Laying down some pain could mean anything from giving someone a scare to them ending up face-down in a downtown alleyway.

"I appreciate the offer, but they were only doing their job. I'm sure all the fuss will die down in a few more days."

Luis nodded. "That's a shame. I was looking forward to putting some manner on those *pendejos*." He put an arm on her shoulder. "Did I ever tell you about the time I pissed my pants during a fight?"

"No. But it's really okay. I'm fine." What was it with people wanting to share their stories of public urination? First it had been Brendan telling her about his partner, Charlie, and now it was Luis. Didn't anyone use toilets anymore?

Luis tightened his grip on her shoulder. "So it's the third round. I have the first two rounds in the bag. The guy is really starting to wobble. I can see that glazed look in his eyes. Then, from nowhere, he hits me with this uppercut. I can feel this wet sensation. I'm thinking maybe he's busted my nose, but I look down. I can't see any blood. It's then it hits me. I've pissed my shorts."

"What happened next?" Sofia was caught up in the story in spite of herself.

"Had to finish him off and get out of there. Landed a big right hand. He went down, and I ran for the dressing room."

Sofia wasn't sure what the proper response to Luis's story was. She settled for "I guess these things happen."

Her cell rang, saving her from any more stories about bodily functions gone horribly wrong. It was Brendan. She took off her gloves and answered it.

"Hey, Brendan, what's up?" she said.

"Where are you?" Brendan sounded annoyed.

"Working out at Jack's in Venice."

"I need you back in the office. Soon as you can."

Now that Brendan had had time to think about it, he had come to the obvious conclusion. She came with too much baggage. It was one thing to train up a regular rookie. It was quite another to train up a rookie who couldn't even go on a stakeout without embarrassing herself, and by extension, Maloney Investigations, all over the Internet.

"I'll be right there," she said. "I totally understand that you can't keep me on."

"Sofia, what the hell are you talking about?"

"That stakeout thing. I get it."

"This hasn't got anything to do with that," said Brendan. "It's about last night."

Last night? She thought last night had gone well. That she'd done the job asked of her. "What about it?"

Brendan gave a long sigh. "Nigel Fairbroad's body washed up on Broad Beach this morning. I have two LA County sheriffs in the office who want to talk to everyone who saw him. Don't worry, it's routine, but the sooner they talk to you the sooner we can all get back to normal."

Sofia stood in the middle of the gym. Her legs felt weak, like she'd been hit with a really good shot. She might have been one of the last people to see Nigel Fairbroad alive. It was an eerie feeling. How could someone be here one minute and then gone the next? She knew people died. Just not like this.

And Broad Beach? Of all the places for a body to wash up. Broad Beach had some of the most expensive beachfront property in Malibu. It was home to studio heads and movie stars. Five million dollars bought a pretty average house in that part of the 'Bu. It was not somewhere usually associated with dead bodies on the beach, even if this particular body was someone who was in same line of business.

She unlaced her gloves. The media was going to have a field day. It might take her off the main gossip homepages. She hated herself for even thinking of that. Besides, it'd be even worse if the media found out she was involved with the death, too.

She grabbed her towel, jammed it into her gym bag next to her gloves, took her car keys out of the side pocket, and headed for the door.

"Gotta go," she shouted over her shoulder to Luis. She hit the door and was back outside in the blazing sunshine before anyone could ask why she was leaving in such a hurry.

9

S ofia pulled the Tesla Roadster into a space a few doors door from the entrance to the building where Maloney Investigations had their office. She sat quietly and took a few deep breaths. She wanted to compose herself before she spoke to the LA County sheriff's department.

Brendan had explained the jurisdictions when she started working for him. Although Malibu was technically a city outside Los Angeles, Malibu didn't have its own police department. Instead, law enforcement was contracted out to the Lost Hills station of the LA County sheriff's department in nearby Agoura Hills. As Nigel's body had been found in Malibu, that made his death a matter for the county sheriff. The LAPD would only become involved if it turned out that he had come to harm somewhere else first.

Sofia had spent the slow crawl back up PCH thinking over everything that had happened the night before. Nigel had certainly seemed distracted. But suicidal? Given that last night had been the first and last time she had met him, and their meeting had lasted only a few minutes, it was impossible for her to know. All she could do was relate what had happened. But he hadn't seemed suicidal to her. Distracted, maybe a little worried, but not suicidal.

She got out of the Roadster and walked into the building. Aidan was at his usual post in the main office, hunched behind his bank of screens. She was thankful that he didn't seem to be still reviewing the footage of her peeing outside the rehab clinic. He raised a hand by way of greeting.

"Brendan in with the sheriff's deputies?" she asked, moving yet another pack of adult diapers from her chair and dumping them under her desk. If he was going to keep this up, she ought to figure out a way to get them to seniors in need.

"Not deputies," Aidan corrected. "Homicide investigators."

"They're thinking homicide already?" said Sofia. "How come?"

"No idea. Why don't you ask them when they talk to you? I'm sure they'll be happy to share. But maybe you should take a bathroom break first."

Sofia reached down and grabbed the pack of diapers. She launched it in Aidan's direction. It cleared the top of his screens just as Brendan's office door opened, and he stepped out with two serious middle-aged white guys in suits. If any of them had noticed the flying pack of diapers, they didn't let on.

"This is Sofia Salgado," Brendan said to the two homicide investigators. "She was running the honey-trap operation on behalf of the vic's wife." He turned to Sofia. "Sofia, do you have a couple of minutes?"

"Sure," she said, walking over.

Brendan did the introductions. She followed them back into Brendan's office. Brendan took a seat behind his desk while the two cops and Sofia perched on a chair and couch respectively. The couch was usually reserved for clients.

She ran through the events of the previous evening from when she arrived at Frank's Grotto until she left and saw Nigel making a hasty exit. The two investigators stopped her a couple of times to ask questions and generally clarify things, but it was all fairly routine. The only time they looked at each other was when she mentioned Bruce Blunt's crude attempt to pick her up and Nigel's super-charged exit.

Finally, they got up, shook Brendan's hand, and thanked them both for their time. Brendan showed them out. Sofia stayed in his office until he came back in.

Brendan sat down behind his desk and went back to reading an open file, making notes as he went. Eventually he looked up. "Was there something else?"

Sofia wasn't sure. The whole thing felt so anti-climactic. A man was dead. A man she had been trying to proposition not twenty-four hours ago. It felt like there should be more. "I don't know."

Brendan leaned back in his chair. He put his hands behind his head, lacing his fingers together. "We were hired to see if the guy had a wandering eye. We did that. Something happened to him afterward. That falls outside our remit. Unless there's something you haven't told me."

"What? No. There's nothing else."

"Then why are you still sitting in my office?" said Brendan.

"It just seems so, I dunno, so incomplete."

Brendan got up and walked over to the window, hands jammed into his pockets. "Life's incomplete. You don't get many nice, neat endings tied up with a bow like on TV. People come into our lives, and then they leave again." He smiled at her. "This line of work isn't any different from that."

10

Once a week, Brendan took Aidan and Sofia out to lunch at Marmalade Cafe in Cross Creek. They got a table in back and went over their current cases while they ate. Today was company lunch/case review day. The problem was that the only case she wanted to discuss wasn't their case anymore. Not only was it closed, the case's main subject was currently being cut open by the coroner in the LA County morgue.

"Okay." Brendan ran his finger down the list of live cases, none of which included any dead TV producers. "Mrs. Wong's missing Pekinese."

Aidan finished chewing a mouthful of blackened chicken sandwich and swallowed. "Posters are still up with the reward. I've spoken to all the local pounds, and there's no sign of our puppy. But there have been a couple of other purebred small dogs that have gone missing in the past few weeks, so chances are they're probably being stolen to order. I can talk to the sheriff's department again, but it's not exactly top of their list right now."

"What about the Palisades? Santa Monica? The Marina?

If someone's stealing dogs, the chances are that they're not just covering Malibu. See if Santa Monica PD has any open cases," said Brendan.

Aidan made a note. Brendan looked over at Sofia who had just taken a bite of salad. "The Sabrina Ross case? Anything?"

Sofia swallowed quickly. She'd been hoping that Brendan would skip the Ross case this week. There was never any significant news on the Ross case. There hadn't been any in almost ten years. She was pretty sure that Brendan kept it on their books as a favor to Sabrina's father. Some agencies would have kept it as a regular source of income, but Sofia knew from seeing one of the invoices that Brendan only charged a hundred dollars a month to keep it open, a fraction of the real cost to Maloney Investigations.

Sabrina Ross had been a young co-ed at Pepperdine University who had gone missing over fifteen years ago after a party at a frat house at USC. The LAPD had conducted a huge search and spoken to hundreds of witnesses. Sabrina's father, a wealthy tech millionaire, had offered a million-dollar reward that had served to bring out every crank and nutcase in America. Not only had Sabrina never been found, there had never been a confirmed sighting of her since she went missing. Most people, Sofia included, had come to the conclusion that she was dead.

Sofia spent one afternoon a week chasing old leads and speaking to people who had likely been spoken to dozens of times before or who had all but forgotten poor Sabrina. It was a thankless task. At any given moment, she could conjure up the last known image of Sabrina, a photograph taken at the frat party that showed a slightly drunk pretty blond girl with a goofy smile hamming it up for the camera. Sabrina had become trapped in time, destined to be forever twenty years of age, not allowed to grow up or grow old. It made Sofia shiver thinking about it. She tried to think of something Brendan could pass onto Sabrina's father, but the pickings were meager.

"I spoke to the lady who thought she'd seen her at a bus stop on the night she went missing, Gladys Hildebrand," Sofia offered.

"And?" Brendan asked.

"She couldn't tell me anything more than what she'd already told the cops. I asked if she'd seen anyone talking to Sabrina or whether she looked upset, but she didn't think so. I'm sorry."

Sofia really was sorry. There would have been no better feeling than to have offered Sabrina's father some glimmer of hope. But the Sabrina Ross case looked destined to remain incomplete.

They spent the rest of lunch going over a half dozen other active cases that Maloney Investigations had on file. Every time a waiter or busboy came round, Aidan would insist on ordering Sofia more iced tea until Brendan finally told him to knock it off. Aidan responded by going into a sulk and playing with his phone, obsessively swiping left and very rarely right as he played with Tinder, his favorite dating app.

"Can you save that for your own time, Aidan?" Brendan said.

Aidan looked up from what to Sofia looked like a stunningly perfect brunette with model looks. When he saw Sofia looking, he smiled and swiped left, effectively deleting her from his list of possible matches.

"What was wrong with her?" Sofia asked.

Aidan rolled his eyes. "Too short."

"She was five eight," said Sofia, who was five foot eight herself. "In heels she'd be your height."

Brendan waved his hand at Sofia, indicating that she should drop it. "Don't even go there. That way lies madness."

"Five nine's my ideal. I'm not going to settle," said Aidan.

"Because you've already left swiped ninety percent of the single women in the Greater Los Angeles area?" said Sofia.

Aidan shot her a withering look. "The saturation point for online dating apps in LA is thirty-six percent. There are plenty more where they came from."

Brendan flagged down a waiter for the check. "I don't know why people can't just meet these days. What happened to old-school romance? You work with some cute girl, you ask her out, and hey, presto."

The whole time he was talking, Brendan was looking at both of them. It wasn't a secret that he had always harbored a desire for Aidan and Sofia to get together. Both of them smiled politely, but as soon as Brendan's attention had turned to paying the check, they simultaneously mimed throwing up.

Sofia thanked Brendan for picking up the check, and the three of them wandered outside. She was still thinking about Sabrina Ross and Nigel Fairbroad and how unfair it was that some people's story came to an end too soon, while others never even got an ending, as she pulled up outside the office.

A glamorous woman wearing a backless black dress and Louboutin high heels with red soles was pacing back and forth on the sidewalk in front of the office. Standing a short distance away was a man with thick gray hair wearing an expensive Italian suit. Sofia was fairly sure he was the attorney who steered so much business Brendan's way. She was also fairly sure that the woman was the freshly-widowed Mrs. Nigel Fairbroad. For a woman whose husband had just washed up dead on Broad Beach, she didn't so much look sad as angry.

Sofia, who was the first back at the office because Aidan drove like a grandma, got out of her car.

"Can I help you?" she asked.

Melissa Fairbroad stopped in her tracks. She lowered her Louis Vuitton sunglasses and took a moment to study Sofia. She had an unforgiving gaze, though that may have been down to too much Botox. Her expression seemed to be frozen at a permanent mixture of shock and annoyance.

"Holy Mother of Mary," Melissa Fairbroad announced loudly to no one in particular. "No wonder he didn't make a pass at you. Talk about sending a girl to do a woman's job. I mean, do you even have tits under whatever that hideous outfit is, sweetheart?"

For once, Sofia was speechless. Suddenly, the prospect of Nigel having taken his own life seemed more likely than it had before.

11

T he man who'd arrived with Melissa Fairbroad walked over, introduced himself as Melissa's attorney, John Stark, and gently guided Sofia away from his client.

"Melissa's spent most of the morning being grilled by the cops," he said to Sofia, as if that made his client's outburst okay.

Sofia could only manage a curt "I see."

Brendan had already mentioned to Sofia that John Stark, Attorney at Law, threw a lot of business in Maloney Investigation's direction, so she knew it was probably best to suck up the abuse, at least until she worked out what they wanted. Melissa didn't strike Sofia as the kind of woman who made casual social calls when she could be at home having her nails done or torturing fluffy kittens.

Brendan and Aidan pulled up in Aidan's canary-yellow Porsche, which was as obnoxious as it sounded. Brendan strode over and shook Starks's hand.

"Come on, let's get you folks inside," he said. "I'm assuming this isn't something you want to discuss out on the sidewalk," he added, shooting Sofia a slightly disgruntled look.

"Sorry," Sofia said. "I don't have a key."

Brendan hustled everyone inside the building as Sofia and Aidan brought up the rear. Having delivered her verdict, Melissa proceeded to completely ignore Sofia, and instead, turned to critiquing the Maloney Investigations office, which Sofia had to admit, tended toward the functional.

"If you were going for shabby chic without the chic, then you totally achieved that result." Melissa clicked along on her Louboutin heels.

Next Melissa turned to Brendan. "John here tells me that you're one of the best in the business. I hope you are, because they are saying that Nigel was murdered, and I'm fairly certain they think I did it. Assholes!"

Brendan winced as Melissa dropped the A-bomb. He didn't say anything to her about it though. Sofia guessed he took less of a hard line with clients than he did with staff. And it wasn't as if he could have gone through a twenty-five year stint in the LAPD, working in some of the city's toughest neighborhoods, without having heard language that would have made a longshoreman blush. Criminals weren't exactly noted for their use of pristine language. Nor were cops.

Brendan looked to John Stark. "You think they're heading in that direction?"

Stark gave a small nod. "They haven't said for definite that they're treating it as homicide. They're calling it suspicious. But I have a contact down at the coroner's office, and while they haven't completed the autopsy yet, word is that he had a couple of bullet-sized holes when he washed up on Broad Beach and scared all the rich folks."

It was a cold way to talk about the woman's recently

dead husband, and Sofia looked to see how she would respond.

"Scared? Pah," interjected Melissa. "It's all movie people living there. The only thing that would scare them is a bad opening weekend at the box office. I doubt they even blinked. Now if it had been a homeless person who had washed up, that would have been different."

Sofia had to concede that, leaving aside Melissa's acerbic delivery, she did have a point. Nobody got a beach house in Broad Beach by being a shrinking violet. Those homes were reserved for people who had, for the most part, clawed their way to the top of their respective professions, no doubt leaving a few metaphorical corpses of their own behind.

"Why don't you all come into my office and take a seat? We can talk this over. Sofia. Aidan. You come in, too. If that's okay with you, Mrs. Fairbroad?" said Brendan.

Melissa's lip curled as she glanced at Sofia. "I suppose that's acceptable. That's really up to John."

Her tone that suggested it was anything but acceptable, but Sofia smiled at her like she didn't notice. She was playing the role of Someone Being Nice to the Client.

"No reason why not. It should save us time down the line," said Stark.

With that ringing endorsement, Sofia followed everyone else into Brendan's office. She and Aidan stood by the window as Stark and Melissa took the couch. Brendan settled in behind his desk and adopted his reflective pose with his hands behind his head, fingers interlaced. She'd used that pose herself on her TV show, but it really only looked right on Brendan.

Stark kicked things off. "I take it the sheriff's department has already been here to talk to you, Brendan?"

Brendan looked straight at him. "Yes. I called them as

soon as I heard about your husband, Mrs. Fairbroad. By the way, my sincere condolences."

Melissa blasted straight past the part about condolences. "Why would you call the cops and tell them I was using you to see if my husband was cheating on me?"

Stark put a hand out toward his client, but Melissa batted it away. "Get off me. I want an answer, and it better be good.

Brendan's expression remained neutral. "Sometimes volunteering information is better than having someone find it out. And believe me, they would have found out sooner or later. At which point it would have looked worse. Of course, I'm working on the assumption that you weren't involved in your husband's unfortunate demise because you have to admit it does look like one hell of a coincidence. You ask us to investigate him because you want to dig up dirt to help a divorce settlement, and the next morning, he turns up dead."

Sofia wondered if Melissa would spontaneously combust. She didn't actually say anything. Well, not words. She sat on the couch, her face red (but still expressionless), her hands balled into fists, knuckles white, and made a noise like a kettle of water coming to the boil. She seemed to be trembling with what Sofia guessed was pent-up rage. If she were still acting, she'd want to use that for Furious Woman.

Stark spoke first. "Let's clear one thing up from the get-go. Mrs. Fairbroad did not kill her husband. They may have been going through a rough patch, but she was not involved in any way with whatever happened to him."

Spoken like a true attorney.

Melissa seemed to unclench a fraction as she listened to her attorney's stout defense.

"But you're not particularly upset that he's gone?" said Brendan. The slightest hint of a smile crossed his face. It was like he'd slipped back into homicide detective mode. "Or at least you appear to be masking your grief better than most people in this situation."

Melissa seemed to levitate from the couch. "I am not going to sit here and listen to this complete bullshit."

"Mrs. Fairbroad, you don't have to listen to me. That's quite correct, but while you are here, I'd appreciate it if you didn't use that kind of language in my office." Brendan fixed her with a stare Sofia didn't see often. She had always thought of it as a hangman's stare, the kind of look he gave someone just before he dropped the hatch from under their feet and let them swing.

Brendan's stare had the desired effect. Melissa sat back down like her knees had given up on her. "I did not kill my husband, Mr. Maloney. I know I don't come across as the most sympathetic person in the world or as a grieving widow."

You got that right, sister. Sofia kept her face expressionless.

Melissa continued, "I was planning on divorcing Nigel. I hadn't been in love with him for quite some time. He irritated me in ways I can't even describe. I'm not happy he's dead. But I'm not going to pretend to feel something I don't or to be someone I'm not."

It sounded way too slick. It was the type of speech that might have been coached out of someone by an attorney like Stark, or that someone practiced in front of the mirror before they went on Dr. Phil. It was, in a word, bad acting.

Brendan dialed down his death stare a couple of notches. "You may not have a choice about pretending, Mrs. Fairbroad. Like it or not, people judge other people by how they react to something like this. The same goes for cops. They see a woman who doesn't seem that troubled by her husband's death, and they start getting real curious why not."

"I think they're already curious, Mr. Maloney," Melissa shot back.

"They have already indicated that Melissa is their prime suspect," said Stark. "She has motive. All they need now is opportunity and forensics that link to her, and they'll be arresting her. I'm certain of it. The pressure's on to solve this fast, even if that means blaming the wrong person. Brendan, you know as well as I do how these things can work when the vic is deemed important enough. Dead white people get attention. Rich, dead white people in the industry get close scrutiny indeed."

Brendan unlocked his fingers. He dropped his hands to his desk, and swept them across the top as if he were trying to smooth out the surface. "So what do you want from us? I can't go back and untalk to the sheriff's department, and to be frank, I'd do the same thing again if I had to. I rely on my good name and a good working relationship with those guys to stay in business. You know how that works."

Melissa leaned forward. As she did so, her skirt rode up a little, which would have given Brendan a flash of her golden-brown, Pilates-sculpted thighs.

Not an accidental move. Still, Sofia had to admire the smooth way she'd done it.

Stark cleared his throat. "We want you to find the killer."

"Now," Melissa said to Brendan, "does that sound like the act of a guilty woman?"

It sounded exactly like the act of a guilty woman to Sofia, and she was fairly sure it did to everyone in the room.

But no one was going to say that. Not out loud. Not in front of Melissa Fairbroad. Or Brendan.

Brendan diplomatically ducked the question. "Can you give us a moment? This kind of investigation is a major undertaking. It's not a decision I can make without speaking to my co-workers, Aidan and Sofia."

"Of course. I understand completely." Stark stood to go.

Melissa looked less understanding but she still followed her attorney's lead.

"You can wait in the outer office," said Brendan. "We won't take long, and you'll have an answer before you leave. That way we can get started immediately, or you can begin looking for someone else. Depending upon what we decide."

12

Brendan looked at Sofia and Aidan in turn. "So? Should we take it or not?"

Sofia was impressed that he was asking them, and that he seemed ready to take their answer seriously. She could get used to that.

Aidan took a big breath of air, filling his cheeks and letting it out again slowly. "It's a big case. Could really kick the business up a notch. Put Maloney Investigations on the map." He must have caught his dad's death stare because he quickly added, "Not that we're not already on the map. Just we'd be even bigger."

Brendan nodded. "Sofia?"

Sofia had been glad he hadn't asked her first. She hadn't been sure. Still wasn't. It was true that it was a big case. If Melissa was telling the truth and they could actually find the real killer or killers, it would be huge. Plus, they would potentially be saving an innocent woman from a life behind bars. The only snag was that Sofia was far from convinced of Melissa's innocence.

What if the agency found another potential suspect, and

Melissa Fairbroad used her money and connections to have the cops railroad that person instead of her? Then another innocent person might end up behind bars. Sofia's head was spinning from the potential ethical dilemmas. She had left her acting career behind so she could actually make a positive difference. This didn't feel like that. Not even close.

"Sofia?" Brendan prompted.

"I don't know. What if she did it? Doesn't that put us in an impossible position? We can't exactly go to the cops if we're on her payroll. They'll be all kinds of nondisclosure agreements. Won't there?"

"We can cross that bridge when we get there," said Brendan. "But typically, yes. There will be a certain amount of client privilege. You know attorneys represent guilty people all the time. It's part of what makes this country great. The right to a proper defense. Even if you're guilty as sin. It's up to the prosecution to do its job."

"You think we should take it?" Aidan asked.

"I think we'd regret it if we don't, and some other outfit comes in and snaps it up. Plus, and I have to factor this in, John Stark has put a lot of business my way since I set up this agency. I get more referrals from him than just about anyone else in this town. If I don't help him when he really needs me, then I'm not sure those referrals will keep coming, and I wouldn't blame him for using someone else next time he knows someone who has a problem," said Brendan.

It was one of the longest speeches Sofia had heard Brendan give. She realized that he was staring at her.

"So?" he asked. "Should we take it?"

13

S ofia walked out of Brendan's office. They'd taken the case. But at least Brendan had let her voice her concerns first.

Despite her objections, which mainly centered around the fact that Melissa seemed to hate her, she had been designated by Brendan as the person to talk to Melissa Fairbroad to get an idea of her movements over the past few days. Then they'd corroborate her story. Reading between the lines, Sofia knew that Brendan really wanted to know if it was likely Melissa actually did it.

"Women are more open with other women," Brendan had told Sofia. She didn't want to be the one to burst his bubble and tell him that more often than not women were the least likely people to trust another woman, so she agreed.

While she talked to Melissa, Brendan was going to thrash out some details with John Stark. Meanwhile, Aidan was going to mine as much information as he could about Nigel and Melissa Fairbroad so they'd have a vague idea as to where to start their investigation. There could be a lot of reasons someone might want another person dead. Divorce was only one of those reasons, and in fairness to Melissa, there were less risky ways to achieve her goal than having her husband killed and dumped in the Pacific.

Sofia sat down with Melissa at a long table tucked in a corner of the larger outer office she shared with Aidan. Melissa had already made herself at home and had a good snoop around.

Before she had even sat down with her yellow legal pad, Melissa had said, "Why do you have like a month's supply of adult diapers under your desk?"

"Those would be my colleague's idea of a joke." If one of them was going to lie, Sofia didn't want it to be her. Trust would be important if she was going to get what she needed from Melissa. Trust started with honesty. "You know, we can deal with dark stuff, so sometimes we play tricks on each other to lighten the mood."

"Uh-huh." Melissa looked thoroughly unconvinced by this explanation. She probably thought Sofia had an incontinence problem.

Sofia uncapped her pen. "How about we start with where you were on the day of your husband's disappearance."

"The whole day?" Melissa said.

"From when you woke up," said Sofia.

Melissa rolled her eyes. Up close, they seemed the only part of her face actually capable of movement. "I guess I got up around nine. Nigel had already left for work. I lay in bed reading for a little while."

"Paperbook or e-book?" Sofia asked.

"Excuse me?" said Melissa.

"If you were reading on an e-reader or a tablet, then Aidan over there should be able to confirm what time it was.

When he's not hiding diapers under my desk, he's a bit of a computer whizz."

Melissa still looked skeptical.

"Basically, anything we can use that backs up what you tell us is a good thing," Sofia went on.

Melissa let out a little sigh. "I have a Kindle. I have mild arthritis in my hands so I can't really hold a large hardback book for any length of time."

Sofia made a note of the Melissa's Kindle account and also of the arthritis. She would confirm with Melissa's doctor, see if he could give them a statement about her condition and how it affected her. That was a good nugget of information to have. If it came down to it, maybe they could argue that someone with severe arthritis in her hands would have difficulty pulling the trigger of a gun. Not that she thought it would come to it, but tiny details that often seemed insignificant at the time could often prove crucial later on.

Where doubt could be shed there was always the chance of an acquittal. It had only been a few minutes but already she was starting to think like one of the defense team. Maybe this case would give her that neat ending that Brendan said was so unattainable.

"Okay," said Sofia. "Then what? By the way, I know this might seem really boring."

"Oh, it is. Believe me," said Melissa.

FOR THE NEXT SIXTY MINUTES, Sofia took note of Melissa's mind-numbing schedule on the day her husband died. It didn't seem to differ from what she did on any other day, which was not much. Or at least not much that was productive or contributed to anything apart from looking good, staying in shape, and spending her husband's money, something Melissa seemed to have a particular aptitude for.

Brendan was still holed up in his office with Stark, so Sofia moved on to asking Melissa, as diplomatically as she could, about her husband.

"Why do you think he was interested in other women?"

Melissa pursed her lips. "Maybe he wasn't, but he sure as hell didn't fuck me anymore. If you call what he did before fucking. He was *so* British. It's that private school repressed thing they have. It does not make for a happy marriage if, like me, you still have a physical appetite."

Sofia wasn't sure what to write down from that answer, so she moved on to another question. "Did he seem worried about anything?"

"Of course. He was a TV producer. Nigel's ulcers had ulcers. I'm amazed his doctor didn't have names for them."

It was like prying information out of a rock. "Was there anything he was particularly concerned about?"

"I just told you, sweetheart, he worried about everything," Melissa said.

Sofia would have to try to circle back to that later. "What about alcohol? Drugs?"

"No, Nigel was never a drinker. He was so strait-laced about that kind of thing. He'd almost faint if someone so much as pulled out a joint when he was around. He really was uptight. You can't believe." Melissa rolled her eyes again.

Sofia wondered why Nigel had married Melissa. They didn't seem to have much in common, but she would have looked good on his arm at events. Had he been that shallow, too?

She forged on with the questioning. "Did he have any new friends?"

"I'm not sure he had any old friends, really. Just work people." Melissa crossed her arms. "Next question."

That might have hit a nerve. Interesting. Sofia tried again "Were there any late-night phone calls? Unexpected visitors? Did he disappear without telling you where he was? Anything that might have seemed out of the ordinary for him?"

"Not really, but then again we led quite separate lives. Had done for years, sweetheart," Melissa said. "Oh, and by the way, I'm sorry for saying earlier that you had no tits. You clearly do, but that outfit really does you no favors."

EVENTUALLY, Sofia ran out of questions. Melissa had already run out of whatever meager supply of patience she had started with. Sofia was relieved to see Brendan walk out of his office with John Stark. Both men were laughing. They seemed to be in a good mood. At least the case was fun for someone.

Melissa looked at her. "Are we done here? Because I am exhausted."

"It's been really helpful," Sofia lied.

Sofia stood with Brendan and Aidan and watched the two leave. Stark opened the door to his Mercedes S class, and Melissa got in.

She really did have amazing legs. Sofia remembered the words of a long ago director "You can do a lot with a good pair of legs." Well, Melissa had.

Stark walked round, got into the driver's seat, backed the Mercedes out of his space, and drove away.

"Well?" Brendan said to Sofia. "She do it?"

"I don't know," said Sofia. "She doesn't have an alibi—home alone all evening. And she looks guilty."

"Not a good look for someone in her situation," said Aidan.

"What do we think Nigel got caught up in?" Brendan asked.

Sofia shrugged. "Something bad."

"In other words, we have no idea," Aidan said. "By the way, Sofia, that recording app that I put on your phone is still running. I heard every word of your interview. For someone who hits the headlines, you really should be more careful about safeguarding your privacy."

Sofia dug out her phone. She clicked on the screen and deleted the app. She also went into the settings and reset her password. The new one read: "AidanIsAnAsshat"

"Long password." Aidan tried to sneak a look at the screen as Sofia angled it away from his gaze.

"Don't worry," she said. "It's easy to remember."

14

Brendan stood in front of Sofia and Aidan with his arms folded, and a wooden toothpick protruding from the corner of his mouth. The toothpick was a sign that Brendan was in full-on work mode. She could already see that whatever reasons he had given them for taking on the case, this was the kind of investigation that he lived for. Life-and-death stakes, just like when he'd been on the force.

She saw where he was coming from. It didn't matter what side you were on, there wasn't much point being in the private investigator business if you weren't prepared to take on the big cases. It would be like a fighter who worked for years and then turned down a shot at the title.

"Okay," said Brendan. "Who knows whether Melissa's telling the truth or not? And, frankly, who cares? What we need is an alternative suspect with a motive. Let's start digging. Start with Nigel's production company."

"Already on it," Aidan said, reading from his cell phone screen. "They have an office down in Santa Monica. Nigel's partner is a guy named Jerry Gonzales." Aidan glanced across at Sofia. "One of your tribe."

"Because he's called Gonzales?" Sofia asked, unable to keep the irritation out of her voice. Sofia's father had been Hispanic, her mom's family a mix of German, Italian, and Scottish, and though she was proud of her heritage, she pretty much thought of herself as plain old American. Her Spanish skills didn't extend much beyond, hello, please, thank you, ordering a beer, and telling someone to get lost in language Brendan almost certainly wouldn't approve of.

"I meant movie folk." Aidan plowed on. "He and Jerry set up the company seven years ago, and they have a first-look deal with Warner Brothers, though they've worked with a number of different networks including Fox and NBC. Some of their big shows have been *World's Fattest Pets*, *America's Hottest Firemen*, and a dating show called *So You Think You're All That, Girlfriend?* They are currently making a show for one of the cable networks called *Swamptrash Survival*."

Sofia tried to look thoughtful. She wasn't going to admit that she had spent many a happy hour vegetating in front of her laptop watching most of those shows, and could, if called upon, have given Brendan and Aidan a rundown of the season highlights of each one and a lot more shows besides. For a while she'd been completely addicted to *America's Top Model*. It was so bad that in between seasons she would go back and watch all the old episodes. Looking back, it may have gone some way to explaining why she didn't have a regular boyfriend. But now she'd finally be able to put her addiction to really bad reality TV shows to positive use. It had all been research for a case.

"*Swamptrash Survival* is about a hillbilly survivalist called Tucker Trimble who teaches a bunch of rich kids how to survive in the backwoods of Kentucky. Tucker goes by the nickname 'TT' and his catchphrase is "I'm gonna make y'all squeal like a pig.'" " said Sofia.

Both Aidan and Brendan looked at her.

"I knew that," said Aidan, adding, "they shoot it up in Topanga Canyon."

Topanga Canyon was within spitting distance of where they were in Malibu. It was home to an eclectic mix of showbiz people, horse owners, old surfers, and folks who still wore tie-dye T-shirts, grew and smoked their own dope, and were generally bohemian. If Sofia had been unhappy living at Nirvana Cove, Topanga would have been on her list of places to relocate. It was as close to being out in the country as possible while still being in touching distance of Los Angeles.

"Okay, so go talk to Gonzales first and whoever else will speak to you at the production company. If he and Nigel were business partners, then maybe there was a falling out," Brendan ordered. "That'd give us something."

"On it." Aidan headed for the door.

Sofia followed him. If Aidan got his way, she'd be stuck in the office answering the phone like some kind of glorified secretary rather than a trainee investigator. The only way she was going to learn was by going out there and actually doing the job.

"Wait up there, junior, this is my turf." She grabbed her bag and raced to catch him as he pushed through the door on his way to the parking lot.

15

Sofia pulled the red Tesla Roadster into a parking spot across the street from the building where Nigel's production company was based. Aidan had spent the drive down PCH from Malibu to Santa Monica in a sulk, furiously left-swiping potential matches on a new dating app he'd discovered. Sofia had flipped on the radio to make it easier to ignore him. The top story was California's ongoing water shortage, which was threatening to turn into a full-blown crisis. Needless to say, one of the shock jocks was proposing that they use "a Sofia Salgado sprinkler system" as a possible solution. This drew a laugh from Aidan, who reached over to turn up the volume just as one DJ said, "Now that girl knows how to process water."

Sofia touched the screen, turning the radio off. They rode the rest of the way in silence.

Sofia and Aidan walked into the reception area and asked if they could speak to Mr. Gonzales. The attractive young receptionist (in Sofia's experience production company receptionists were always young, female, and attractive) gave Sofia and Aidan a broad smile, and said, "Sure thing."

There was a hurried phone call, presumably to Jerry Gonzales. When the receptionist put the phone back down, she seemed on edge. She kept stealing glances across the lobby at them.

The receptionist's phone rang. She answered, keeping her voice low, her eyes never leaving Sofia. Sofia and Aidan had identified themselves as being from Maloney Investigations. Jerry Gonzales wasn't obligated to talk to them. Sofia fully expected that any moment the building's security would arrive and ask them to leave.

Finally, the receptionist got up and leaned over the reception desk. "Ms. Salgado, would you and your colleague like a beverage? Fiji water? Juice? Coffee? Or if you want something else, I can always have someone run down the street and fetch it."

Aidan shot her a 'what the hell?' look. PIs usually didn't get such a warm reception. Especially not when they were here to ask someone if they'd been involved in the murder of their business partner.

"Do you have any iced tea? Peach flavor. A big jug if you can manage it." Aidan smirked.

"We're fine," said Sofia.

"I can totally get you peach-flavored iced tea!" The receptionist was busy pushing the boundaries of just how perky one person could be. She looked at Aidan. "A jug. That's what you said, right?"

"He was joking," said Sofia. "It's hard to tell because he's really not funny."

"Okay." The receptionist's brow crinkled into an uncertain expression. "Just let me know if you change your mind. It's really no trouble. No trouble at all!"

Aidan leaned over to Sofia. "Why are they being so nice? It's freaking me out."

Before Sofia could answer, the elevator door opened and Jerry Gonzales swept out, flanked on either side by an assistant. He was casually but expensively dressed in tan pants and a royal blue Ralph Lauren polo shirt. He looked as if he had just stepped off the first tee at Riviera Country Club in Bel Air.

"Sofia Salgado!" he said, reaching out to shake her hand. "I'm a big fan. No. Scratch that. I'm a *huge* fan." He turned to Aidan. "Wanna know how you spell superstar? S-O-F-I-A. S-A-L-G-A-D-O. That's how you spell superstar. Am I right?"

Sofia wished the ground would open up and swallow her whole. Gonzales was treating this like a talent meeting rather than the start of a privately funded homicide investigation. Out of the corner of her eye, Sofia caught Aidan smirking. He was having a good morning.

"Could you say that again? I didn't quite catch the spelling," Aidan said.

As Sofia got to her feet, her elbow accidentally-on-purpose caught Aidan in the ribs, and he grunted. Gonzales and his assistants didn't even register it. They were too busy staring at Sofia with dollar signs in their eyes. They clearly thought she must be here as the first stop in resurrecting her former career. Maybe they thought she was angling for a guest spot next to Tucker Trimble on *Swamptrash Survival*. More likely, they were already envisioning a celebrity rehab show like the one her former agent had pitched before Fred ran him off.

Jerry Gonzales leaned in closer to Sofia. "Look, let's not discuss things in the lobby. Why don't you come up to my office? We can talk there."

"I think that would a really good idea," said Sofia.

Over the past few days, her celebrity status had pretty much always worked against her. If now it was working in her favor, who was she to argue with that? She allowed herself to be guided back to the elevator by Jerry. Aidan had to fall in behind. She was praying he kept his mouth shut about why they were here until they got into Jerry's office. They could drop the boom on him there.

"Sorry." Gonzales finally acknowledged Aidan's presence. "I haven't asked your name."

"Just call me Aidan," said Aidan, shaking Gonzales's hand.

"You're Sofia's....manager?" said Gonzales.

"Well," said Aidan. "I try to manage her. But she kind of likes to go with the flow."

Still with the pee jokes. Was he ever going to run out? Sofia sighed. Now *she* was making them, too. This wasn't good.

They all crammed into the elevator that would take them up to Gonzales's office.

Inside the elevator everyone resorted to the standard default 'stare straight ahead and don't speak' elevator mode. Sofia wondered where it had come from. Maybe it was the lack of personal space that led to people closing down. At least it got Aidan to shut up.

The doors opened. She followed Gonzales and his assistants down a corridor into an office with yet another attractive receptionist and into a wide corner office with a pretty amazing view of the Santa Monica Pier. Gonzales motioned for her and Aidan to sit down, and his assistants withdrew.

It was time to drop the boom on him.

"Mr. Gonzales, I'll get straight to the point. We're here to speak to you about the murder of your business partner, Nigel Fairbroad," said Sofia.

She wasn't about to mention they were working for Melissa. Not just yet.

Jerry Gonzales did a double take. He stood and looked around his office. "Okay, where are the cameras? Is this like one of those candid camera-type deals? I have to say that if it is, then it's in poor taste, and that's from the guy who brought the world *So You Think You're All That, Girlfriend?*"

Aidan stared Gonzales down. "This isn't a joke. Nor are there cameras. We're here to ask you a few questions about your deceased partner. It'll take a few minutes."

Aidan actually did menacing fairly well. Sofia glimpsed Brendan as he must have been in his younger days—intimidating and in control. She sometimes forgot that beyond all the diaper gags and the patronizing tone, when it came down to it, Aidan was actually pretty good at what he did. Being an arrogant asshole and being good at the job weren't mutually exclusive—something she'd learned far too well in the movie industry.

Jerry Gonzales's demeanor changed instantly, and he sat back down. All the dollar signs were gone from his eyes. "I thought you quitting the business to play at being a private cop was a joke. Or research for a role. Not real."

She ignored the jibe. She'd been insulted by better men than Gonzales. She needed to start asking him serious questions, but she didn't want to dive in by asking Gonzales to account for his whereabouts. That would be fastest way to getting thrown out of his office. In any case, the sheriff's department would cover that territory better than they could. It was better to start general. "Mr. Gonzales, did you notice any change in Nigel's behavior over the last few weeks or months? Did he seem anxious? Upset? Was there anything he confided to you?"

Jerry Gonzales picked up the phone on his desk. "Hi, Jasmine, can you get my attorney on the phone?"

So much for the direct approach.

Aidan shot Sofia a 'what's the deal with this guy?' look. "Did you have any fallings out with Mr. Fairbroad? Having to work with someone every day can create tensions."

"Who are you?" said Gonzales. The question seemed to be aimed at both of them. "I mean I know who Half Pint over here is. But who are you?"

"Aidan Maloney of Maloney Investigations. We're a firm of private investigators who have been asked to look into the circumstances surrounding your business partner's untimely demise. I take it you've heard the rumors circulating that he was shot before he was dumped in the Pacific."

Gonzales looked like he was thinking about how to answer Aidan's question. In the end, he just nodded.

"If there's someone out there who wanted to harm him, your life may be under threat," Aidan said. "The sooner whoever did this is brought to justice, the better for everyone."

"Nice speech, Mr. Maloney. Are you a washed-up actor, too?" said Gonzales.

Sofia hadn't expected him to exactly welcome them with open arms, but she hadn't expected quite this level of hostility, either. Not only that, but Gonzales hadn't uttered a single word of regret that his business partner of so many years was dead.

"Mr. Gonzales, you don't seem troubled by the fact Nigel was shot and fed to the sharks by a person or persons unknown. That might strike people as a little odd." Aidan sounded just like his father had when talking to Mrs. Fairbroad. It was eerie.

Gonzales let out an audible sigh. "Nigel and I hadn't been getting along. That's hardly a secret. You know what this industry is like for gossip, so you'll find that out soon enough. But the idea that I am somehow involved in what happened to him? That's laughable."

Sofia sensed this was about as candid as Jerry Gonzales was about to get. Mr. Fairbroad had seemed like a nice enough guy, and nobody seemed to care that he'd been murdered. She felt bad for him.

"I make dumb TV shows," Gonzales went on. "I do it well, and I make a ton of money doing it. That's it." He paused. A smile flitted across his face. "Wait. You're not working for that pyscho wife of his, are you?"

Neither Aidan nor Sofia answered. "She's trying to muddy the waters, right? Throw suspicion on someone else."

If he wasn't going to answer their questions, they didn't have to answer his.

"All we're doing is trying to find the truth of what happened to Nigel and why," Sofia said. "Nothing more, nothing less."

"Sure you are." Gonzales's tone oozed sarcasm.

His phone buzzed and Jasmine came on, sounding less perky than before. "Your attorney is on line one, Mr. Gonzales."

"Tell him to hold for a second. I'm just finishing up here." Gonzales clicked a button, and the line went dead. "Oh, this is just too perfect. I assume you've met Melissa Fairbroad, so you must have some idea of what I'm saying."

Aidan got up from where he was sitting. "No, Mr. Gonzales, I really don't. Why don't you tell me?"

Gonzales leaned away from Aidan's looming form. Sofia wished she were big enough to loom over someone like that.

"Don't be coy," said Aidan. "If you have something to say, why don't you man up and say it?"

Gonzales stood up and walked round his desk, past Aidan and Sofia to his office door. "Let's say that Melissa wasn't exactly an ideal wife and leave it at that. I'm sure even the Half Pint Detective can work out what that means."

Sofia didn't rise to that bait.

Gonzales opened the door, making sure the door was between him and Aidan. "You can show yourselves out, but don't talk to any of my employees on the way or I'll call the Santa Monica Police Department and make a complaint. Understand me?"

"Perfectly," said Sofia as she stepped through the door. Aidan followed her. The door slammed behind them.

"Well," said Aidan, "that went well, don't you think?"

16

They got back into Sofia's Roadster. For having been all but thrown out of the office, Aidan seemed pretty upbeat.

"He's hiding something." Aidan closed the passenger door.

"So is our client," Sofia said.

"I thought that was a given," said Aidan. "Hollywood wife living in Brentwood. Stressed-out husband who probably hasn't had an erection since the last Eagles reunion tour."

"They toured last year," said Sofia.

"Whatever," said Aidan. "She was probably fooling around with her tennis coach or some yoga dude. That's where we ought to look next. Women like that always have something on the side."

"Generalize much?" Sofia pulled out of the parking space and joined the traffic on Ocean Avenue. "What if he's right? She had the motive. What if she killed him because we came up blank running the honey-trap? When she realized she couldn't base a divorce on infidelity, she flipped out, and decided to take the easy route."

"Except it's not the easy route, is it?" Aidan shot back. "If she planned on offing her hubby, she's not going to go out and hire a PI firm to draw attention to the problems in their marriage first. That puts her straight in the frame. It's dumb, and she doesn't strike me as dumb. Insanely hot, obnoxious, and slightly unhinged." He seemed to lose his train of thought. "She has a dirty mouth, too. I kind of like that."

"You're gross," said Sofia. "But, hey, she's single now, so there's nothing stopping you. She probably meets all the criteria in your stupid checklists."

Aidan seemed to consider her suggestion seriously. "Nah, my old man would flip out. Plus I have a date lined up for tonight. Right age. Right height. UC Davis grad, smart but not too smart."

Sofia already pitied the unfortunate young woman. "You wouldn't want to be with a woman who was *too* smart."

"Exactly." If Aidan detected the sarcasm in Sofia's voice, he didn't let it show. "It would be a complete disaster."

"Kind of cuts down the dating pool pretty substantially for you," Sofia continued. "I mean, there must be a lot of women who are smarter than you."

Aidan glanced over at her. "Like *you* go for brainiacs? That dude you were seeing who tends bar at Frank's Grotto is hardly a rocket scientist. Dude could be in a dark room and wouldn't even notice if someone turned on the light."

"I'm dating him for his, err, other qualities," said Sofia. A defensive tone had crept into her voice, and she wished she hadn't said anything.

"Which other qualities?" Aidan said.

Sofia had to actually stop and think. "He's really sweet."

Aidan laughed. "What? Like a Labrador puppy? You

accuse me of being superficial, yet you're only hooking up with that guy because of his puppy dog looks."

"That's not true," Sofia protested.

Aidan shot her a look of sheer disbelief.

"Okay, maybe his looks are a factor," said Sofia, back-tracking.

"See?" said Aidan. "People want what they want."

17

I f the Fairbroad family residence was anything to go by, there was a lot more money in TV shows called things like *So You Think You're All That, Girlfriend?* than Sofia had thought. Their house was located near the top of a quiet street in Brentwood, an upmarket neighborhood sandwiched between Malibu to the north and Santa Monica to the south.

The house itself was set back from the road, shielded from public view by a tall bougainvillea hedge and electronically controlled metal gates. Aidan had already checked the house out on the property website Zillow and emailed Sofia the details before he left to get ready for his hot date with the latest unfortunate woman he'd be rejecting shortly for some minor imperfection.

According to Zillow, the Fairbroads had purchased the house seven years ago. Its current value was estimated to be approximately four point six million dollars. For that amount of money, unimaginable to most people in the world, they got an architect-designed four-bedroom, three-bath home of just under five thousand square feet set on a pretty spacious half acre lot—with a lap pool, large decks, and a spa area, complete with wet bar, cabana, and hot tub.

Sofia parked on the street. She'd decided not to call ahead. She hoped to catch Melissa at home and hopefully slightly off guard. That way she stood a better chance of Melissa being honest about the infidelity Gonzales had hinted at. Brendan had impressed upon them that they could help Melissa best if they could build a complete picture of her life. Money could be a motive for divorce, but so could a jealous, and possibly impatient, lover who wanted Nigel out of the way so he could a start a new life with Melissa, the rich widow. Sofia had to find out if that lover existed.

She rang the buzzer on the keypad next to the gates and waited. A few moments later, a woman answered.

"Yes?" It wasn't Melissa. This woman had a strong Hispanic accent.

"Hi, it's Sofia Salgado from Maloney Investigations in Malibu. I'm here to speak with Mrs. Fairbroad."

There was a silence. Sofia waited several minutes, but no one replied.

Eventually she hit the buzzer again. If Melissa wasn't home, then having a chance to talk to the woman she presumed was a housekeeper or cleaner would be the next best thing. In any case she didn't want to turn back without having accomplished something.

"Yes?" asked the same woman. "What do you want?"

"I'm supposed to be meeting Melissa here. I'm working for her. Would it be possible for me to wait inside rather than standing out on the street? I'd really appreciate it. If she's not back soon, I'll leave her a note and come back tomorrow." Sofia added a parting shot. "I'm afraid she'll be unhappy with me if she finds me loitering on her sidewalk."

There was another silence. The voice on the other end probably knew just how easy it was to make Melissa angry. The gates swung open. Sofia walked through and up the driveway to the front door.

The front door opened before she even reached it. A middle-aged Hispanic woman stood at the door. She peered at Sofia over half-moon glasses attached to a gold chain around her neck.

"Thanks for letting me in." Sofia walked past her and into the double-height front hallway. Ahead of them was a sweeping, curved staircase. On the right hand side was a large living room, tastefully decorated, complete with a marble fireplace that looked like it had never been used. Across from the living room was what looked like a home office with bookcases crammed with leather-bound books and a giant mahogany desk with a captain's chair. Sofia guessed that this had been Nigel's office.

"You're the housekeeper." Sofia framed it as a statement rather than a question. "Sorry, Mrs. Fairbroad told me your name, but it's slipped my mind."

"Perla," said the woman.

Sofia put out her hand. "I'm Sofia."

Perla shook a little tentatively. "I know who you are. My daughters watched your TV show."

Finally, thought Sofia, her fame was working for her. "Oh, really? What are their names?"

Partly she wanted to get Perla on her side, but she had always taken an interest in people who had taken an interest in her. There was nothing more awful to Sofia than someone who treated the people with contempt who made their career possible and paid their bills. She had seen lots of actors complain about fans over the years, and she had vowed to never become one of those actors.

She still remembered how exciting it had been when she had first moved to LA with her mom and sister and saw people she recognized from movies and TV. Even if it wasn't that magical after she stepped behind the curtain, that didn't mean she had to ruin the illusion for everyone else.

"Marie and Jennifer," said Perla.

"Sweet," said Sofia. "How old are they?"

"Marie just started college at UCLA, and Jennifer is graduating high school this year." Perla seemed to be starting to warm up.

"You must be so proud," said Sofia.

"They're good girls," said Perla with a smile. "And you, you are real detective now?"

"Yup," said Sofia. "Not just playing one on TV. But I'm still in training and I'm more an investigator rather than a detective."

"That is nice," said Perla uncertainly.

Sofia figured that with the small talk out of the way, this was her chance to get some inside information. "Maybe I got the time wrong. Did Mrs. Fairbroad say how long she was going to be?"

Perla shrugged. "Another hour. She went to the spa."

Sofia would have guessed that Melissa would be at a meeting with Stark planning her defense. Or making arrangements for her husband's funeral. A spa visit was an odd choice for the top of her 'To Do' list on the day she was widowed, but it kind of figured.

"What spa does she go to?" she asked Perla.

"I don't know the name," said Perla. "I think it's down on San Vincente and South Bundy."

Sofia's knowledge of Brentwood's finest day spas was less than complete, but she figured there couldn't be that many spas on the corner of San Vicente and South Bundy. "I think I know the one. So, Perla, you must be pretty upset about Mr. Fairbroad?"

"Oh, yes," said Perla. "He was a very nice man. It's so scary what happened to him."

At least someone cared that Nigel had died yesterday. But Sofia didn't have time to go there. She needed to cut to the chase before Melissa returned from whatever she was getting done, but it was a delicate topic. She couldn't exactly come straight out and ask whether Perla thought Melissa had killed her husband, or whether she'd been cheating on him. "Did you notice any strange visitors over the last few days? People hanging around outside? Anyone who looked out of place? Someone who came to work on the house?"

Perla took a moment to think it over. "It's a quiet neighborhood."

She had that right. Pacific Palisades was about as white bread as it got, even compared to somewhere like Santa Monica. Sofia didn't have the exact crime statistics for the area, but there was a reason why the LAPD cops referred to West Los Angeles as West Latte Division. Sure, they had crime here, but it was nothing when compared to other parts of the city.

"What about Mr. and Mrs. Fairbroad? Were they getting along? Did you hear them arguing?" Sofia held her breath. This could go either way. If Perla told Melissa that Sofia had asked about her relationship with Nigel, she was likely to go off the deep end, and Maloney Investigations could lose this gig entirely. But Perla might have good information, so she had to ask.

Perla didn't respond. Sofia stayed silent and counted to

ten in her head. Slowly. People hated dead air time. Especially awkward silences. If she backed off and let Perla stew, she bet she'd fill it.

Right on cue, Perla said, "You don't say anything to Mrs. Fairbroad?"

Perla was looking at the floor rather than Sofia. That was a pretty good sign that something had been going on in the house.

"Absolutely. I won't repeat anything you say to Mrs. Fairbroad." Sofia chose her words with care. She wouldn't say anything to Melissa, or her attorney, but she'd have to share anything relevant with Brendan and Aidan.

Perla waved for Sofia to follow her. They walked through into a large, lavish, and spotless kitchen. The cabinets looked handmade, the appliances were all top of the line Subzero and Miele brands, and the counters were polished granite. Typical kitchen for these parts.

"You want coffee?" Perla asked.

"No, thank you." Melissa could be back at any second. Sofia needed to hurry things along without spooking Perla. "So, Mr. and Mrs. Fairbroad?"

Perla shrugged. "They always argue. Ever since I work here."

"How long have you worked for them?"

"About five years," said Perla.

"And they've always argued?"

"Never this bad," said Perla.

"So it got worse over the past few months?"

Perla opened a cupboard, took out a mug and poured herself a cup of coffee from a pot on the counter. "Yes, the past few months."

"What kind of things were they arguing over?"

Perla blew on the coffee before taking a sip. "Money.

Mrs. Fairbroad spending too much of it. I don't think Mr. Fairbroad spent money on himself. Just this house and a nice car. A couple of weeks ago, Mr. Fairbroad came home early, and there was a credit card bill. He must have picked it up and seen what was on it, because as soon as she walked in the door, he shouted at her. He said she needed to stop her crazy spending. She got angry. She said it was her money, too. Then he said that she didn't make any money. Like that until she leaves. She almost broke the door when she close it so hard."

Sofia made a note to ask Aidan to run a more detailed credit check on the Fairbroads' finances. Arguing about money was hardly unusual. She'd read that it was the number one source of friction in most marriages, but it was still a good lead. Something else occurred to Sofia. "Was he mad about the amount of money she was spending, or what she was spending it on?"

Perla thought it over. "Both. She practically lives at the spa, goes three, sometimes four times a week. Very expensive."

In itself, there was nothing unusual about a woman like Melissa spending so much time at a spa. For a wealthy, married woman without a job and a busy husband, living in an area like Brentwood, it was probably fairly typical. Some women probably went most days. But going to the spa right after your husband was murdered? When you were probably the cop's number one suspect? That didn't seem like normal behavior to Sofia. And even if it could be explained away by someone hanging onto their usual routine in order to deal with the shock of such an event, it sure as hell wasn't smart.

If Melissa was charged, and it got as far as a trial (which it almost certainly would if the DA wanted it to), her actions would be used against her by a jury. Any prosecutor worth his salt would ask the same question of a jury that Sofia was asking herself now. What normal person whose husband has just been killed skips off to keep their regular spa appointment?

18

Sofia had been wrong when she'd figured she could find the spa without too much trouble. She counted at least two day-spas, a beauty salon, and a hair salon all within a block of the intersection of San Vicente and South Bundy streets in Brentwood. There were also several high-priced boutiques, any number of fancy restaurants and upmarket cafes, and a bunch of other places where Brentwood housewives with too much time and too many credit cards could blow through thousands of dollars without having to walk more than a few hundred yards.

The first spa that Sofia checked out haughtily refused to tell her whether or not Melissa Fairbroad was a client, claiming client confidentiality like a doctor on TV. Sofia waited for the manager to leave to deal with a major crisis (likely, a broken nail) and slipped the receptionist fifty bucks. Client confidentiality was suspended long enough for her to learn that this spa wasn't Melissa's preferred pampering hangout.

The second spa was called BOS, which stood for Brentwood Organic Spa. Sofia pushed through the polished glass door and into the plush reception area. A bunch of over-stuffed white and cream-colored couches and chaise lounges were scattered around the reception area. Not seeing any staff, or customers, Sofia perched on a chaise.

A few minutes passed before a door opened, and a young, blond man appeared. He was dressed in long, flowing white robes and carrying an iPad. He looked at Sofia, then at the screen, and back at Sofia.

"I'm sorry. Can I help you?" he asked.

"I hope so," said Sofia. "I'm trying to track down my friend Melissa Fairbroad. I was supposed to meet her, but I guess she must have forgotten our appointment because her housekeeper said she was down here, maybe getting a facial."

The blond man's gaze shifted past Sofia to the street outside. She turned to see what he was looking at just in time to watch Melissa Fairbroad drive slowly past in a pearl-white Benz convertible with the top down. "Looks like you just missed her."

"Damn," said Sofia. "Looks like I just did."

The phone on the desk rang.

"If you'll excuse me," he said, putting his iPad down on the counter in front of her.

He stood with his back to her as he picked up the hand-set. She plucked her cell phone from her pocket and made a show of holding it at arm's length and peering at the screen. She looked past it at the iPad.

From years spent in producer's offices, she had acquired an uncanny ability for reading papers, documents, and more recently, screens, upside down. It was amazing what people left in plain sight for the upside down reader.

On the iPad screen was what looked like a list of the day's appointments. She picked out Melissa Fairbroad's name, a time of 1 p.m. and next to it the words "Chakra Massage," then "Therapist: Moonbow."

"I'll see if he's available," the blond was saying to the person on the other end of the line. He turned round and grabbed the iPad from the desk. "He's available tomorrow morning. How does ten suit you? Okay. Perfect. We'll see you then."

He ended the call, put the handset back and turned back to Sofia. "Is there anything else I can help you with?"

"Yes," said Sofia, steeling herself to do something that she found more embarrassing than urinating in public while being filmed. "My chakras are really." She stopped, trying to think of the correct term. "They're really blocked. You wouldn't have anyone available to ... unblock them, would you?"

The blond guy didn't even blink. He raised a finger in the air as if testing the direction of the wind. "You're in luck. Moonbow's two thirty just cancelled. I can see if he's available."

19

S ofia sat by herself in a small, white room and drew a line under the heading for her new list: "Things I Assumed I Could Go My Whole Life Without Saying".

1. "My chakras are really blocked."
2. "Of course I don't think keeping your stuffed dead cat in your bedroom is weird." (Dating related)
3. Please stop putting adult diapers on my desk.

She had already changed from her regular clothes into a flowing white robe similar to the one the guy manning the reception area had been wearing. She thought she looked a little like Jesus or early Princess Leia.

She had also been given tea that tasted like feet and was supposed to 'open' her chakras, to make the massage more effective. As soon as she'd been left alone, she had dumped the tea into a nearby plant. She couldn't be definite, but she was pretty sure that plant's leaves were starting to turn black at the tips. Better the plant than her.

The door opened. Sofia had to bite down on her lower lip to keep from laughing as Moonbow swept into the room wearing long, flowing purple robes that accentuated his dark blue eyes. In his early forties, he had thick, graying hair tied back in a ponytail and a moustache that wouldn't have looked out of place on a Western gunfighter. In fact, he looked kind of like Sam Neill, but taller. He would have been sexy in jeans and a cowboy shirt, but the robes detracted from that effect.

Without saying anything, he stood with his hands on his slim hips and closed his eyes. He took a deep breath, and exhaled slowly. His hands came up and moved in a circle as if he were doing Tai Chi. Even though he looked weird doing it, Sofia had to admit that he had sexy hands—strong, with long fingers.

"Stand up for me, please," he said.

Sofia stood.

"You have a thick aura," he said in a slightly stoned-sounding California accent, his eyes still closed. "Your fifth chakra is badly constricted. You also need work done on your manipura or lustrous gem, that is to say, your third chakra."

Sofia was starting to regret her decision to book the session. She didn't let just any guy near her lustrous gem, never mind a forty-something dude in purple robes.

Moonbow opened his eyes, and she was impressed by his eyelashes. He had really great eyelashes for a guy.

Rather than looking at her, he stared off into the distance and took another deep breath. "Please remove your robe, lie down on the table, and we can begin."

What the hell? She was pretty sure if Moonbow's hands

wandered near her lustrous gem she'd be more than capable of dealing with it. She hadn't spent all those hours sweating it out at the gym for nothing. She was also pretty sure that this might be the only way she might get the information she needed from Moonbow about Melissa Fairbroad. She certainly wouldn't find out anything if she ran out screaming.

"There is a towel here." Moonbow lifted a large white bath towel from a hook and handed it to her. The towel was warm. "I'll be back in a moment."

Moonbow disappeared back through the door. Rather self-consciously, Sofia took off her robe, lay face-down on the table, and placed the towel over her ass. She had kept her cell phone, and set it on the chair. It was going to record whatever conversation took place between them. If Moonbow killed her, at least there would be proof. Aidan would probably think it was pretty funny if she died in some kind of chakra-opening accident.

A few moments later, the door opened again, and footsteps slapped across the floor. She saw purple sandals through the face rest. She assumed they belonged to Moonbow. She noted, somewhat randomly, that he had the most perfectly pedicured toenails of any man she'd known. Not that she spent a lot of time checking out men's feet, but moustache notwithstanding, he clearly spent a lot of time on personal grooming.

Moonbow began massaging her shoulders and lower back. She had to admit that it felt pretty damn amazing. He kneaded a couple of knots below her shoulder blades. He might have looked a little weird in his purple robes, but he definitely had some kind of magic touch. The stresses and strains of the last few days melted away. She had to remind herself that she was here for another reason before she sunk into a blissful stupor right there on the table.

She wasn't exactly sure how to ask him about Melissa. After all, if Melissa found out that Sofia had been asking people about her, she might not be too happy about it. But that was her job.

Sofia figured that she'd work her way round to Melissa. It would be less suspicious that way. "So how long have you been clearing chakras, Moonbow?"

As soon as the words were out of her mouth, she realized how dumb they sounded. It was the massage equivalent of asking your hair stylist where they planned on going on vacation, or a cab driver if he'd been busy.

"It's better if you remain silent while I work," said Moonbow.

"Sorry." So much for getting info on Melissa.

"Ssshhh," said Moonbow.

Moonbow continued to work his way down her spine, and Sofia decided she had no choice but to relax and enjoy the massage. He seemed to be discovering knots and muscle tension she hadn't known she had. She was starting to see why Melissa was such a frequent visitor. At a hundred bucks for a half hour, Chakra massage was serious money, but it seemed totally worth it.

As Moonbow seemed to be winding down, she decided to take the more direct route. "I can't believe Melissa's been keeping you a secret from me all this time."

"Oh, you mean Mrs. Fairbroad?" said Moonbow.

Finally, thought Sofia, she was getting somewhere. "Yeah. Terrible news about her husband."

Moonbow didn't say anything. Sofia wondered if he'd heard her. "They think he was murdered."

Moonbow lifted his hands away suddenly, and she missed them.

"Okay," he said. "You can get dressed again. If you need another appointment, talk to Leo in reception."

She heard him walk to the door, open it, go through, and close it behind him. She hadn't even had the opportunity to ask Moonbow if he'd managed to unblock her lustrous jewel.

20

Sofia practically floated out to her car. She didn't know about her chakras, but she felt more relaxed than she had in months. It was like being stoned, without the cloudy head, paranoia, or craving for pizza.

As she hit the clicker to unlock the Tesla someone shouted her name. She turned to see a blond woman in tight Lycra running gear pushing a baby stroller toward her. She had no idea who the woman was.

"I thought it was you." The blond mom took Sofia's hand in hers like they were old friends. "It is so good to see you getting your life back together." She lowered her voice to a breathy whisper. "Addiction is a cruel disease."

There was no point in trying to tell a woman she had never met before that she wasn't an addict. She would think that Sofia was in denial.

"Thank you," said Sofia. "That really means a lot."

The blonde gave her hand another squeeze. "Stay strong."

"I will," Sofia told her, using her old acting chops to look sad.

Out of the corner of her eye, Sofia saw the front door of the Brentwood Organic Spa open and a man walk out. He was dressed in a gray chalk-striped suit and white shirt with black tasseled loafers. If it hadn't have been for the moustache, she would never have guessed it was Moonbow, obviously back in his civilian clothes. He looked a lot better dressed like a normal person. He had his cell phone pressed to his ear.

Sofia moved so that the woman with the stroller was between her and Moonbow. "I really appreciate your concern."

"Oh, you're quite welcome. I was an actress before I met my husband, so I know how tough the business is on women. Especially strong, independent women like you."

"It sure is," said Sofia, her eyes fixed on Moonbow, who was looking out into the street.

There was something different about him. It wasn't just that he had ditched his purple robes for a suit. His whole demeanor seemed to be different. The way he stood, the way he walked, his posture, everything. It took a moment before it clicked what she was looking at. It was like watching an actor who had completely nailed a character, right down to the tiniest gestures, suddenly emerge from their trailer at the end of a day's shooting and suddenly be themselves again. Moonbow had talent.

"Was it alcohol or pills?" the blond mom was asking her.

Moonbow stepped off the curb as a white Benz convertible pulled up. He got into the passenger seat next to Melissa Fairbroad. She leaned over and kissed him. On the lips. It was a long, lingering kiss rather than a friendly peck. *Uh-oh.*

"It's none of my business, right?" the blond mom was saying. "I shouldn't have asked you that."

"No, it's fine," Sofia said, completely transfixed by Moonbow and Melissa's canoodling in broad daylight. Jeez, at least she could have been smart enough to put the top up on the car.

"Stay strong," said the woman. "I believe in you."

21

Once Sofia was away from the worried mom and back in her Roadster, she called Brendan and told him that she'd just seen Melissa Fairbroad kissing her massage therapist, Moonbow, in the middle of the street in broad daylight. That seemed like important news.

"You're sure it was her?" Brendan sounded skeptical.

Sofia didn't blame him. If she hadn't seen them together with her own eyes, she would have been skeptical, too. "Yeah. Right out in the middle of Brentwood like she didn't have a care in the world."

"I'll let Stark know," said Brendan.

"Why?" Sofia was still worried that their client might not like the idea of her own PIs spying on her.

"Because he's the best guy to tell her to start using some common sense. If she keeps up like this, it won't matter how good her legal team is," said Brendan.

Sofia heard him move the phone away from his ear long enough to shout through to Aidan, "Hey, Aidan, we're gonna need a background check on a massage therapist by the name of Moonbow working out of a place in Brentwood called the Brentwood Organic Spa."

Brendan came back on the line. "You get any name for him other than Moonbow?"

"Nope," said Sofia.

"She isn't doing herself any favors." Brendan seemed to be thinking aloud. "Locking lips with some dude in public means she's either innocent or dumb, or both."

"If she was involved with someone else, maybe he went after Nigel so he could be with her," said Sofia.

"Now you're thinking," said Brendan. "That's exactly the kind of muddy-the-waters thinking Stark is going to need if he's going to get his client off the hook."

Brendan had a point. They hadn't been hired to solve the murder so much as to offer enough doubt so Stark could do his job with a jury—assuming the cops went after Melissa after all.

"Do you want me to come back to the office now?" Sofia asked.

"No," said Brendan. "Aidan told me that they're shooting that TV show of Nigel's up in Topanga. Why don't you head up there first? It's on your way. Just ask around. When did anyone last see Nigel? How did he seem? Had he fallen out with anyone? Was he sleeping with any of the crew or with someone back at the office? Y'know, the usual kind of stuff."

"You mean gossip?" said Sofia.

"Precisely," said Brendan.

22

A narrow road with switchbacks and steep drops, the road up into Topanga Canyon demanded all of Sofia's attention. The set of *Swamptrash Survival* was actually an old ranch up in Topanga Oaks. Sofia stopped off at the Topanga Creek General Store to pick up dinner, a bottle of water, and lunchmeat for Fred. She asked the cashier for directions to the ranch, paid for her groceries, and headed back out to the parking lot.

Out front, an elderly lady was holding up a sign protesting the Kuwait War. Her placard said something rude about President Bush. The first one. Sofia wondered if the frayed cardboard sign was some kind of environmental homage to recycling. Or a deliberate attempt to highlight the fact that invading foreign countries had become a recurring theme of American foreign policy. Or if the elderly lady had smoked a little too much of Topanga's finest herb and really thought it was still 1991. After all, unlike the rest of the city, Topanga didn't seem to change that much. It still looked pretty much the same as when Sofia had seen it when she, her mom, and sister had first moved out to California almost twelve years ago. That was much of its charm.

Sofia turned off Topanga Canyon Boulevard and headed up a steep hill. At the top of the hill, she took a left, following the cashier's directions. The road narrowed and ended at a gate. Sofia got out. She worried she'd taken the wrong turn until she saw a production company sign tacked to one of the gate posts. She opened the gate, got back into the Roadster, and drove down a bumpy, rutted track with oak trees on either side.

Six hundred yards farther, the track began to slope down. A hundred yards after that, the oak trees thinned to reveal a wide meadow filled with vehicles, including a half dozen or so Winnebago trailers. That was a film set.

She parked the Tesla with the rest of the crew cars and headed for the trailers. If she was going to get anywhere here, she knew from personal experience the people she had to speak to first, and get on her side or at least not piss off, were the production's Teamsters.

They weren't hard to spot. She spotted a likely candidate standing by the main production trailer, smoking a cigarette. He had a biker's beard and a huge barrel chest and looked like a Teamster. It helped that he was wearing a T-shirt emblazoned with the letters IBT Local 399, which was the local Teamster's union that covered members working in the motion picture and television industry in the greater Los Angeles area.

"Hey," said Sofia, always ready with a witty opener.

The teamster took a long drag on his smoke. "What's up?"

"Not too much. I'm trying to find out what happened to Nigel Fairbroad. Maybe you can answer some questions?"

"You a reporter?"

"Private investigator, though I used to be in the business. You know Jimmy Artane?"

Jimmy Artane had been the Teamster captain on *Half Pint Detective* until he'd had a massive heart attack on set one day and had taken early retirement. A huge bear of a man, he'd come from a family of Teamsters that went back several generations. Despite the Teamsters' sometimes militant reputation, he'd been well respected by everyone. He looked after his union members but would bend the rules where he had to in order to help the production company. If you were fair with Jimmy, he was fair with you. If you crossed him, then you'd better look out.

"Sure," said the teamster. "How's he doing?"

The question pulled Sofia up short. It had been a couple of years since she last spoke to him. She made a mental note to go see him and his family as soon as this case was finished.

"I haven't talked to him in a while," she said. "Last I heard though he was making steady progress. Think he had a couple of stents put in."

The Teamster pushed his sunglasses back up onto his forehead. "This stays between us?"

"Absolutely." Sofia was suddenly optimistic. People tended not to ask for confidentiality unless they actually had something significant to tell you.

"Now looky here. What do we have here? I'm guessing fresh meat. Finger lickin' good, too."

The southern drawl came from behind her. Sofia turned to see Tucker Trimble standing there, staring unashamedly at her ass. He was barefoot and bare-chested. The only clothes he had on were a pair of army green camouflage cargo pants and a battered John Deere baseball cap. Greasy brown hair ran down to his shoulders, and he was sporting thick, dark stubble. A long hunting knife dangled from a strap around his waist. He looked just like he did on the show, although the TV didn't capture his smell.

Tucker put his hand out to Sofia. "Tucker Trimble, but you can call me TT. That stands for Tucker Trimble. TT, see? Not titties, though I do like me some nice titties." Tucker moved his laser-like gaze from Sofia's face to her chest. His small, pink tongue darted across his lips for emphasis. Clearly, Tucker was either still in character or not the fizziest drink in the refrigerator.

He sidled up next to her and dropped his hand right onto her breast and started kneading it like it was bread dough. The Teamster leaned forward as if he was about to do something, but Sofia had always found the best way to deal with an unreconstructed sexist, or any man who regarded women as pieces of meat, was for a woman to establish firm boundaries on her own. She brought her right knee up as hard as she could into Tucker's groin.

Tucker let out a decidedly unmanly shriek of pain and doubled over. Sofia took a step back as Tucker fell to his knees. She resisted the urge to follow up with a swift rabbit punch to the back of his head. She'd made her point.

"Touch me again, and I'll take that hunting knife from you and make sure you're singing falsetto in the church choir," she told him.

Tucker moaned. He raised one hand, palm out, in a gesture of surrender.

Sofia glanced over at the Teamster. "Please tell me he's an actor in character."

A lot of the cast of reality TV shows were people who

deliberately hammed it up for the cameras, often with the producer's encouragement. Regular people behaving normally didn't usually make for great Nielsen ratings.

The Teamster shook his head. "Nope. Tucker here is the real deal. Straight outta Kentucky."

Tucker rocked back and forth on his knees. He swept the hair from in front of his face and managed a grimace she thought was probably supposed to be a smile. "Oooh, I like 'em feisty. Yes, sir."

Sofia saw that Tucker was not a man who recognized boundaries easily. "I'm not joking about cutting them off."

"Okay, okay," said Tucker. "I'll be a good boy."

"Promise?" Sofia said.

"Redneck's honor," he replied, spitting on the palm of his hand and reaching out to shake.

Sofia backed up. "It's okay. I'll take your word for it."

A production coordinator sporting a headset plugged into a walkie talkie wandered over toward them. "We need you on set if we're going to get the gator wrestling scene in before lunch."

The production coordinator stopped as she noticed that the show's star was on his knees in the dirt.

"You okay, Tucker?" she asked, giving Sofia a wary look.

Slowly, Tucker got back up. He rubbed his groin. "The show must go on, right?"

He half smiled at Sofia. "Think I might be safer wrasslin' a gator."

Sofia returned his smile. "Maybe you're not as dumb as you look."

She resisted the urge to go and immediately wash the breast he had touched, and instead stood impassively watching him.

The production coordinator took Tucker by the elbow

and gently guided him off toward an area where two small alligators were sitting in a large metal pen, presumably ready for their close up.

Sofia wasn't sure who to feel sorrier for. On one side was an animal with a brain the size of a shriveled walnut completely driven by primal urges that could be traced back to the earliest prehistoric swamp, and on the other the two alligators. In the end, she decided her sympathies lay with the gators. After all, no one had bothered to ask them if they wanted to become reality television stars. They probably didn't even have an agent.

Now that Tucker was gone, the Teamster was positively beaming at Sofia. "About time someone put Tucker in his place."

"Not popular on set?" Sofia asked.

"He was fine when he started. But as soon as the show started to do well, his true character started to show."

"Which is?" said Sofia.

The Teamster rubbed at his beard. "Between us?"

"Strictly," Sofia said.

"He's a complete asshole," the Teamster said. "I've worked with some real prima donnas in my time, but this guy is off the charts. Rude, demanding, racist, sexist, terrible personal hygiene. You name an unappealing quality in a human being, and he possesses it."

"The swamp trash thing isn't an act then?" Sofia said.

"No, he's the real deal. Done prison time, too. The PR people for the show have managed to keep that under wraps."

"Prison? Back in Kentucky?"

"I don't know all the details, but I think so," said the Teamster.

Sofia made a mental note to have Aidan look into it, if he

hadn't already. If there was dirt to be found on someone, Aidan would find it. As annoying as he was, and he could be really, really annoying, when it came to investigation, he was good at what he did.

"Did he and Nigel have any run-ins?" said Sofia as one of the alligators reared up and lunged against the bars of its cage while Tucker poked a stick at it from outside.

The teamster looked around, making sure no one else from the crew was close enough to overhear. "A few, yeah. Every time the ratings jumped, Tucker wanted something else. A new trailer. A personal assistant. A bigger fee."

"Did Nigel give him what he asked for?" Sofia asked.

"Pretty much," said the Teamster. "He drew the line at the personal assistant when Tucker held an open casting for that position at his hotel."

Sofia hated to imagine what a Tucker Trimble open casting call involved. "Did Tucker ever threaten Nigel?"

"Lady, Tucker threatens everyone. Don't get me wrong, a lot of the time he can be as nice as pie, but if he's not getting his way ... Well, you saw what he's like."

Over by the gator pen, Tucker was dancing around and generally acting like a clown for the crew. Sofia was sorely tempted to open the pen, push him in and let them fight it out. Pretty much the only thing stopping her was a worry that the alligators might come down with a bad case of food poisoning if they chowed down on Tucker.

"Did he ever threaten Nigel?" Sofia pressed.

"Are you asking me that or are you asking if I think he killed him?" the Teamster said.

"Both, I guess," said Sofia.

"I didn't ever hear him threaten Nigel directly. But did he kill him? I don't know anything that suggests he did. Is he capable of it? I'd say he is. But then a lot of people are capable of a lot of things. Doesn't mean they do them."

Back over at the gator pen, Tucker pulled his knife from its sheath and spun it around in his hand. He looked over in Sofia's direction and winked.

23

Brendan threw an 8 x 10 black-and-white photograph down onto his desk. Sofia reached over and picked it up. In her previous career, an 8 x 10 inch photograph usually signified an actor's headshot and had a resume stapled to the back. What she found herself looking at now was a close-up of a man's hand. Or, more precisely, what was left of a man's hand. Three of the fingers were missing, leaving ragged, bloody stumps where his middle, index and pinkie fingers would normally have been. Sofia had already worked out that it had to have been the left hand because part of his wedding ring was still intact, bound round a fragment of bone like a piece of macabre Gothic jewelry.

Sofia handed the photograph off to Aidan, feeling sorry for Nigel again.

Aidan took a look. "Poor guy. Must have put his hand up just before he was shot."

"Yeah, gun was probably less than two feet from him when it was fired. As clear a defensive wound as you're likely to see. He didn't stand a chance." Brendan cleared his throat.

"By the way, we haven't officially seen this. I had to call in a few favors downtown to get access to this stuff."

Aidan handed the photograph back to his father, and Brendan placed it back in a folder with the other information he'd been given from Nigel's autopsy.

"Whoever did this," Brendan said, "was either a professional, or at least had the stomach of one. Or, and this is equally likely, it was someone really ticked off at Nigel. It takes a lot to pull the trigger on an unarmed man who's trying to shield his face with his hand."

"Maybe they thought he was trying to grab the gun," Sofia said.

"That's good," said Brendan. "I like that. I don't believe it, but it's a possibility. If they do tie the weapon to Melissa, then Stark will have to try to construct some kind of self-defense case. Them fighting over the gun and it going off ... Well, it's LA, you might find a jury who'd buy that. Hell, if they could acquit OJ in this town, then anything's possible."

Sofia knew that the OJ Simpson case was a sore point for Brendan, as it was for most former or current LAPD officers. If they'd been serving at the time, they were all a hundred percent convinced of his guilt. "So Melissa is still the prime suspect?"

"So far," said Brendan. "If I was a betting man, I'd say they're waiting to get the green light from the DA before they arrest her, and the fun really begins. I'm not sure they're convinced she pulled the trigger, but they're fairly certain she's involved somehow."

Sofia's mind immediately flashed on Moonbow getting into Melissa's Benz outside the spa and their passionate greeting.

"How about you give us a full report of your day, Sofia?" Brendan asked.

"OK. But it may not all be good news for Melissa's defense." Sofia took out her notes. She ran through her day, including what the housekeeper had told her about Melissa and Nigel's arguments about money. She told them about her visit to the spa and her up close and personal encounter with Moonbow. She skated over the chakra massage. She'd tell Brendan later, but Aidan would only use it as a way of getting a week's worth of double entendres and jokes about how handy a blocked chakra would have been back in the parking lot of the rehab place. Then went on to the kiss she'd witnessed between Melissa and Moonbow.

Aidan looked annoyed. "Hard to believe the guy's real name is Moonbow."

Sofia shrugged. "It's California. I knew a kid in school whose name was Celestial Spring Jakowski."

"And you complained about your mother and I giving you a good Irish name," Brendan said to Aidan.

Aidan put his hands up. "I'll never complain about that again."

It was rare to hear Brendan mention his late wife. She had died of cancer when Aidan was a teenager, and Sofia had often wondered if Aidan's search for the unattainable perfect woman was his attempt at avoiding a real relationship and therefore not getting hurt again. Not that she'd ever say that to him. Or at least not until he stopped leaving adult diapers on her desk. It was difficult to have an adult conversation with a grown man who thought incontinence was hilarious.

Brendan brought them back on task. "What else, Sofia?"

She told them about her visit to the set of *Swamptrash Survival* up in Topanga and brought them up to speed with her Tucker Trimble encounter. "Trimble definitely had his runs in with Nigel from what the Teamster captain on the show told me, and he has a record back in Kentucky."

"Aidan," said Brendan.

"Already on it," said Aidan.

"Good work," said Brendan. "Though I'd advise that kneeing someone you're interviewing in the groin may not quite be textbook procedure."

"He started it," said Sofia. She wasn't going to apologize, but she did feel bad about it. Not because she'd hurt Trimble, or his testicles (she could only hope that she might have taken him out of the shallow end of the gene pool with her single blow), but because it did lack a certain amount of professionalism. But her breasts were her own private breasts, and she wasn't going to apologize for protecting them.

"Aidan, what do you have?" Brendan asked.

Aidan picked up a fat pile of papers next to his chair and theatrically dumped them on Brendan's desk. He was the data king, sure, but he had a bit of the drama queen about him, too.

Brendan picked up the papers and began sifting through them. He'd scan a page before handing it off to Sofia. "Give us the highlights."

"The big story is that there was a ton of financial activity over the past six months," Aidan said. "Nigel was moving money around at warp speed. Shifting five and six figures sums between accounts. Taking out new credit cards like they were about to stop offering them. Moving balances to new cards to pay off old ones. Also credit card charges in weird places out of town."

"Like hotels?" Sofia asked.

"Hotels. Spas. Flights to Europe. I went back two years

and up until six months ago their spending patterns were pretty predictable," Aidan said. "Then it changed."

"The hotels could have been Melissa and Moonbow?" said Sofia.

"That was my first thought," Aidan said. "But I checked the reservations, and they were for Nigel."

"Maybe he was having an affair, too," Brendan said. "He finds out that Melissa's cheating and decides that what's good for the goose is good for the gander. That kind of a deal."

"Possible," said Aidan.

"So all this money that was being moved around. Did he have financial problems?" Brendan asked.

"That's how it looks. Oh, and about two months ago he set up a life insurance policy using that new credit card money. Melissa's the sole beneficiary," Aidan said. "For a million dollars. He had to go get a medical before the insurance company would sign off on it."

"He passed?" said Sofia.

"With flying colors," said Aidan.

Brendan picked the black-and-white morgue picture up from desk and studied it. "We know the poor guy didn't die from natural causes. That's one thing we can be certain of."

"So Melissa's set for a while," said Sofia.

"And Moonring," said Aidan.

"Moonbow," Sofia corrected him.

"Whatever," said Aidan.

It wasn't looking good for their client. Melissa seemed to have one motive stacked on top of another. From a secret lover to a fractured relationship with her husband and a nice, juicy insurance policy that would pay for a lot of spa visits. Brendan was right. The cops were running behind, but they'd catch up, and when they did, Melissa, and probably Moonbow, would be taking the perp walk in the full glare of LA's voracious media.

Brendan's thoughts must have been running along similar lines. "Let's keep digging on Trimble. All we need is enough to put doubt in the minds of a jury. If Trimble has a record, and he banged heads with Nigel, that might be enough."

"You think?" Aidan asked.

Brendan shrugged. "Not really, but it's all we got. Let's call it a day. You kids go have fun. I'll see you in the morning."

Aidan almost jumped from his chair. Sofia was pretty sure he had at least one, and possibly two or three, Tinder dates awaiting him. Somewhere, several unfortunate women were doing their makeup and getting ready for a date with a man who would inevitably find some minute flaw that would give him grounds to dismiss them as a future second date/girlfriend/partner. Either they wouldn't be educated enough, or they'd be too educated. They'd be too bossy or too passive. Or they'd have a tattoo or a piercing somewhere other than their ears, or some other feature from a long list of Aidan's non-negotiables. That would lead them to being nexted, which was the term Aidan actually used when he'd decided a woman he was seeing was no longer worthy of his time. But right now that wasn't what was bothering Sofia.

She cleared her throat. "What if she actually is guilty and our doing this means that she gets off, or even sends someone who didn't do it to prison?"

Next to her, Aidan rolled his eyes and let out an exasperated, "Oh, boy."

Brendan smoothed his hands across the desk. He took a moment before he spoke. He seemed to be choosing what he said with care. "Sofia, we're not going to go out and frame Tucker Trimble or anyone else. We're not going to plant a gun on him or pay someone to give false testimony. Who does or does not get convicted—if it even comes to that—is a matter for the courts. All we're doing is gathering evidence that may strengthen our client's defense."

Sofia understood exactly what Brendan was saying. She even agreed with it. The American justice system wasn't ideal, but it was a hell of a lot better than vigilantism. People got their day in court. The evidence was heard and assessed by a jury of their fellow citizens. That was all great. But it didn't change the fact that someone with the money to hire a good attorney and someone like Maloney Investigations stood a pretty good chance of beating the rap, whether they were guilty or not.

Brendan seemed to sense Sofia's continued discomfort. "Think back to the OJ Simpson trial."

"Sure." In fact, she had gone through a period when she was about fifteen when she'd read pretty much everything to do with it, and watched all the documentaries she could find about what had been dubbed America's 'trial of the century' where football superstar OJ Simpson had been acquitted of murdering his ex-wife, Nicole Simpson, and her friend, Ron Goldman. She'd even pestered Brendan for weeks with questions about it, which, looking back on it, must have been pretty annoying.

"Okay, so when the defense pulled out those tapes of an LAPD detective using racial slurs, was that fair or not?" Brendan asked.

Sofia remembered the release of the Mark Fuhrman tapes as being a pivotal moment in the racially-charged case. Fuhrman, one of the LAPD's lead investigators, had found key evidence against OJ Simpson. He'd also been caught on tape using racial epithets while helping a woman researching a screenplay about the LAPD. OJ Simpson's defense team had used the tapes to claim that Fuhrman was a racist cop, and he had planted the evidence to convict OJ Simpson, a black man.

"Well, the judge admitted it as evidence, so then yeah," said Sofia.

"Exactly," said Brendan. "We do our job, and we let the system do its job."

"Great." Aidan jack-in-the-boxed out of his chair. "That's settled then. See you tomorrow."

"Sofia?" said Brendan. "Does that make sense?"

Just because it made sense didn't make it right.

24

The sun was sinking down into the waves of the Pacific Ocean as Sofia walked barefoot along the beach. She usually came down here when she needed to clear her head. Feeling the cool sand between her toes and listening to the crash of the waves usually helped her sort through the events of the day and get some perspective on things that troubled her. Tonight, though, it didn't seem to be working.

She understood what Brendan had said about allowing the legal system to do its job. She just wasn't sure it made her feel any better. She had turned her back on a career that millions of people around the world would have killed for. Or at least a career that millions of people around the world thought would be worth killing for (the reality was a little different). But she had done it because she wanted to make a difference in the world. To do something that left the world a better place. And now she was confronted with a situation where, justice system or not, she might be quite literally helping someone get away with murder. That had to be leaving the world a worse place.

Although she'd had the briefest encounter with Nigel Fairbroad, he had seemed like a decent enough man. He hadn't been sleazy. He hadn't hit on her. In fact, he'd helped her out of an awkward situation. Now he was dead. Not movie dead. Real, gone forever, mutilated, and dumped into the sea dead. Never to return. Life over. And the only thing her job demanded of her was that Nigel's death didn't adversely affect Melissa. And she didn't even like Melissa.

It didn't sit right. It didn't seem fair. Not that the world was fair. She knew enough to know that. She wasn't that naive. The world was indifferent and random and beautiful and cruel, often all at the same time. So why did she feel, for the first time since she had started working at Maloney Investigations, that she'd made a mistake? That maybe this wasn't the job for her after all?

She could, if she wanted, always go back to acting. Walking away when her career was on an upswing wouldn't count against her. Not in Hollywood. As far as the movie and TV industry was concerned the word *no* was pretty much the sexiest word in the world. If you were in demand, saying "no" made you more desirable, not less.

The opportunity to go back might not last forever. Eventually there would be a new young actress who would take her place. But she definitely still had a window where she could return to her old working life with no questions asked. It wasn't like she'd be going back to some horrible job, either. She'd been paid ridiculously well for basically dressing up and playing make believe, a job which was sometimes even fun. Her hiatus would make her more interesting to producers and casting directors. All she had to do was say the word, and she could be back in a world of six-figure paydays, where she didn't have to lift so much as a finger, and people would kiss her ass all day long. And she wouldn't have to worry about whether she was making the world better or worse.

"Hey!"

Sofia glanced back over her shoulder to see Jeffrey Wiener scrambling along the beach toward her. His face was red, and he was struggling to catch his breath.

She stopped walking and waited for him to catch up.

"Didn't you hear me calling you?" said Jeffrey between gasps for air.

"Sorry," said Sofia. "I was kind of distracted."

He shot her a sympathetic smile. "Tough day at the office?"

She had forgotten that when he wasn't busy manipulating everyone he came into contact with and generally trying to bend people to his will, her former agent could actually be a sweet guy.

"Something like that." Even if she had wanted to share the details, she wasn't at liberty to. Brendan had drilled the need for client confidentiality into her from the first day. In any case, a gossip like Jeffrey would be the last person she'd share Melissa Fairbroad's problems with. Telling an agent a secret was like taking out an ad in the *LA Times* and hoping no one read it. Okay, she thought, hardly anyone did read the *LA Times* anymore, but telling an agent anything you didn't want spread all over town faster than wildfire was still a bad idea.

Jeffrey stared out over the ocean. "I never get tired of this view."

Sofia smiled. "Me, either."

He glanced over at her. "I guess we both have a lot to thank a little show called *Half Pint Detective* for. And each other. You know I have clients that I'm closer with than my wife."

She wasn't sure that she liked where this was going. "You've been divorced three times."

"That reinforces my point," he said. "It's a bond, Sofia. Especially between an actor and their agent. I mean directors, producers, they come and go. And writers, don't get me started on those schmucks. But actors. You guys really have to put yourselves out there. Open up. Expose your heart and soul, the core of your being, to the world. And I'd like to think my job is to make sure that through that process you feel completely safe. Like I'm your safety net, ready to catch you if you fall."

Sofia, who'd been standing next to Jeffrey as they both enjoyed the sunset, turned to face him. "Jeffrey, why are you giving me your signing speech?"

"My what?" said Jeffrey, unable to meet her eye.

"You know, the speech you give every single person when you want them to sign agency papers so you can represent them," she said.

He dropped his hand onto his chest. "I am hurt that you reduced my words of friendship and kindness to a business pitch."

His eyes seemed to be filling with tears. Either he really was upset, or it was the salt in the air.

"I'm sorry, Jeffrey," Sofia said. "I thought that you were trying to ..." She trailed off. What had she thought he was trying to do? For once, he did seem to be genuinely emotional. "It's been a hard day."

"You mean to say that playing a detective and actually being one are two different things?" he asked, his eyes still moist with tears.

"I guess they are," she said. "I mean, I knew it would be, but the reality of it's starting to sink in." She reached out and put her hand on his shoulder. "Listen, I appreciate your concern. I really do."

"Good," he said. "Because I have an offer for you. I spoke to the network again this morning, and they're prepared to really break the bank to get you for *Celebrity Second Chances*. Of course we'll have to keep the figure to ourselves because they don't want the other talent to know, but they really want to make this happen."

The transformation was remarkable. Within a matter of seconds, his tears had disappeared, and he'd transitioned from concerned friend to talent agent. It was like watching a science fiction TV show where regular human beings transformed into reptilian lizards, only a Hollywood agent in full-on sales mode was even more unsettling. Suddenly the prospect of representing a cold-blooded murderer seemed a lot less daunting than it had minutes before.

"That does sound like a great offer, Jeffrey," she said. "And I really appreciate you getting it for me, even though I'm not actually in the business anymore, and you're not my agent, but I'm going to have to pass."

She turned away and walked back down the beach toward her little blue trailer. Jeffrey chased behind her for a few hundred yards spouting on about things like gross profit participation and how this would be the perfect platform for an eventual return to TV drama and movies, and how there could be a book deal, too. At one point, she was fairly sure he said something like "these days something like drug addiction really offers a terrific cross-media business opportunity to someone with the right platform," and she had to stop to stare at him in disbelief. After that look, he gave up.

BACK AT HER TRAILER, another scavenger was waiting for her. Perched on the railing, Fred the seagull cocked his head as she walked up the steps and let out a loud squawk. She unlocked the front door and propped it open to let in the sea air. She poured herself a glass of wine from a bottle in the refrigerator, put bologna into a bowl, and took it outside for Fred. She sat on the porch sipping at her wine and watched Fred peck at the meat, dropping pieces on the porch floor.

"You're a messy eater, you know that, Fred?" she told him.

He squawked once in answer. It sounded like "whatever."

Taking out her phone, she checked her voicemail. A message from her mom. She was still worried about the rehab clinic incident. A message from her sister asking if Sofia could babysit the niece and nephew for the weekend. And a new message left moments before from Jeffrey apologizing for his behavior but asking her to keep an open mind about the *Celebrity Second Chances* offer. She deleted that one.

Fred had already wolfed down his dinner bowl and was eyeing her wine. "Nope, dude, that's all you're getting. I think you'd be a mean drunk."

Fred squawked again and flapped his wings, but stayed put.

Sofia picked up her wine glass, went back inside, and began to fix dinner for herself. While she waited for the water to boil for her artichokes, she called her mom. Her stepdad picked up.

"Hey, Sofia," he said. "Your mom's out at her book club, but I'll tell her you called. Everything okay?"

"Great," Sofia said. "How are you?"

"Fine. Played golf this morning, did some gardening. Y'know, the usual stuff."

Her stepdad was a man of few words, which was probably just as well because her mom could talk the hind legs off a donkey. He promised he'd pass on the news to her mom that she was great, and not in need of rehab, celeb or otherwise, and hung up.

Next, she called her sister and said she'd be happy to babysit on Saturday so Emily and her husband could go away. They needed the time alone. As she was telling Emily she was available, Sofia heard what sounded like ground warfare in the background. She loved her niece and nephew to bits, but they were, to put it politely, a handful. Her nephew, Van, spent most of his time dismantling things to try to figure out how they worked, and her blond, pony-tailed niece, Violet, was obsessed with mixed martial arts to the point where her elementary school was threatening to expel her if she put one more of her classmates into a choke-hold or performed a move she had invented that involved leaping off of desks. She called it "the flying death claw."

"So, Mom is worried about you," Emily said.

"There's no need. I'm fine."

"How's the job?" her sister asked.

"Good," Sofia said. "Challenging, but good. Better than acting."

"You know I hate you for having the life I wanted and then giving it up, right?" said Emily, cheerfully.

"I know," said Sofia. Emily had made peace with that long ago, and Sofia suspected that she was much happier with her perfect husband and hell-on-wheels kids than Sofia ever was with acting.

"Okay, see you Saturday."

BY THE TIME Sofia had eaten dinner and walked back out onto the porch, Fred had flown off.

She looked up at the dark sky and the few stars able to shine through the light pollution and smog. She picked up her phone and scrolled down to Jose, the barman from Frank's Grotto. She tapped out a text asking him to come over but deleted it. It was late, she was tired, and she had a busy day ahead of her tomorrow. Plus, she wasn't sure if he'd respond to a late night booty call, and she'd had enough humiliation for one week.

She went back inside, took a hot shower, and went to bed. She read for a little while and fell asleep thinking about why someone might have wanted to kill Nigel Fairbroad. She had a little list going:

1. Life insurance money.
2. To run away with Moonbow and live life with wide open chakras.
3. Because they needed gator feed.

25

A idan was already at his desk by the time Sofia arrived at the office at a little before eight o'clock. She picked up the new bag of adult diapers from her chair and walked over to Aidan.

"Don't you think this joke is getting a little old?" she said, smacking the diapers down on his desk.

Aidan looked up from his screen. "Not really, no."

She perched on the edge of his desk. "So how was your date? Or were there dates?"

He held up three fingers.

"Three dates," she said. To think that she'd spent the night home alone after having dinner with a bird.

"First one was a SIF," Aidan said. "So that one was short."

"What's a SIF?" Sofia asked.

"Secret Internet Fatty. I should have guessed when she said she was curvy and didn't have any full body pics," Aidan said.

"You're a disgusting sexist pig. You know that, right?" said Sofia.

Aidan stood up and headed over to the coffee maker. "You want one?"

"No, thanks."

"So you'd date a fat guy who lied about being overweight on his profile?" Aidan said, pouring himself a mug of coffee.

"Maybe or maybe not, but I wouldn't call him names."

"I didn't call her names," said Aidan.

"You just called her a secret Internet fatty!"

"No, I didn't. I said that to you, not her. And you're totally lying. If your date ended up being a SIF, you'd come home after and call all your girlfriends and bitch about how what an awful night you had and how come guys are such lying douchebags, so don't make out like you're somehow superior."

"I absolutely would not," Sofia protested, although he might have been right. "What about the other two lucky ladies?"

Aidan took a sip of coffee and walked back to his desk. "Number two was a bust."

"How come?" Sofia braced herself for his response.

"Didn't shave her legs," he said with a shrug.

Okay, that was kind of gross. Sofia kept going. "That was it?"

"You heard what I just said, right? I mean if she doesn't shave her legs, she probably doesn't shave her, you know what, either," said Aidan.

"So?" Sofia said.

"What do you mean 'so?' " Aidan shot back.

"Don't you think it's weird how guys expect women not to have hair down there now? It kind of creeps me out, the idea that grown women should look like they haven't hit puberty yet."

"Yeah, well you're not me," said Aidan. "Or any one of ninety per cent of male dating partners in LA."

"Thank God," said Sofia. "So what about lucky contestant number three? Too skinny? Too tall?"

Aidan put his coffee down and smiled. "Nope."

"So what was wrong with her?" Sofia asked.

"Nothing."

Sofia couldn't believe what she'd just heard. Since Aidan had started online dating and applied his ridiculous set of criteria, he must have been on hundreds of dates and hadn't found anyone he couldn't find fault with. "Wait. What? Nothing?"

Aidan shrugged. "Nope. She was damn near perfect."

"But not completely perfect?"

"I don't know," Aidan said. "It was a first date. I'm seeing her again on Saturday."

Sofia checked her watch, grabbed a piece of paper, and jotted down the time. Aidan looked at her, puzzled.

"What are you doing?" he asked.

"Logging the time that this momentous news broke to the world: the moment when Aidan Maloney didn't find fault and went for a second date," said Sofia.

"You jealous?"

"No, but I am going to stop shaving my legs just to be on the safe side," said Sofia.

Aidan spun around on his office chair. "Believe me, you have nothing to fear. You fail the Aidan Maloney gold standard in pretty much every main category."

Sofia held up a hand. "Please, don't tell me. I'd like to hold out some tiny glimmer of hope for us."

She leaned over his shoulder. "So have you actually been doing any work this morning or are you simply basking in the glow of finally getting a second date for once in your miserable existence?"

Aidan hit a button, and the left hand screen on his desk filled with an image of a man Sofia recognized as Moonbow, minus his purple robes and moustache and a few years younger. He was wearing prison blues, standing behind a ruler showing his height and holding up a white piece of card with what Sofia guessed was a prison inmate number written on it. He looked cuter without the moustache. She could see what Melissa saw in him.

"Meet Bobby Rogers," said Aidan. "Born in Philly on August 8th, 1965. High school dropout but not dumb. Made a ton of money in the eighties selling timeshare property in Florida. Only problem was that he didn't actually own the holiday condos he was selling."

"If it was timeshare, the people who bought them didn't either." Sofia had been approached by timeshare salesmen before.

Aidan laughed. "Anyway, he got caught by the Feds and sentenced to seven years. Got out after five. Moved onto selling tech stocks out of a New York boiler room operation. Would have taken another fall but was smart enough to rat out some of the other players. Still copped two years, which turned out to be a great deal because the guys he ratted out got twelve."

"So how did he get from that to Moonbow?" Sofia asked.

Aidan stretched his arms out wide. "California, dude. Land of last chances and total reinvention."

"So, he could have met Melissa Fairbroad and seen the chance for a big score after they got the husband out of the way?" Sofia said. "From what I've seen, it wouldn't have been that hard to persuade Melissa that offing Nigel was a good plan. She didn't seem to like him much."

"It's entirely possible." He held up his index finger. "But hold that thought because…"

He reached down and clicked his mouse. Moonbow, aka Bobby Rogers's face disappeared and was replaced by a picture of Tucker "TT" Trimble. He was also holding up a prison number but, unlike Bobby, Tucker looked pretty much exactly the same. The same facial hair, the same straggly hair, and the same mad-dog scowl.

Sofia studied Tucker's mug shot. She guessed that the TV show had one thing right. If it did come to a major breakdown in society or a post-apocalyptic scenario, Tucker would probably be one of the last survivors, along with rats and cockroaches.

"So what was Tucker in for?" she asked Aidan, although the question she really wanted an answer to was why a production company would hire someone with a criminal record for a show where he was put in charge of a bunch of teenagers. Not just any old show either: one with knives, guns, and all kinds of other instruments of wilderness survival training.

"Might take less time if I told you what he wasn't in for," Aidan said. "His jacket's pretty impressive."

He opened a desk drawer, pulled out a manila folder, and passed it to Sofia. She opened it and started reading. Aidan hadn't been lying. It was a pretty extensive record. Most of Tucker's convictions were for some kind of assault. He wasn't a thief or a fraudster like Bobby Rogers. From the newspaper reports Aidan had also assembled, it seemed Tucker had an extremely short temper and love of substances, legal and illegal. Going by one report from his hometown back in Kentucky, he also appeared to have a problem with any kind of authority in general and cops in particular.

Flicking to the final pages of the file, she read a long profile of Tucker written for the first season of the TV show. His colorful past was mentioned, at length, but it had been spun so that he would come off to the casual reader as a likeable tobacco-chewing, moonshine-distilling redneck rogue whose numerous run ins with the law were more *Dukes of Hazzard* than *America's Most Wanted*. Much was made of Tucker's having found Jesus during his last spell in prison and wanting to make recompense to society at large by passing on his backwoods survival skills to troubled teens. Sofia's favorite quote from Tucker was "I can relate to screwed-up kids because I was one." But Tucker's screwed-up adolescence had extended into his late thirties.

Still, as Jeffrey had been trying to impress upon her last night, the great American public did love a tale of redemption. Even more so when it came gift wrapped in homespun, folksy sentiment. Sofia wasn't buying it, and neither was Aidan, but it had clearly worked for Tucker Trimble's fans.

"Fun guy, right?" Aidan said as Sofia handed the file back.

"Oh yeah, a regular comedian in camo."

"You ever watch the show?" Aidan asked.

"A little." She'd watched it before, but she wasn't going to watch it again, not after meeting Tucker in person.

"He's actually pretty good with the kids," Aidan said. "Kind of relatable in a weird way. There was this one episode in the first season where this girl with an eating disorder had a complete meltdown. Tucker stayed out with her the whole night in the pouring rain. It was pretty much the first time in the kid's life that someone hadn't given up on her."

Sofia had always wondered what Aidan did in the evenings when he wasn't finding fault with the single female population of greater Los Angeles. She guessed that his spare hours were filled with bad reality TV shows. Like hers.

"You're saying he's innocent?" she asked.

Aidan shrugged. "No, I think he could be our man. I'm just saying he's not all bad."

The main office door opened, and Brendan walked in. Sofia was going to leave Aidan to break the good news. They had not one but two strong potential suspects in Moonbow and Tucker.

Moonbow's connection to Melissa made him less than ideal, but if he was linked to Nigel's murder, Sofia was sure that Stark would advise Melissa to talk to the cops first and sell him down the river. Sofia doubted Melissa would hesitate for a second if it came down to a choice between her lover and life behind bars. No one was *that* good at opening a woman's chakras.

Brendan walked over to the coffee machine and poured himself a cup. He looked distracted. Sofia could usually gauge his mood pretty easily. He was good at putting on his game face in front of clients and strangers, but working with someone every day, you got to read in between the lines. If Brendan was in a good mood, he was full of good mornings. If he was having a bad morning, he tended to go quiet and was best avoided, at least until he'd had his first cup of coffee.

"I have to make a phone call," Brendan said before disappearing into his office and closing the door.

Sofia looked at Aidan. He gave her an 'I don't know what's up with him either' shrug.

A few minutes later, Brendan's office door opened again, and he stuck his head out. Sofia was pretty sure she smelled cigarette smoke. Brendan had been an on-off smoker since she'd known him. He was also pretty secretive about it because Aidan really didn't like his old man smoking. Brendan sneaking a cigarette in his office qualified as a bad sign.

"Stark wants to see us at his office in an hour," Brendan said.

Sofia exchanged another look with Aidan. He looked as worried as she felt. Another bad sign.

"Problem?" Sofia asked.

"You could say that," said Brendan. "Melissa Fairbroad was just arrested. I've spoken to a couple of people downtown, and the word is they're going to charge her with first-degree murder."

26

Melissa's attorney, John Stark, Esq., had an entire floor of a gleaming office building in Century City. Sofia understood why Maloney Investigations was eager to keep him happy. He must have had at least a dozen other attorneys working for him, not to mention dozens more paralegals, admin, and support staff.

Walking out of the elevator, Aidan, Brendan, and Sofia were greeted by a sparkling reception area manned by two female receptionists. Sofia had barely settled into one of the plush couches before Stark himself appeared and personally escorted them into his large corner office.

"I thought having Aidan and Sofia here would save us time later, John," said Brendan. "I hope you don't mind."

Stark took a seat behind his desk. "Not at all. We need every hand on deck right now." He took a dramatic pause. "I'll be honest with you, Brendan. It's not looking good. Last night the sheriff's department had a tip to go search a boat Nigel Fairbroad had at Marina Del Rey."

"We know who called it in?" Brendan asked.

Stark shook his head. "Came via an anonymous tip line.

I have my suspicions about who it may have been but I'll get to that a little later." He glanced over at Aidan. "I'm guessing from what Brendan told me on the phone this morning that you probably have the same name in mind as I do."

"The wife?" said Aidan.

Stark shrugged. "She has plenty of motive, but she's not my first choice, obviously. Listen, before we dive in, do you guys want anything? Water? Coffee?"

They all declined. Sofia guessed that Aidan and Brendan were as keen as she was to know what the anonymous tipster offered up to the sheriff's department.

"Okay," Stark said. "So the sheriff's department go to check out the boat."

"Was this the one Nigel was dumped from?" Sofia asked. This was the first she'd heard of Nigel owning a boat, never mind one in Marina Del Rey.

Stark shrugged. "Good question. It's looking that way, but last night was the first time anyone had bothered to take a look."

Sofia felt a little better when both Brendan and Aidan looked as she confused as she was. How could the cops not have checked out Nigel's boat when he'd been found washed up on Broad Beach having presumably been dumped out at sea? If his body had been thrown into the ocean from a dock or pier, the tides would have likely brought him ashore pretty quickly if his body hadn't been weighed down.

But not if he'd been dumped on the beach in Malibu and hadn't washed up. That seemed unlikely. Almost every stretch of the Malibu coastline was overlooked by multiple homes or used by surfers or beach bums. You couldn't so much as toss an empty beer can on a Malibu beach without incurring the wrath of at least one wealthy resident. Dumping a body would have been noticed.

"Seems kind of shoddy," said Brendan.

"I agree with you, but now I'm thinking it might have been better if it had stayed like that," said Stark.

"That bad?" Aidan prompted.

"Oh yeah," Stark said. "So the cops get down there, climb aboard, and go below deck. They find empty shell casings, a gun that's the same caliber as the casings, and blood stains, which is exactly what the civic-minded member of the public who called it in told them they'd find."

"How does that link it to Melissa?" Sofia asked.

"Her prints are all over the gun," Stark said.

No one said anything for a few moments as it sunk in. That put Melissa at the scene of the crime. It would be tough to claim she had nothing to do with it now. And it just got harder for Sofia to convince herself that they were doing something good by helping her out.

"The blood?" said Brendan finally.

"They're waiting on the forensics, but odds on the blood will match to Nigel," said Stark.

"With any luck it won't match Mrs. Fairbroad, too," Aidan said.

The wife below deck with a handgun. It was just like the game Clue, and all the other suspects had been crossed out. The situation couldn't have been worse. Unless someone found a video tape of Melissa pulling the trigger and shooting Nigel. Sofia didn't rule out that possibility.

"They have anything apart from blood?" Brendan said. "He had three fingers blown off. There would be bone fragments, a chunk of gold from his wedding ring, something."

"If they did, they haven't mentioned it so far," said Stark.

"It'll come out in disclosure if they have."

Brendan shook his head. "There's neat and then there's too neat."

"No such thing as way too neat for a good prosecutor in front of a jury," Stark said. "They'll get up in court and claim Occam's Razor. The simplest explanation is almost always the correct one. Melissa shot him on the boat, took it out, dumped the body over the side, and hoped that would be that."

"And left the gun lying there with her prints all over it?" Sofia asked.

Stark looked over at Brendan. "Brendan? You handled your fair share of homicides when you were on the force. How would you explain that one?"

Brendan got up and walked to the window. "Criminals are dumb. Or they panic. She was a first timer. Maybe she did as much as she could to cover her tracks, and then the horror of it sunk in. Or maybe she planned on going back and getting the gun. Either way, it doesn't change the fact her prints are on that gun and that gun matches to the slugs the coroner pulled out of Nigel's body."

"Why not dump the gun with the body?" said Sofia. "A gun won't wash up. It'll sink to the bottom."

"Brendan just gave you the answer," Stark said. "She panicked. Or she forgot. Or maybe on some subconscious level, she wanted to be caught. Like he said, the prosecution doesn't have to explain away a screw-up by the defendant any more than it has to justify why someone makes a full confession. The evidence is the evidence. It is what it is."

"But isn't it obvious that whoever called in the tip has to be involved somehow? Otherwise how would they know to tell the cops to look where they did?" Sofia said.

For the first time since Brendan had said they were

taking on Melissa Fairbroad as a client, Sofia felt the right-eous indignation that she thought the job ought to have given her. Melissa might have played a part in her husband's death, Sofia wasn't naive enough to think otherwise, but that still didn't change the fact that she might be being rail-roaded. By the cops. Or possibly by the real killer.

Stark leaned forward, his elbows resting on his desk. His phone rang. He picked it up, gave the briefest of answers to whatever question he'd just been asked, and turned his attention back to Sofia. "We all know the person who called in the tip is involved. Now we have to prove it. He's our best hope to show that Melissa Fairbroad is innocent."

"It could have been someone who went onto the boat to steal something or someone trying to return a piece of borrowed rope or someone who smelled something funny and went to investigate," said Brendan. "It's a good lead, but we don't want to pin everything on it."

He was right.

"But to know that, first we have to find them." Brendan glanced over at Aidan. "Aidan's been doing some digging."

"Glad to hear it," said Stark. "What did you turn up?"

Aidan reached into his briefcase, pulled out two files and laid them down on the desk. "I'd bet that the tipster is one of these two."

Stark opened each file in turn and took his time leafing through the contents. "Trimble I knew about. Melissa mentioned that he and Nigel'd had some run-ins."

"Bet she never mentioned Moonbow," Sofia said, her comment earning an irritated glance from Brendan.

Stark looked up from the files. If he had been annoyed by how Sofia had spoken about his client, it never showed. Sofia imagined that maintaining a poker face came with the job.

"You're correct," he said quietly. "She omitted that particular relationship. It's regrettable, but understandable. Often people want to keep certain private aspects of their life private. Even from their attorney."

"Now she knows that someone dimed her out, she might be more forthcoming about Bobby Rogers," said Brendan.

"I'm sure she will," Stark said. "So out of these two, Brendan, who do you think?"

Brendan stuck his hands in his pockets. "We don't want to forget that it might be a third individual, but if I had to pick from just these two, I'd say if she was involved, my money would be on Rogers. If she has nothing to do with it, then Trimble."

Stark took a deep breath and slowly exhaled. "She wasn't involved. I know that might be hard to believe seeing as she's not the most sympathetic person in the world. But that's the truth."

"You mean that's what she told you," Brendan said.

Stark nodded. "That's what she told me."

"But then she didn't tell you about her affair either," Sofia said.

Stark smiled. "That's true. But I believe her when she told me that she wasn't involved in what happened to Nigel."

"Would you have told us if she'd admitted to you she did it?" asked Sofia.

"Of course not," said Stark, the smile still flickering on his face. "Look, keep digging. See what else you can turn up on Moonbow and Trimble."

"And if we can't find anything beyond what we already know?" asked Sofia.

"Then I'll do my best with it when it comes to trial. But in this case, I'm not sure my best will be enough," said Stark.

27

Brendan drove them back to the office. The mood was downbeat. Melissa's fingerprints on the gun made Stark's job an uphill task. They could throw her conman lover and Tucker Trimble into the mix, but a jury would fixate on the gun. Sofia knew that she would. Melissa looked guilty.

Back in the office, Aidan had barely sat down at his desk when he leapt back up again, heading for the door.

"What is it?" Sofia asked, running after him.

"You know how Nigel's boat is moored at Marina Del Rey?" Aidan said. "Well, guess what, that's where Moonbow has been renting an apartment. Exact same complex."

Sofia grabbed her jacket. "I'm coming with you."

For once, Aidan didn't argue.

NIGEL HAD KEPT HIS BOAT, a thirty-four foot motor cruiser called Imperial Sunset, in the Dolphin Bay complex in Marina Del Rey. Marina Del Rey, or simply The Marina as it was known to locals, was a small upmarket community made up of large apartment complexes favored by singles and divorcees. It sat just south of Venice Beach and north of LAX airport.

Dolphin Bay was a large apartment complex built back in the early eighties that also offered boat docks. It was gated and had security guards to make sure only residents, boat owners, and their guests could drive in. It was a pretty fancy address for a professional chakra-opener.

Sofia pulled her red Tesla into one of the visitor's parking spots near the apartment's leasing office. She and Aidan got out. They had an apartment number for Moonbow, but Sofia had already called the Organic Spa to book a fake appointment and worked out that he wouldn't be home for at least an hour. In the meantime, she and Aidan would try to take a look at Nigel's boat and see if any other boat owners were around and willing to talk.

It was a pleasant day as they walked toward the slips. Warm but not hot, probably in the high sixties—T-shirt weather. A few cotton-wool clouds scrolled across an otherwise perfect blue sky. With the pressures that came with his job, Sofia saw how having a boat down here, even if he rarely had the time to take it out, would have been a great retreat for Nigel. On a day like today, it was hard to imagine this part of the city as being at the center of anything as gruesome as a murder.

Aidan's cell phone rang. He looked down at the screen. "Excuse me," he said, stepping away to take the call.

From the smile on his face Sofia suspected it wasn't work-related. He finished his call and walked back over.

"Sorry about that," he said.

"Second date?" she said.

He didn't say anything.

"So what's the lucky gal's name?" It was so unusual to

see Aidan being evasive that she wasn't going to miss the opportunity to give him as hard a time as he gave her when it came to dating.

"Why do you want to know?"

"Come on, just her first name. It is a woman, right? You've not Eve for Steve or anything?" Sofia knew that would get a reaction from him. She had never heard Aidan say anything straight-out homophobic, but like most straight men he could get touchy about any suggestion that he was less than a hundred percent hetero.

"Sofia. Her name's Sofia," Aidan blurted out.

Sofia put her hand over her mouth to stifle her laugh while Aidan looked embarrassed. "Seriously?"

"It's a pretty common name," he said, bristling.

"It's not that common."

"Well, it's not special," Aidan countered.

"You might want to save telling her that for the fourth date. Women love hearing how not special they are."

"You're a riot," said Aidan.

Before Sofia could tease him any further, she spotted someone, the face obscured by a white captain's hat up on the deck of a nearby boat.

"Excuse me," she called out.

The person stopped moving and looked over, then took off a hat and shook out a long mane of streaked blond hair before straightening up and leaning on the brush that had been swabbing the deck. As soon as the figure turned, Sofia realized it was a woman because she was sporting pretty impressive silicone boobs. At least she assumed those boobs were silicone given how little they moved. She bet that, in the event of the boat capsizing, they could double as flotation devices. From Aidan's slack-jawed expression, he seemed to be thinking something very different.

"Put your tongue back in and let me do the talking," Sofia told him.

She strode down the gangway.

"Hey!" she said brightly, harnessing as much former child star perkiness as she could muster. "Or should I say ahoy?"

Next to her Aidan muttered, "I can't believe you just said 'ahoy.' Who are you, Gilligan?"

The silicone blonde ran gleaming red-polished finger-nails through her mane. "You're not reporters, are you?"

"No, ma'am," said Sofia. "We're investigators. It will only take five minutes tops. I can see you're busy." One of the first tricks she had picked up from Brendan was to give people a time limit. Most people were prepared to give you five minutes of their time even if you ended up taking more. "We'll ask you a couple of questions, and then we'll get out of your hair. By the way, who does your hair? It's fantastic."

"Oh, Giorgio in Santa Monica," said the blond boat owner.

"No kidding," said Sofia, nudging Aidan to follow her up and onto the deck before the blonde changed her mind. "My hairdresser moved to Phoenix of all places, and I haven't been able to find anyone I like since."

"You'll be lucky if you can get in with Giorgio," she said. "But tell him I sent you."

Sofia put her hand out. "I'm Sofia, and this is Aidan. We're from Maloney Investigations."

The blonde's expression seemed to freeze a little. "You're not police office officers? When you said investigators…"

Sofia had said investigators for precisely that reason. As soon as people heard the phrase "private detective" they got creeped out. She left the private off when she could. "If it makes you feel better, Maloney Investigations is run by

Brendan Maloney. He's a retired homicide detective with the LAPD, and Aidan here is also retired LAPD."

The blonde seemed to notice Aidan properly for the first time and shifted into flirt mode. "You don't look old enough to be retired."

"I was injured in the line of duty, took early retirement," said Aidan, openly ogling the woman's boobs.

Sofia had realized over the years that big boobs to a man were the equivalent of a moving pocket watch to someone about to be hypnotized. Both objects made their eyes glaze over and made people very open to suggestion, no matter how ridiculous the suggestion might be. She was pretty sure that, if requested, Aidan would cluck like a chicken and flap his wings, possibly jump right off the boat, if he was suitably distracted by a pair of 34 triple Ds.

"Injured?" the blonde pouted. "How terrible. Are you okay now?"

"He's great," said Sofia. "He's just started seeing a woman with the same name as me. What are the odds? Anyway, can we ask you a few things?"

"Of course," said the blonde, her eyes never leaving Aidan.

"Right," said Aidan, ripping his gaze from the woman's chest. "You probably heard about a boat owner called Nigel Fairbroad."

"Oh, yes," said the blonde. "Poor man. I can't believe something like that could happen here."

This was a great start.

"So you knew him?" said Sofia.

"Well, I wouldn't say *knew*. I didn't actually realize it was him until I saw his picture on the news and made the connection. He was the guy with the cute accent I'd say hello to when he came down to take his cruiser out for a spin. He was always so polite, but then British people are kind of like that."

"Can you remember the last time that you saw him, Ms...?" said Sofia.

"Carolyn. Carolyn Reynolds," said the blonde.

"So can you recall the last time you saw Nigel, Ms. Reynolds?" asked Aidan.

"Okay, this is freaky," said Carolyn, warming to the topic now that she had gotten going. "But I'm fairly sure the last time I saw him was the, you know, the night he disappeared. I might even have been the last person to see him alive."

Given that he was shot in the face, Sofia kind of doubted that.

"Really?" said Aidan. "That's something. Have the police spoken to you?"

"Oh, yes," said Carolyn. "They took a statement when they came down this morning, but between you and me, they didn't seem all that interested in what I had to tell them."

"And what did you have to tell them?" asked Aidan.

"Just that I saw Nigel the night before he was found dead, and that he took his cruiser out, but that I never saw him bring it back in," Carolyn said.

Sofia couldn't believe the cops who spoke to Carolyn wouldn't have been interested in a detail like this. Someone who was dumped into the Pacific taking his boat out hours before he died wasn't exactly a minor detail. But it did leave one question.

"Was he alone when he took it out? Or did you see anyone with him?" Sofia asked.

"The cops did ask me that. I don't know. I mean I can't say for sure. I heard him talking, but he could have been on his cell phone. I didn't actually see anyone." She looked at

Aidan and Sofia in turn. "I'm sorry. I wish I could say for sure."

"Don't worry about it," said Aidan. "You've been really helpful. You didn't by any chance catch any of what he was saying? Maybe he called this person he was speaking to by name?"

Carolyn took a step and leaned again on the brush. She bit down on her lower lip and looked up, obviously trying to conjure up her memory of that night. "Yeah, you know, I think he did."

Sofia traded a glance with Aidan. Neither of them had any great hope that coming down here would yield anything, so this was a bonus. If she had overheard the name Moonbow or Bobby or Tucker, then Stark could use that to link them to what happened. After all, Carolyn couldn't say for sure if he'd been on the phone or talking to someone who was in the boat with him.

"I'm sure he mentioned the name Melissa. It kind of rung a bell because that's his wife's name. He'd mentioned her to me before."

Sofia's heart sank. Nigel mentioning his wife's name was exactly the opposite of helpful to them. She looked over at Aidan. His expression had changed, too.

"Did you tell the cops that?" Aidan said.

"Oh yeah," said Carolyn cheerfully, happy that she'd recalled this additional detail for them. "Now *that* they were interested in."

I bet they were. Sofia gave her a weak smile.

"They asked if I remembered if he was talking to her or about her, but honestly I couldn't say for sure," Carolyn continued.

Aidan shifted gears. "But you couldn't say for sure whether you saw Melissa Fairbroad?"

Carolyn shook her head.

"Would you recognize her if you did see her? Had you noticed her down here with Nigel before?" Sofia asked.

That prompted another shake of the head. "Nope, and before you ask, I hadn't seen him with any other women either, which was kind of surprising."

"Why was that surprising?" Sofia asked, her curiosity genuine.

"He was a producer. I mean, those guys are usually pretty bad for horn-dogging around. I used to do a little acting so I know how that whole deal works. Y'know, the casting couch."

Sofia couldn't recall having seen Carolyn in anything, or run into her at any castings, though she doubted that they would have been up for the same roles. Carolyn had about twenty years on her, and at least three cup sizes.

"What about other people? Did he come down here with friends?" Aidan asked.

"Not that I remember, no. He kind of kept himself to himself for the most part. The only person he really had any time for was Dave. Dave has the cruiser next to Nigel's. Nigel used to ask him about boat stuff. Dave's ex-navy. What he doesn't know about boats isn't worth knowing," said Carolyn.

"Thanks, Carolyn. That's been really helpful. Listen, could I get your number in case we forgot to ask you something and need to get in touch?" Aidan took out his cell phone and handed it to Carolyn. "You can punch it in for me right here."

Carolyn smiled and took Aidan's phone. "You always ask witnesses for their phone number?"

"Just the pretty ones," said Aidan.

Sofia suppressed the urge to roll her eyes. If this was the

kind of cheesy line Aidan used on his Tinder dates, then no wonder he'd struggled to get a second date. *Just the pretty ones. Gag.*

"You're welcome aboard any time, Mr. Maloney." Carolyn handed his cell phone back, and her hand lingered against his about two extra seconds. Sofia was horrified to see that Aidan's corny line had worked so well. It just made women in general seem stupider.

SHE AND AIDAN walked farther down the dock. Nigel's cruiser was sealed off with yellow crime scene tape. She was happy to push some boundaries but climbing aboard a crime scene wasn't one of them. The sheriff's department would probably have collected all the forensic evidence they needed, but they still wouldn't take kindly to a couple of private investigators climbing all over their crime scene. In any case, the evidence would have to be released to Stark during the discovery process.

Dave, the ex-navy man, was on deck as they approached. Sofia introduced herself and Aidan. Dave seemed affable.

"You were on that TV show?" he said to Sofia.

"Guilty as charged," said Sofia.

"My grandkids loved that show," Dave said.

"That's great," said Sofia.

"And now you're a PI?" Like everyone else in the world, Dave seemed flummoxed by Sofia's career change. It was as if she had run away from the circus to become an accountant or something.

"Yup, thought I'd try doing it for real instead of playing one on TV. Carolyn said you were in the Navy," said Sofia, hoping to move the conversation away from her puzzling career change.

"Twenty-five years," said Dave, proudly.

"I appreciate your service, sir," said Aidan.

It came off a little ass-kissy but Sofia felt that it was a definite improvement on his "just the pretty ones" line.

"I had a great time," said Dave. "I'd recommend it to anyone." He smiled at Sofia. "If you're ever thinking about another career switch...."

"I'll keep it in mind." Sofia found herself warming to him. He seemed pretty normal for LA. She was pretty sure Dave thought Tinder was something you used to start a camp fire. If he'd been twenty years younger, she might have used one of Aidan's cheesy lines or asked him for his number.

"We're working on behalf of the Fairbroad family," said Sofia. It sounded better than saying they were working for Melissa, the black widow likely to be put on trial for Nigel's murder. "Carolyn said that Nigel used to speak to you. We were wondering if you were here the night he was killed."

"I wasn't. I wish I had been. Maybe I could have done something," Dave said. "Nigel was a pretty nice guy. For a limey."

Sofia was about to ask Dave where he had been, but stopped herself. It could have come off as accusatory, and they needed him on their side. "Did Nigel seem worried about anything? Did you see him with anyone the past few weeks?"

"Never saw him with anyone down here," said Dave. "Though a few days before he was killed I heard him having an argument with a man on his phone."

"You have any idea who it was or what the argument was about?" Aidan asked.

Dave shook his head. "Not a clue, but it did seem pretty heated. I remember it because Nigel was always pretty soft-spoken. Y'know a real English gent. He seemed pretty steamed about something."

"But you don't remember any details of his end of the conversation?" Sofia pressed.

"I try not to eavesdrop on other peoples' conversations, young lady," said Dave, fixing her with a steady gaze. "In the Navy, with everyone living right on top of each other, you learn to tune out stuff like that. Makes life a lot more straightforward if you don't stick your nose into everyone else's business."

The last comment seemed pretty pointed. Sofia let Aidan ask Dave a few more questions about when he'd last seen Nigel, thanked Dave for his time, and walked back down the dock. Carolyn had changed into a hot-pink bikini that didn't leave much to the imagination. She waved at Aidan as they walked past her boat and made the universal call me sign by holding her hand up to her ear, her thumb and pinkie extended.

"You going to call her?" Sofia wondered if Carolyn was exactly five foot nine.

Aidan ignored the question, waved at Carolyn, and kept walking.

28

S quinting in the sun that glinted off the water in the marina, Sofia stood at the entrance to Dolphin Bay apartment complex. She pulled up the number of the Brentwood Organic Spa and hit the green call button. "Hi, is that Leo? ... Yeah, hi, Leo. I was wondering if Moonbow is available today."

At the mention of the name Moonbow, Aidan made a jerking off gesture. For someone who had been born and raised in Southern California, Aidan was remarkably intolerant of anything even vaguely New Age. Still, Moonbow was a con man, reinvented New Age persona or not.

"He's not?" Sofia said. She gave Aidan a thumbs-up. If he wasn't at work, then maybe he was in his apartment.

"No, it's okay. It was Moonbow I wanted to see... Yes, he is pretty popular. Okay, well thanks anyway. You've been very helpful." Sofia killed the call before Leo could ask her any more questions or try to schedule an appointment with another masseur.

"You sure you want to do this?" said Aidan.

"I'll be fine," Sofia said. "What's he gonna do? Close my chakras?"

"The guy did five years in the pen. He'll know how to handle himself. Plus, even if he is inside, he's going to be super edgy after Melissa was arrested."

Part of Sofia knew Aidan had a point. Moonbow would be jumpy. As a convicted felon, if he got caught up in this, and they could stick a conspiracy charge on him, he'd been looking at a life sentence. Life without possibility of parole, even the hint of it, was enough to make anyone dangerous. At the same time, Sofia didn't want to punk out now. This was her chance to prove herself. Not just to Brendan and Aidan, but to herself. If she was going to make a career out of this, she'd have to be prepared to take risks, including with her personal safety.

"Just trust me, okay?" she said to Aidan.

Aidan shrugged. "It's your funeral."

"Thanks for your kind words of encouragement."

WITH AIDAN WAITING around the corner, next to the building's two elevators, Sofia walked down the corridor and stopped outside apartment 412, residence of one Bobby Rogers, aka Moonbow. She knocked, and stepped back, her hands shaking with nerves.

Aidan had been reluctant to let her be the one to take a shot at talking to Moonbow. But she had persuaded him that this was the way to go. Her reasoning was that a womanizer and con artist like Moonbow was more likely to be disarmed by an attractive young woman than by an ex-cop like Aidan. If she couldn't get anywhere, then Aidan could always try.

Sofia doubted Moonbow would open up to Aidan.

Fraudsters and con artists tended to be pretty tuned in and adept at reading people, and he'd see right through Aidan. She had already decided to approach the meeting like an improv exercise. She was playing the part of Woman Interested in Opening More Than Her Chakra While Pretending She Doesn't Know Aidan is Listening. The first part would be easy, the second not so much.

Heavy footsteps approached the apartment door. The peephole went dark, then there was the sound of two locks being thrown back and a chain being taken off. The door opened to reveal Bobby Rogers in a purple velvet tracksuit. She hadn't seen a man who wore so much purple since she'd looked at pictures of Prince before he changed his name to a squiggly symbol.

Moonbow stared at her. A flicker of recognition crossed his face, and he was definitely on guard.

"Can I help you?" His voice was barely above a whisper.

She hoped the voice was part of his whole Moonbow persona. Con artists and fraudsters were just actors playing a role, and Moonbow was the character Bobby Rogers had created. Moonbow was a lot less violent than Bobby, so she hoped he'd stay in character.

She avoided making direct eye contact. "I don't know if you remember me. We met the other day at the spa where you work in Brentwood. Sofia." As she said her name she looked up at him with doe eyes.

He didn't seem that impressed, but she forged on.

"You really opened up my chakras, and I looked up your address." She ran the tip of her tongue slowly across her lips. "I was wondering if you could do something about my lustrous jewel. It's been really ... throbbing."

She cringed as she delivered that last line. It was like dialogue from a really bad porn movie, but if she'd learned anything about men, it was that there was no such thing as being too obvious. With the bartender from Moonshadows, she had flirted mercilessly for weeks before he'd finally taken the hint and she'd managed to access his lustrous jewels.

He looked her up and down, but it wasn't the kind of look she was expecting from a man she'd just propositioned. Moonbow was proving to be a hard guy to seduce, though she doubted it was because he didn't get the subtext, but more that he had his guard up. Or maybe Melissa Fairbroad was all the woman he needed. Or he had a thing for older women. Or he just didn't believe her and planned on doing to her what he may have done to Nigel. She took a deep breath and waited. Woman Who Needed Her Chakras Opened had said her piece.

"Okay," he said after what seemed like an endless silence. "But it's going to cost you. I'm four hundred for the hour. But for that, I clear everything, and I'll polish up your lustrous jewel so that it's box fresh."

Cost her? She was supposed to pay him? Then the penny dropped. What he did at the spa may have been legit, okay weird, but legit, but clearly he was offering women like Melissa and now Sofia a different kind of service out of hours.

Moonbow was a gigolo. And Sofia had just propositioned him. Worse, Aidan had heard every word. This was going to make her rehab accident look like nothing.

Well, she had come this far, and it would all be for nothing if she didn't get inside his apartment.

"That's fine. Can I come in? I feel kind of weird talking about this while I'm standing in the corridor."

"Sure thing," he said, opening the door a little wider and stepping back so she could walk past.

The apartment's decor was like a mash up of *Austin Powers: The Spy Who Shagged Me* and late seventies San Fernando Valley ranch house. Purple featured heavily, as did sheepskin rugs and lava lamps. Sofia kind of had to hand it to Bobby Rogers. He'd gone for a full-on method acting approach when creating this Moonbow character. He wasn't just playing the role—he was living it, ceiling mirrors and all. *Oh my God, he actually has a mirror on the ceiling.* She thought such things were the stuff of legend, but they actually existed in real life. She was glad Aidan didn't have a camera on her, too.

Now that she was inside the apartment, she needed to stall for time, and fast.

"Could I have a glass of water?" she asked, feeling completely lame as the words came out of her mouth. Surely, if she was going to stay in character, she should have a more elaborate request. A hookah pipe. Nipple clamps. A gimp mask. Something that suggested an overly-sexed yet frustrated Hollywood type, which a glass of water, even if it was Fiji water or coconut water that had been harvested by dusky maidens in the Caribbean, kind of didn't.

"Sure. Make yourself comfortable," said Moonbow, disappearing into the kitchen.

"Thanks," she called after him, glancing quickly around the living room and opening her handbag.

She crossed quickly to a purple chaise lounge. She reached down under it, feeling for a ridge or shelf. "It's a lovely place you have here."

When he didn't reply, she panicked a little. Her heart was knocking against her ribs. All she needed was a few more seconds. A trickle of sweat ran down her back, but she got it done.

She straightened up as he walked back in with a glass of

water that she had no intention of drinking. Who knew what he might have put in it?

"I know who you really are," she said, planting her feet wide like she'd been taught at the boxing gym. She might have to fight her way out of the apartment, and she wasn't sure if Aidan would get through the door in time if Moonbow got angry that he'd been duped. She imagined that con artists reacted particularly badly to being conned themselves. It was probably a matter of professional pride.

Moonbow put the glass of water down on a coffee table shaped like a kidney bean. He straightened up, clasped his hands together and cracked his knuckles. It was a gesture way more nightclub bouncer than New Age massage therapist. Bobby Rogers was coming out to play. She didn't want to play with him, but she had to put up his guard, make him do something or her trip here wouldn't yield the results she needed.

"So, who am I then?" Moonbow said.

"Your name is Bobby Rogers. You were born and raised in the city of brotherly love. Didn't finish high school, did a year of community college, then found your true vocation by committing fraud and scamming people. That led to a couple of felony convictions. Your longest time down was five years. You got out, moved west, and reinvented yourself as Moonbow. A pretty good cover for a gigolo servicing frustrated housewives and divorcees of West Los Angeles."

Moonbow listened with a smile. His eyes told a different story. They narrowed to slits, the pupils pieces of jet-black coal. His arms were loose by his side, but his hands had clenched into fists. She hadn't been too worried about him attacking her before because it would be an incredibly dumb thing to do. Then again, criminals, even smooth ones like Moonbow, got caught because they did dumb things.

She backed up a little, making sure she had a good six feet between her and Moonbow. "I also know you are involved with Melissa Fairbroad. You've been having an affair."

Moonbow raised his hands. She stepped away, the back of her legs bumping against the coffee table. She almost lost her balance and fell right onto the bean. She waited for him to strike. He didn't. His fists unclenched, and he slowly clapped his hands.

"Bravo," he said. "If there was a law against trying to make something of your life, I might be worried. But this is America. I paid my debt to society. As for being a gigolo, anything that happens between myself and a client is strictly between us. As soon as we become sexually involved, it's a personal relationship, not a business one. My relationship with Melissa is none of anyone's business except ours."

As defenses went, it was fairly impressive. If she'd thought Moonbow would be spooked, she'd been wrong. He didn't seem in the slightest bit troubled by Sofia knowing his true identity.

"The LA County sheriff might see it a bit differently."

"You're assuming they don't already know." Moonbow's smile grew broader.

He was bluffing. He had to be.

"I spoke to them late last night. If you don't believe me, then you always call them and ask. I'll wait while you do."

"Did you tell them you were sleeping with Melissa?" Sofia said.

"Of course I told them. They were going to find out anyway. If I'd lied, it would have made me look guilty. You can believe me or not, but I had nothing to do with what happened to Melissa's husband."

He seemed pretty sure of himself. Sofia would give him that much. "What were you doing that night?"

"On the night Nigel was killed, I was all tucked up in bed with someone who will swear I never left her side."

"Melissa?" As soon as she asked the question, she felt like an idiot.

"No, not with Melissa. Let's just say I'm pretty popular with women of a certain age and background," said Moonbow. "I give them what their husbands can't."

He was clearly waiting for Sofia to ask what that was. She wasn't about to give him the satisfaction. It didn't take a detective to work out what Moonbow provided to the rich housewives of Brentwood.

She started for the door. Moonbow stood his ground, making sure she would have to walk past him to reach the hallway. She tensed, her body on high alert, ready to strike out should he make a move. She kept her back to the wall, and made sure she was facing him as she pushed past. He eyed her like prey but didn't make the slightest move.

She was at the door when he spoke. "By the way, I knew who you were when you came to the spa. So don't leave here thinking that you got one over on me, because you didn't."

It could be true. It could be a bluff. She really didn't care either way. Someone like him wasn't going to admit that anyone had got the drop on him.

"Thanks for your time, Bobby," she said, opening the apartment door.

His smirk fell away. "You take care now."

It sounded like a threat.

She walked out into the corridor and closed the door behind her. Her legs felt like jelly, and her heart was still racing but she had done what she came to do.

Mission accomplished.

29

Aidan waited for her by the elevator. His jacket had ridden up a little, and his right hand rested on his gun, a .357 Smith and Wesson Magnum revolver. He pressed the call button. The elevator door opened. He stepped in and pushed the button to hold the door open for Sofia. She moved next to him.

He stared straight ahead as the elevators door closed.

She nodded toward his weapon. "Were you worried about me?"

He kept staring ahead as the elevator slowly descended to the ground floor. "I figured you and your throbbing lustrous jewel could handle themselves."

Sofia hated to think what he'd leave on her desk at work tomorrow. "It's a chakra term."

"I bet it is," he answered.

The elevator stopped, the doors opened, and they stepped back out into the apartment block's lobby.

"Where'd you place the device?" Aidan asked as they pushed through glass doors and into the sunlight.

"Under the couch," Sofia said. "I didn't have time to find a better location."

"Cool," said Aidan, pulling out his cell, swiping across the screen and pulling up the surveillance app that linked to the tiny wireless microphone that he'd given to Sofia to place inside Moonbow's apartment. "Everything gets sent to cloud storage, so we can either listen live or review it in the morning. We won't be able to use any of it as evidence, of course, but at least it might give us the inside track if he is involved with what happened to Nigel. You spooked him a little, I think, so he'll probably reach out to his buddies."

"I dunno, he seems pretty careful."

Aidan shrugged. "We'll see. Hey, can you drop me back at the office now?"

"Sure," said Sofia as they reached her car and got in. "You in a rush?"

Aidan glanced over at her. "I have a thing later."

"With the other Sofia?" Sofia asked, pulling the Tesla out onto Mindanao Way.

"How come you're so fascinated with who I'm dating?" said Aidan.

"Just being polite. Showing an interest."

"What about you?" Aidan said, changing the subject. "Is that dumb-as-rocks barman polishing your lustrous jewel?"

She refused to take the bait. "Tonight I'm having dinner with the family out in La Canada."

Her mom had insisted that she attend. Sofia was pretty sure her mom still wasn't convinced by her explanation of why she'd been caught urinating in public. She'd decided it was best to go and let them see she was fine. Otherwise, they'd think that she was going through some kind of life crisis.

"Lucky you," said Aidan.

It beat another evening in with Fred the seagull and a glass of wine, but she didn't tell Aidan that.

30

Sofia went straight back to the office and spent ten minutes checking emails and answering calls. A lady up near Zuma Beach wanted help finding a missing cat. A husband was worried that his wife, a former Playboy model (Sofia knew that because he'd mentioned it *six* times in the space of a four-minute voicemail message), was cheating on him and wanted Maloney Investigations to do surveillance on her the following weekend when he'd be out of town on business. Finally, there was a message from Sofia's mom reminding her about the family dinner and asking her not to be late because she'd gone to a lot of trouble, and if the turkey was left too long in the smoker, it would get dry, and Tim (her mom's second husband) would complain, and then she'd have to kill him, which would ruin an otherwise perfect family dinner.

Across the office, Aidan finished setting up the surveillance app on his computer. Basically everything the microphone in Moonbow's living room caught would be uploaded. It'd give them something to do tomorrow morning, but Sofia wasn't holding out much hope. As soon as he was finished, Aidan grabbed his jacket from the back of his chair and made a beeline for his car. Looked like he wanted to be punctual for the Other Sofia.

Sofia stuck her head into Brendan's office. He was on a call so she handed him the messages from Playboy guy and Lost Cat Lady, and let him know she was leaving.

It was only three in the afternoon, but it had been a long day and she wanted to try to beat the worst of the traffic heading from the west side back to the valley. Not that traffic was ever light. It was just varying degrees of bad. She thought about swinging back home first but decided against it. Tonight, Fred would have to either go hungry or mooch off someone else for his dinner. Or forage like seagulls did before humans moved onto the beach to feed them.

She headed north, picking up Malibu Canyon Road just before she reached the campus of Pepperdine University. From there she could get on the 101 before picking the 134 and taking the 2 freeway to La Canada.

Malibu Canyon Road was quieter than she'd expected. It was single lane for miles, so a lot of regular commuters avoided it. If you got stuck behind a slow-moving vehicle like farm machinery or a big rig hauling timber, you were pretty much screwed because there were no places to pass safely. But she got lucky and zipped along, loving the road and her little Tesla.

The only real way to deal with LA traffic was to adopt a Zen master attitude. And Malibu Canyon was a pretty drive. As she piloted the Roadster through the sweeping curves and steady climb, her mind drifted back to Nigel Fairbroad. She was still struggling with the idea that someone she'd met, if only briefly, had been murdered. She wondered what his final moments had been like.

Something about the night he'd been killed didn't make sense. Pieces were missing. Big pieces.

When she had met him at Frank's Grotto and tried to pick him up, he'd seemed on edge. The way he'd blown her off, how he'd been constantly checking his cell phone, and his sudden departure were the behaviors of a troubled man.

Had he been alone in the boat? If his boat had been returned to its berth in Marina Del Rey, and he had already been dumped overboard by then, it didn't seem likely. Either a person or persons unknown had been with him in his own boat the whole time, or someone in another boat had intercepted him along the way, boarded Nigel's cruiser, killed him, threw him overboard, and returned Nigel's cruiser to its rightful slip. If that was the case, there had to have been at least two people involved. If the person was already in the boat when it left the marina, then there only had to be one.

Leaving Nigel's last moments aside, Sofia thought about each of the suspects. Even though they were on Melissa's defense team, she saw exactly why the cops had her as the prime suspect. Out of everyone, she had the strongest motive. With Nigel out of the way, Melissa would be free to enjoy her life with Moonbow and a big pile of cash. Not only would she inherit the house and the rest of Nigel's money and whatever shares he had in the production company, but there was also the matter of that hefty new life insurance policy. A million reasons right there.

Moonbow seemed eerily calm for a felon who could still end up arrested for a murder one charge. It could be ex-con bravado, but Sofia didn't know anyone who could be that calm unless they were a complete sociopath. He had made his alibi sound pretty watertight, but that didn't mean it was. Maybe another frustrated Brentwood wife had fallen for him. All he needed was for her to swear blind he was with her, and if she was credible, it would be hard for the cops to prove otherwise without firm evidence. Maybe Melissa's team would get lucky and find CCTV footage to disprove it.

Tucker Trimble was the wild card. She didn't doubt he was capable of murder. He had a well-known, hair-trigger temper and previous convictions for violent crimes. He was also wildly unpredictable. Plus, she knew from her own experience what fame could do to someone, especially sudden fame. Fame was usually fleeting, but most people assumed it would last forever. When they found out their fifteen minutes were nearing an end, most people tended to react badly. If Tucker felt that Nigel was threatening his position as star of the show, there was no knowing what he was capable of doing. With his wilderness survival skills, he had plenty of experience killing things. It may not have been that much of a step for Tucker to go from hunting game to taking a human life. From what she'd seen of the TV show, he was proficient with all manners of weapons.

The roar of an engine behind her brought her attention back to the road. She had to pay attention now because the canyon road narrowed up ahead. A white Cadillac Escalade zoomed up close behind her, coming from nowhere. Its hood filled her rearview mirror and the driver stayed inches from the Tesla's rear bumper. Another tailgater.

"Jesus, buy me dinner first," she said.

She pressed her gas pedal, pulling away to get distance between her car and the Escalade. The driver of the Escalade laid on his horn. One way or another, he was determined to get past her. She glanced in her rearview mirror, trying to glimpse the driver, but the Cadillac was too close and too tall.

Round the next corner, the road widened again. She hit the gas, pulling away, and taking the corner at speed. The

Cadillac fell away—it couldn't take curves like a sports car without flipping over. After she rounded the corner, she slowed, and pulled off the road and onto the dirt. The Cadillac came round the corner and sped past.

She tried to get another look at the driver but the Cadillac was moving too fast, and the side windows were tinted. She waited for a few more seconds and pulled back out onto the road. It was probably just an impatient commuter, eager to get home, and happy to bully someone else off the road if it got them into their driveway a few moments quicker. Who knew, maybe there was a big game on that they didn't want to miss. Or maybe they hated Tesla drivers. Or didn't like it that a young woman was driving an expensive sports car. Or they were just an asshole. After all, LA was often called the asshole capital of America. People wanted what they wanted. They wanted it yesterday. And if you or someone else was in the way then that was kind of too bad.

She rolled her neck and tried to relax. Hard to do when she was heading for dinner at her mom's house, and some road warrior had just tried to turn her into jelly. But she was a traffic Zen master. She could do this.

31

Sofia had always been a believer in the power of visualization. Not that she believed if you closed your eyes and dreamed of a Porsche that you'd open them to find one sitting in your driveway. If only. And right now, as she merged from the 2 onto the 134 toward La Canada she couldn't really close her eyes anyway—even if that was what most LA drivers seemed to do when merging. Sofia did believe that if you tried to visualize something in life going well, it was a lot better than dreading it. Even if everything ended up being crappy, there was no point in suffering the crappiness before it happened.

With that in mind, she took a few moments to conjure up a vision of a relaxing dinner with her family. She'd park her Roadster in the driveway, next to Emily and Ray's minivan and Tim's Benz. She'd walk to the front door. Her mom would be waiting with a glass of chilled white wine and a hug. Violet and Van would come running over and hug their Auntie Sofia, wrapping themselves around her legs. She'd hunker down and be showered with kisses as they told her how much they'd missed her.

Eventually Ray would shoo them away. They'd skip off hand in hand to play as everyone looked on dotingly. Tim would appear from his den and give her a hug, and she'd follow the family to the dining room where the table was already laid out. After everyone got caught up, Sofia's mom would order everyone into their seats. They'd enjoy a lovely dinner with no arguments and no one quizzing Sofia about her continuing single status or why she had turned her back on a great acting career to go work as a "gumshoe" (her mom's term for Sofia's new job).

After dinner they'd all go outside and sit by the pool as Violet and Van played quietly. Tim and Ray would clear the dishes (a sign that this really was a dream) and tidy up. Sofia would get to spend quality time with her mom and sister.

"Holy crap on a cracker!" Sofia shouted, turning hard on the steering wheel to avoid getting sideswiped by a hulking black Ford SUV that had come from nowhere. Today, she had won the asshole driver jackpot. Double prizes.

The Tesla was halfway over into the breakdown lane. The black Ford had slowed down. Sofia checked her rearview mirror. The driver was a big white guy with huge arms and biceps that strained the fabric of his blue T-shirt. His face was obscured by an LA Dodgers ball cap and a pair of wraparound sunglasses.

The guy seemed a lot more malevolent than the Cadillac driver had been—more intent on threatening her than on just passing by. He accelerated suddenly. The huge grill of the Ford bore down on the back of the Roadster. If he swerved this time, she would have nowhere to go except into the concrete barrier that ran down this side of the freeway. The Tesla was a really safe car, but against an old Ford tank it would be squished like a bug. So would Sofia.

She jammed down on the gas pedal, and the Tesla

zipped ahead. Grateful for the car's sprightly acceleration, she found a gap and pulled back into the inside lane behind a gardener's truck. Checking her mirror again, she saw that the Ford had moved over a couple of lanes. The driver of the Ford tailgated a Porsche, riding hard on the bumper until the Porsche driver was bullied out of the way and moved over.

The Ford driver threw a look over at the Tesla. He slowed and moved back over a lane so he would be next to her. He kept glancing over. With every glance, he would adjust his speed. He wasn't trying to get in front of her, or behind her. He was aiming to stay parallel but a little behind.

Sofia knew exactly the position he was aiming for. He was trying to get his front wheel in line with the rear wheel of the Tesla. That was the position you needed to be in if you wanted to fishtail someone off the road. Your front wheel next to their rear wheel. You'd hit them hard, then you'd keep going straight. They'd spin round a hundred eighty degrees where, on a busy freeway like this one, they'd be hit by oncoming traffic.

Fishtailing was one of a number of maneuvers, along with J-turns and how to properly run a road block, Sofia had been taught by Hollywood stunt driver and former Nascar driver Dale Arnott. She'd met Dale while shooting a movie in South Carolina after she'd insisted on doing her own driving stunts. He'd spent a week teaching her all kinds of stuff on an abandoned airstrip outside of Charleston. He'd been clear that she couldn't use her newfound skills out on the public highway, but she figured that under the circumstances, Dale wouldn't mind her making an exception.

As soon as the Ford got close, she scooted ahead a little. All the while she counted off the miles until she hit the exit for La Canada. Right now, the counter stood at seven. The Ford driver would make his move long before that.

By now he was barely looking at the road ahead. He slammed on his brakes as he came up too fast on a couple driving a green Prius with a 'Hilary for President' sticker. They didn't appear to notice him until he honked his horn, then they moved out into the outside lane with a completely bemused look.

The Ford accelerated again. This time Sofia couldn't move ahead of him. There was a dark blue Lexus in front of her, the driver doing something she had never seen on an LA freeway—the speed limit. She spotted Iowa plates. Now it made sense.

She checked her mirror. If she couldn't accelerate out of the way, maybe she could brake.

No dice. There was a big rig behind her. It was about twenty feet off her rear bumper, and she wasn't sure if that would be enough. She'd never survive a big rig driving up her tailpipe.

She still had six miles to go until she made the La Canada exit, and two miles to go before she hit the exit before that. There was only one thing for it.

She waited until the Ford was almost in position. As he tensed his arms to spin his wheel, she did the same, moving into the breakdown lane. The Tesla shifted under her, the rear jostling from side to side. The Ford made his move a fraction of a second later.

Sofia hit the gas and scooted down the breakdown lane, passing the blue Lexus on the inside. The driver of the Lexus, 'Mr. Speed Limit,' looked over in horror. People didn't drive like that in Iowa.

The Ford driver obviously hadn't reckoned on making contact with fresh air. Plus, the SUV was top heavy. It began to slide, drifting into the breakdown lane. To wrestle back control, the driver must have hit the brake. Sofia saw his panicked face in her rearview. He pulled his steering wheel back the other way, frantically trying to correct his oversteer. As moves went, it was amazingly dumb, especially with a car with such a high center of gravity.

The black Ford wobbled all over the place, threatening to roll over completely. There was the wail of an air horn as the big rig driver tried to slow. But he was carrying more weight than the SUV was. There was no way he could brake as quickly.

Sofia hit the accelerator. Her car leapt ahead of the Lexus and she moved into the inside lane. Behind the Lexus, the big rig had clipped the rear side of the Ford SUV, sending it spinning. The big rig, still unable to stop, slammed into the front of the Ford.

There was the teeth-grinding sound of metal on metal. The Ford flipped. The big rig kept moving, pushing the Ford like a broom sweeping trash. The Lexus driver finally located his accelerator and scooted up and out of the way. Sofia pulled over into the breakdown lane and came to a stop.

She popped on her hazards, opened her door, and got out. Looking back down the freeway, she watched the big rig finally coming to a stop. A few agonizing seconds later, the door of the black Ford SUV screeched open, and the muscular driver pushed his way out and climbed down. He was way shorter than Sofia would have thought, maybe five four. The big rig driver leapt out of his cab.

From what Sofia saw, no one had run into the back of the big rig. Traffic behind it was stopped, but by some miracle, it had ended up being contained to a two-vehicle crash. The big rig driver went over to check on the Ford driver. The

Ford driver pushed him angrily out of the way. He glared down the freeway at Sofia and reached down to his waist-band as several lanes of traffic behind the big rig came to a honking standstill.

She could take an educated guess at what the Ford driver was about to pull out. It wasn't going to be his insurance details. One near-death experience was good enough for an evening. She jumped back into the Tesla, slammed the driver's door, and smashed down on the accelerator, using every ounce of the Roadster's zero to sixty in three point nine seconds to get the hell out of Dodge.

Sweat trickling down her back, her heart still racing, she reached the La Canada exit. She took the exit fast and headed up the ramp. She thought about calling Brendan, or the cops, but decided against it. At least for now. She wanted to gather her thoughts first. If anyone had been trying to drive her off the road, she'd figured it would be Moonbow or Tucker Trimble. Not some dude she'd never seen before with muscles on his muscles and a look of chronic constipation.

32

"You're late."

Sofia's mom stood framed in the doorway. Sofia leaned in and gave her a hug. "Sorry, traffic was really bad. There was an accident on the 2."

Her mom leaned in to give her a hug. "Well, you're here now. That's all that matters."

Sofia's mom pulled away from the hug but kept her hands on Sofia's arms. She seemed to be studying her face. "I'll always love you. No matter what. You understand that, don't you, Sofia?"

Oh God. The only time her mom came out with stuff like this was when she'd been hitting the wine a little too hard. That usually didn't happen until after dinner, so this was not a good sign of what lay ahead. And, judging by the pained expression on her mom's face, she hadn't been convinced by Sofia's explanation of how she came to be videoed peeing outside a prominent Malibu rehab clinic. Her mom was looking at her like people looked at a dog—right before they took it to the vet for the last time.

"And I love you, too," Sofia said.

From somewhere in the bowels of the kitchen, a timer beeped. Tim shouted through. "Janet! Is this for the broccoli or the potatoes? Should I have turned the grill on?"

Saved by the timer. Her mom rolled her eyes and let go of Sofia's arms as Ray, Sofia's brother-in-law, appeared from the bathroom down the hall clutching a white box with red cross emblazoned across the front. First aid kit.

"Everything okay?" Sofia asked Ray.

"Tim! The grill should have gone on an hour ago. Shut the Golf Channel off once in a while and get a clue," said her mom as she disappeared into the kitchen.

"Flesh wound," said Ray, giving Sofia a hug. He also did the release and arm grab. "You look tired. You getting enough sleep?"

"Long week, that's all," said Sofia.

"I thought the only people who're supposed to look that exhausted are parents," said Ray.

"Violent and Van still a handful, huh?" Sofia said, trying to change the subject.

"A handful? That's a good way to put it. I'll remember that the next time Van takes apart the principal's transmission or Violet chokes out one of the boys she sits next to at lunch. A handful."

Most people would have assumed that Ray was merely exaggerating for comic effect, putting an over-the-top spin on some spirited hijinks. Sofia knew better. There was a reason why Ray locked up all the tools in his garage and searched his son's room for screwdrivers like a prison guard, and why Violet's semi-official family nickname was Violent.

They were sweet kids, but they were also, to put it politely, a little quirky. Six-year-old Van wanted to know how everything in the world worked, and thought the best way of achieving this knowledge was by taking things apart to see (household appliances, flies, automobiles), while seven-year-old Violet was going through a phase where she was obsessed with every kind of unarmed combat, or as she had precociously decided to describe it, "The Science of Fear."

"Van did what? How...? And Violet ... again with the chokeholds?" Sofia asked.

"Hey, sis." Emily walked in through one of the sliding doors that led out to the pool. She was wearing a red swim suit and had her hair up in a towel. She looked fantastic, as always. She walked over and gave Sofia a peck on the cheek.

"Please don't tell me I look tired," Sofia said.

"I'm too exhausted to notice if anyone else looks tired," said Emily. She turned to her husband. "Ray, can you...?"

"On my way," said Ray, disappearing through the door Emily had just come in through.

"Did one of the kids hurt themselves?" Sofia asked her sister.

"Huh?" said Emily.

"The first aid kit?" Sofia said with a nod to Ray as he headed through the door and toward the pool.

"Violet scraped her knees trying to climb up on the roof. It's fine though. She's busy running around, asking if anyone wants to taste her blood to see if they're a vampire," said Emily. "I had to send two neighbor kids packing before they did."

"What was she doing on the roof?" Sofia asked.

"High board isn't high enough for the 'flying death slam.' I mean, duh!" said Emily. "Thankfully, Ray got to her before she could actually jump off. He has the reflexes of a panther."

Tim wandered down the corridor from direction of the kitchen. "Hey, Sofia. How you doing, kiddo?"

He enveloped her in a big bear hug. Tim had gotten together with her mom five years ago, so while he was technically her and Emily's stepfather, he'd never actually been a father figure in the study-hard, eat-your-vegetables role. Sofia liked him. He was pretty straightforward. He loved her mother, and he loved to play golf, loved to watch golf, and loved to talk about golf. That was pretty much it. He had a happy-go-lucky demeanor and didn't seem to get upset about much. If Sofia hadn't known better, she would have suspected he was on some kind of medical marijuana prescription. He really was that mellow.

"Good, Tim, thanks. How are you?" she said.

"Great. Just great. Hey, did you see that accident on the 2? Just flashed up on the news," said Tim.

"Must have just missed it." She hoped her mom hadn't overheard her words. She had used the freeway crash as her excuse for being late. "Was anyone hurt?"

"Don't think so," said Tim. "Freeway's going to be backed up for hours. Y'know you can always stay over with us if you don't want to make the drive back."

"I would," said Sofia, "but I have work in the morning."

"Oh yeah, how's that going?" Tim asked. "Put any bad guys behind bars yet?"

Sofia smiled. People had as many misconceptions about being a private investigator as they did about acting. Both jobs involved long stretches of boring work, like sitting in a car outside someone's house or sitting in a trailer while the crew got set up to shoot a scene, but everyone assumed they were both glamorous and exciting all the time.

"Working on it," she said brightly. Actually, this was one case where her work could actually result in someone being sent to prison. She hoped it was someone really guilty as opposed to whomever the DA could make a case against. By now she knew enough about the criminal justice system to appreciate the difference between the two.

"I'd better go say hi to my niece and nephew," she said to Tim as he walked past and opened a cupboard to reveal a floor-to-ceiling temperature-controlled wine cabinet full of bottles. Besides golf, Tim had also amassed a pretty serious wine collection, though Janet had been doing her best to trim it down to more manageable proportions since they'd gotten married and she'd moved into his home in La Canada.

An afternoon of swimming, not to mention trying to climb up onto the roof to execute the Flying Death Slam, seemed to have tired out Violet and Van. Ray was kneeling next to Violet, putting a Band-Aid on her knee. Van was still in the pool, facemask and snorkel on. Both kids flew to Sofia.

"Auntie Sofia! Auntie Sofia!" they screamed. At least that part of her optimistic visualization had worked.

A soaking wet Van threw off his mask and snorkel and launched himself at her. A slightly less wet Violet did the same. Sofia knelt down and pulled them in for a hug.

"You know," she said, looking at each one of them in turn, "you both look like perfectly normal children."

Van gave her a goofy, gap-toothed smiled. "Hey!"

Violet hugged her so tight around the neck that Sofia feared this might be an attempted choke hold.

"My teacher says I'm special. Mom told me to tell her that normal's boring."

"That's always been my motto," said Sofia.

"No kidding!" said Janet.

Sofia looked up to see her mom, decked out in an apron that read "Wine! How Classy People Get Wasted" and holding a wine glass. "Children, dinner will be ready in a half hour, so you two need to go dry off and get changed."

"Go on," Ray prompted them. "Get in the shower. And, Van, no messing with the plumbing, okay? That's Daddy's job."

Ray glanced over at Tim.

"All my tools are locked up in my toolbox," Tim said. "Should be safe to let them into the bathroom."

"Okay, Dad," Van said, scampering off after his sister to cause who knew what kind of damage. Apart from choking people out and dismantling pretty much every object that came within reach, they were, at least as far as Sofia was concerned, actually pretty good kids. They weren't sneaky or malicious or spoiled. They were just high energy, the way kids had always been before someone came along to tell everyone active kids were suffering from ADHD and needed to take Ritalin. Then again, Sofia wondered if she'd be less tolerant of their behavior if she had to deal with them every day. But Emily and Ray seemed to manage.

"So, Ray, how's business?" Sofia asked.

"Pretty good. Plumbing's pretty recession proof. I mean, if you have a leaky pipe or your toilet stops working, you still need to get it fixed, right? How you finding the new gig?"

Ray had been the only one in the family who had been unconditionally supportive of Sofia turning her back on showbiz. He'd already told Emily, who was the one in the family who'd actually wanted to be an actress, that he would never have married her if she'd been doing that job when they met. Ray was a no-bullshit, blue collar guy who pretty much regarded the entire entertainment industry with a mixture of horror and disdain. He felt that it wasn't the real world in the same way that sticking your hand into a blocked toilet was. Sofia agreed.

Tim appeared with a fresh beer for Ray and a bottle of wine. He handed Ray the beer and shook the bottle in Sofia's direction. "Refill?"

She put her hand over the top of her wine glass. "Driving home later. This is it for me."

Sofia guessed that it came down to the fact that you pretty much had to drive to get anywhere in LA, but she'd always been amazed at the number of normally law-abiding and otherwise responsible citizens who would happily slam down a couple of cocktails and three glasses of wine at dinner and then merrily get behind the wheel. Her max was a glass of wine that she took her time over, and not even that most times.

"No problem," said Tim, wandering back into the house.

"So are you still okay to take the kids on Saturday?" Ray asked.

"Yeah, should be." Sofia planned on taking them down to the beach and pretty much letting them loose. The beach would usually tire them out enough that she could feed them and put them in front of a movie with ice cream. "You have anything special planned?"

"I'm going to take Emily up to Santa Barbara, but don't tell her because I want the place to be a surprise," said Ray. His cell phone rang. "Sorry, I better get this."

Ray stepped away to take the call as Emily came out.

"Where are the rug rats?" she asked Sofia.

"They went to take a shower," Sofia told her. "Tim says he locked up the tools, so don't worry about it."

Emily took the chair next to Sofia's. "So how's Aidan?"

Here we go.

Both her sister and her mom had gotten it into their

heads that Aidan had a thing for Sofia, and that the thing was mutual. Sofia's years of denials had only served to reinforce the idea, and now, it had become a thing. She wasn't sure if it was a running joke or whether they actually believed that one day she and Aidan would get together.

"I think he might have finally found someone he likes," Sofia told her sister.

Emily's eyebrows shot up. "No kidding."

"Yeah," said Sofia. "He's even got as far as a second date."

Emily, who was pretty familiar with Aidan's Tinder/Internet dating obsession and his crazy checklist, seemed genuinely surprised. "Wow. How are you with that?"

Sofia couldn't help but roll her eyes. "Fine. Why wouldn't I be?" As soon as she said it, she realized how defensive she'd sounded.

Emily held up her palms. "No reason. Just taking an interest."

"I work with the guy. That's it. There's never been anything between us, and that's not going to change."

"Let me guess. You're talking about Aidan?" They turned to see their mom coming toward them, wine glass in hand.

"He's dating someone," said Emily. "Sofia's *fine* with it."

"I *am* fine with it," said Sofia.

Emily and her mom exchanged a look. Her mom reached over and put a comforting arm on Sofia's shoulder. "We know, darling."

33

To Sofia's great relief, the dinner topics consisted of pretty much everything apart from her love life, the sheer folly of her career change, and, minor miracle, no one mentioned the incident outside the rehab center or the brief but intense media storm that had followed. Ray and Tim discussed golf and baseball, and their mom told Emily and Sofia about the round-the-world trip she was planning for next year. Emily said she was thinking about taking a part-time job in Ray's office helping out with the paperwork. Ray was a good plumber, but less good at getting paid on time and the day-to-day business admin side of the operation.

For her part, Sofia relaxed and enjoyed eating a meal that she hadn't cooked herself. Her mom was a pretty phenomenal cook. She planned everything with military precision, but could improvise her way round a recipe if she needed to. Sofia thought that she would make a pretty amazing restaurant owner if she'd wanted to open one. She had the right mix of food knowledge and planning and operational skills. Plus, she took absolutely no crap from anyone. Woe betide the person who crossed Janet.

While the grown-ups ate dinner, Van and Violet had been relegated to a smaller children's table over by the fireplace. They ate like ravenous wolves, demolishing the food while arguing about which would be the best instrument to kill someone, a fork or a knife. Despite it seeming obvious that the knife would be the winner, Violet mounted a spirited case for the fork on the basis that a three-pronged fork, if shoved into a person's neck with sufficient force, had a good chance of puncturing more than one major blood vessel. As dinner discussions went it was, Sofia thought, more interesting than golf, book keeping, or world travel.

Sofia helped her sister to clear the plates. Emily doled out ice cream with strawberries and Hershey's chocolate syrup to the kids and sent them into Tim's den to eat it. They could watch TV, but Emily told them that the adults had something to talk about so they had to stay in there—unless someone was bleeding. Overhearing her sister's comment, Sofia had a bad feeling about what the adults might be talking about.

Before Sofia could make her excuses, thank her mom and Tim for a lovely evening, and escape, the doorbell rang. Her mom went to answer it. Sofia was definitely picking up lots of looks between everyone else, as if they were in on a secret that she wasn't. Not good.

Her mom came back into the dining room with a tall, white-haired man wearing half-moon glasses and a tweed sports jacket with leather elbow patches. As soon as she saw him, Sofia knew he was a shrink. It was pretty obvious. No detective skills required for that.

"Sofia, everyone, can we all sit down?" her mom said.

Holy crap on a cracker. They were staging an intervention. Her life was officially a sitcom.

34

Any moment, Sofia was expecting Jeffrey Weiner to pop up from behind the couch with a camera crew and release forms for everyone to sign to agree that their contribution could be used on screen. Luckily, that didn't happen.

But it dawned on Sofia about ten minutes into the intervention that she was in a no-win situation. She couldn't admit to an addiction problem she didn't have. But the more she denied that she had a problem, the more everyone looked at her like she was in denial and this was all part of the process.

The whole thing was ridiculous. Apart from a glass of wine after a hard day at work, she was about as clean living as anyone in LA could get. She rarely even took aspirin when she had a headache.

After a while of everyone telling her how worried they were about her, Sofia got tired of it. She really wanted to drive home, feed Fred if he was still hanging around, go to bed, and pretend the day hadn't happened. It would be a bonus if no one tried to run her off the road on the way.

The main evidence that they seemed to have to prove she had an addiction problem was that her behavior had changed over the past year. She guessed that this was mainly about her career change. Other than that, her mom and the therapist seemed fixated on the whole peeing in the street outside a rehab clinic incident.

Lance Sterling, the therapist, who came off like a skinny version of Dr. Phil, called it, "the clearest cry for help I've seen in over twelve years of dealing with addiction." After he said that, he leaned in, touched Sofia's knee in a way that totally creeped her out, looked her in the eye, and said, "Sofia, you were actually outside a rehab facility. Peeing. In broad daylight."

She glowered at him. "I know that. It was a surveillance operation. I needed to pee. There was nowhere else to go."

At that point, Lance shot her a pitying look and handed the discussion back to her mom. After a few more minutes, Sofia finally lost patience and did something she'd hoped she wouldn't have to. She called Aidan to get him to corroborate her story.

To make sure that no one suspected that Aidan was covering for her, or in the words of Lance Sterling "facilitating self-harming behaviors," Sofia put Aidan on speaker. Risky, but she didn't have much choice.

"Hey, Aidan, how's it going?" she said when he answered. Judging by the background noise, he was in a bar or restaurant with his date, the Other Sofia.

"Good. You skip out on dinner with your crazy family?" Aidan's voice made it clear that he wouldn't blame her if she had. That made him right, and annoying.

"No, I'm right here. So are they. And I have you on speaker. Why don't you say hi?"

"Um, okay. Hi, Sofia's family! By the way, I meant crazy

in the good way. You know like quirky, off-the-wall, kooky," Aidan said, each word digging the hole a little deeper.

Everyone in the room with Sofia pretended not to have heard him call them all crazy. Sofia wasn't sure how to shut him down. He was like the Energizer bunny once he got going.

He must have half covered his cell but everyone in the room heard him say, "Sorry, Sofia, it's work. Why don't you order another drink and I'll be right with you? Shouldn't take too long."

"He's dating a girl named Sofia," Sofia explained to everyone in the room.

Her mom shot Lance a look before staring up at the ceiling. "Don't need to be a shrink to work *that* one out."

Lance looked uncomfortable. At first he'd tried to over-rule Sofia's call to Aidan until Emily had intervened on her behalf after Sofia had threatened to scoot her caught-peeing-outside-rehab ass into her car and leave them to it. It made for a pretty bad day when almost being run off the road by a psychopath in an SUV wasn't the worst thing that happened.

Aidan came back on the line. "Whatever this is, can we make it quick? I'm kind of busy here."

"It won't take long," said Sofia. "All I need you to do is explain to my family exactly what happened outside the rehab clinic when those guys from TMZ were there."

"Wait. You called me out of office hours, with your entire family on speakerphone, to ask me to tell them what happened outside the rehab clinic when it's all on film."

Terrific. Suddenly Aidan had switched to private investi-gator mode and was starting to sound genuinely interested.

"Do you mind if I ask why they want this information? I mean, couldn't you tell them?"

Sofia took the opportunity to stare at each of her family in turn. Janet gave her a concerned smile. Tim kind of nodded to her mom with an I-do-what-I'm-told-round-here look, Emily and Ray were good enough to look embarrassed, and Lance practiced his stare off into the mid distance while hoping that someone would get to the point before the next ad break, apprentice TV shrink look.

"Yes, I could," said Sofia through gritted teeth. Thank God she hadn't Skyped or FaceTimed him so he couldn't actually see what she was looking at. "But they'd like to hear it from a trusted, independent source. So..."

On the other end of the line, Sofia heard rustling followed by a howl of laughter. The howl stopped, and then Aidan said, "Hey, sweetie, could you get me another drink, too? This might take longer than I thought. But I'll catch you up after. It's pretty funny."

Sofia hated to think how that conversation with the Other Sofia was going to go.

Janet leaned over to whisper to Tim. "Second date and he's already calling her sweetie." She shot a look at Sofia and said in a slightly sing-song voice. "This is what happens when you dawdle. The bee loses interest, gets impatient, and flits over to the next flower. In this town, if you snooze, you lose."

Flowers and bees? Really? With any luck, Aidan hadn't overheard that part.

"Sofia is a flower?" said Aidan.

Sofia wasn't going to catch any breaks here.

"Which Sofia?" said Janet pointedly.

"Hey, Janet," said Aidan.

"Hello, darling," said Janet.

"I was talking to Half Pint Detective Sofia," said Aidan. "You there, Half Pint?"

"I called you. Of course I'm here," Sofia said.

"Can I ask you a question?" Aidan didn't wait for her to answer. "Is your family by any chance staging an intervention?"

Lance leaned in toward Sofia's cell phone, which she had set down on the coffee table so that everyone could hear. "We prefer to use the term pro-active spiritual re-connection. Intervention can sound overly aggressive."

"Wait. Who's that?" said Aidan. "Tim?"

"This is Lance Sterling, Aidan. I'm a licensed psychotherapist assisting Sofia and her family."

There was another howl of laughter from Aidan. This one went on longer. He seemed to be laughing so hard that he was struggling for air. Sofia hoped he choked on it. "Oh, man. It is. This is too good."

"Aidan, could you please tell everyone what actually happened? That I'd had too much iced tea, I needed to pee. You were a jerk off, and I ended up having to go in the street," Sofia snapped.

"Hey, no leading the witness, Half Pint," said Aidan.

"This is not funny," said Sofia.

"Oh, thanks, sweetie," said Aidan. It sounded like he took another sip from his drink.

"Again with the sweetie," Janet whispered to Tim. "Her name is Sofia. Can you believe that?"

Tim looked at his watch. "Is this going to take much longer? The Golf channel has—"

Janet glared at him, and he shut right up.

"Just tell them." Sofia practically spat the words out.

"Okay, okay," said Aidan. "Sofia drank too much iced tea and didn't have a plan as to what she'd do on a long stakeout if she had to pee. I wouldn't relieve her, so she relieved herself on the street. The TMZ guys happened to be there for the same reason we were. To see if a particular actor had skipped out of rehab to go score. Sofia doesn't have any kind of addiction problem that I know of. Seeing as how I'm a private investigator and spend more time with her than is healthy, I'm pretty sure I would have picked up on it if she had. Plus we had to take pee tests a couple weeks ago because some paranoid client demanded it. I can send you a copy of the results if you need it. Sofia is as pure as the driven snow. Or at least as far as drugs are concerned."

The living room fell silent. Thank God Aidan had finally put her out of her misery, and too bad she hadn't remembered that pee test earlier. Then she wouldn't have had to call Aidan.

Emily was the first to recover. She mumbled an apology.

"Yeah, me, too," said Ray, nodding like a bobblehead doll.

Tim shot Janet an exasperated 'I told you so' look.

"I'm sorry too, Sofia," Tim said. "This was probably the last thing you needed right now. What with the new job and everything." He gave Sofia's mom another look. "But your mom only asked Lance over here to help because she cares about you."

Lance, who had sunk back into the club chair at Aidan's words, suddenly perked up, leaning forward and placing his leather-patched elbows on his knees as he affected a professorial posture. "As I'm here already, if any of you wish to discuss any communication problems you're having, I'd be happy to help facilitate that discussion. No extra charge."

Everyone in the room except for Janet answered at the same time. "No!"

Lance looked deflated. Here he was all ready to get his therapist teeth into a nice juicy addiction problem and medically all it boiled down to was Sofia's weak bladder.

"Are you sure? Because I definitely sense some deep-seated issues here. It's pretty much the norm for most families that there are tensions. I'd be happy to help facilitate..."

Tim cut him off, raising a hand, and saying, "We really appreciate the offer, don't we, Janet?"

"Yes, absolutely," said Sofia's mom. Her face had flushed, but Sofia couldn't tell if it was from embarrassment or from the wine she'd been slugging down like a thirsty long-shoreman while preparing dinner. She must have been working herself up for the intervention.

From the cell phone on the coffee table, Aidan's voice piped up. "Can I go back to my date now? You don't need to cross-examine me or anything?"

Sofia had all but forgotten that Aidan was still on the line and listening to everything being said. She was already dreading facing him in the office tomorrow. Lustrous jewels and an intervention all in the same day. He had fuel for weeks of jokes now. "Yes, thanks, Aidan. You're all done."

She hung up and tried not to think of how he was going to spin these events for the Other Sofia.

Tim got up from his seat. "Lance, I'll show you out, and again, we really appreciate you coming out here."

Lance looked crestfallen as he got up to a chorus of mumbled thanks and followed Tim out of the room and to the front door. Everyone else in the room sat in silence. They mostly seemed to be waiting for Sofia's reaction.

More than anything, she felt embarrassed. She also felt angry that her mom had thought she was capable of having a drug problem. At least she presumed that was what she'd thought. And she was angry that everyone else in the family had gone along with it. Though, to be fair to them, Janet was a force of nature when she got an idea in her head.

If their mom hadn't been a force of nature, they would

still be back in Indiana rather than out here in California. Not that there was anything inherently wrong with Indiana. The people were a lot nicer and way less fake than people in LA. But no one could argue that there wasn't something to be said for living somewhere the sun shone pretty much year round and where the temperature, at least out on the coast, remained at a pretty steady seventy-five degrees. Plus, there was Fred.

When Emily, not Sofia, had expressed an interest in acting that went beyond the lead in the school play, it had been Janet who had packed her two girls into their ten-year-old station wagon and driven them out to LA. They'd set up camp, like so many aspiring families, at the Oakwood Apartments in Hollywood while Emily did the round of agents and auditions. It had been a sheer quirk of fate that Sofia had been home sick on the day that Emily had gone to the audition for a new kids TV show called *Half Pint Detective*, and somehow got cast instead of her older sister.

Now that would have been rich territory for Lance the therapist. Older sister wants to be an actress and younger sister quite literally stumbles into her sister's dream. Sofia was still amazed with how well Emily had dealt with it. It probably helped that Sofia's fame had allowed Emily to see what it was really like and realize that it wasn't what she'd dreamed of. In the end, Emily hadn't been any more impressed with the world behind the film industry than Sofia had been. But still, it had been Emily's dream and Sofia, the one who hadn't been that interested in any of it, had been the one who ended up going to the ball and dancing the night away.

It had been to Emily's eternal credit that not only had she not made an issue of it, she had been super supportive from the very beginning, helping Sofia run lines, working as a stand-in when they needed someone there to help light scenes, and generally just being awesome. At the same time, Sofia and their mom had gone out of the way to try to include Emily as much as they could and for Sofia not to be seen as the special or chosen daughter.

They were always a team, and Sofia figured their closeness came down to the fact that there had pretty much always just been the three of them. They'd had to stick together in order to get by. There hadn't been room for any major fall outs. Sofia wasn't about to change that now.

She stood up as Tim walked back into the living room. Apart from when someone had written them for her, Sofia didn't think she was very big on speeches. Especially not heartfelt ones, but the occasion seemed to call for her to say something.

"Guys, I really do appreciate that you were worried about me enough to organize this. Okay, it was a little weird." She paused. "Okay, a lot weird, but it came from a good place, so no hard feelings."

As she took a breath, an almighty bang came from the den. While everyone else froze, Ray jumped to his feet. He took off running toward the den. He really did have the reflexes of a panther.

"Van? Violet? You guys okay?" Ray shouted.

Sofia, who had completely forgotten what she had planned on saying next, was close behind as Ray pushed opened the door into the den. Smoke and dust floated into the hall. First Van and then Violet emerged. Van's hair was standing straight up, and they both looked pale. Other than that they didn't appear to be injured.

Behind the two kids, the flat-screen TV that had been mounted on the far wall lay face-down on the floor. Pieces of screen lay in a mosaic pattern across the carpet. Two chunks of missing plaster indicated where the TV had been fixed to the wall by brackets, and a butter knife showed what had been used to pry it away.

Van looked around at the assembled adults. "Sorry!"

"What happened?" Emily asked the kids. "Are either of you hurt?"

"It was my fault," said Van. "Violet was helping me take it off the wall, and it got too heavy."

Before anyone could reprimand him or his sister, Van turned to Sofia. "Hey, Auntie Sofia, are you a drug addict anymore?"

35

With the day she'd had, Sofia decided not to take Malibu Canyon Road back to Nirvana Cove. Instead she took the 10 freeway to PCH, figuring that the heavier the traffic, the less likely someone was to try to run her off the road or otherwise stage a mysterious accident.

She got back to the Cove around eleven in the evening and parked the remarkably unscathed Roadster in the upper parking lot. She patted its fender to thank it for its splendid performance that day, then walked down the path toward her blue trailer.

The path was pretty quiet. She stayed alert to any sudden movements from the shadows, or anyone following her. If someone was happy enough to try to force her off the road, it was fair to say that they wouldn't stop at more conventional means. Not that she had any idea why someone would want to harm her. After all, if it was connected to the investigation into Nigel's death, they'd still have Brendan and Aidan to deal with. Maybe they figured she was the one who would be most easily scared. Or it was completely unrelated. Probably that.

No matter the reason, she planned on letting Brendan know about it when she went to work the next morning. He'd know how to handle it. She hoped that he wouldn't over-react and take her off the case.

As she turned into the narrow lane where her trailer was, she froze. There was a light on inside. She was pretty certain she hadn't left any lights on before she left.

Ducking into the shadows, she crept toward her trailer. As she got closer she saw a figure on the porch. Her heartbeat thudded in her ears. She swallowed hard and didn't move.

Narrowing her eyes, she tried to get a better look at the figure on the porch. It was a man. He was tall. Definitely over six feet. And really well built.

She started as his hand reached up and out. He held his palm open. Something moved next to him. Fred the seagull inched along the railing to the man's outstretched hand.

Sofia walked from the shadows. "You scared the crap out of me, Gray."

The man turned to her. "Hey, Sofia. Didn't see you there."

She walked up the stairs and onto the porch. Gray leaned in and gave her a hug. "Sorry, Adrianna's at my place, and she's refusing to leave. I can't afford to make a scene so I came down here. You weren't around so I thought I'd hang with Fred until you got back, give him something to eat."

Gray Cole was a full-blown, one hundred percent A-list Hollywood movie star. He was lusted after by women around the world. He was also Sofia's neighbor. He'd been one of the first people she met when she'd moved into Nirvana Cove and they'd become firm friends.

Gray was one of the few people who completely under-stood her decision to turn her back on showbiz. Part of the reason he understood was because Gray had, over the years, become adept at presenting one face to the public and media, while his private life was very different. Unlike Sofia, Gray had already reached the global level of fame that ruled out the kind of major life change that she had chosen. Gray was trapped by celebrity, his every move reported and dissected. As he'd told her on more than one occasion, "a gilded cage is still a cage," or in his case a gilded closet.

Hollywood might have moved on from the days when the studios went to great lengths to make sure no one knew certain leading men were gay. But it hadn't moved on that much. While no one was going to have their career ended by coming out, if they'd cultivated the image that Gray had, their brand would certainly take a hit, as would the type of roles they'd be offered and what they'd be paid. Gray Cole could have come out, but he chose not to torpedo his career.

Part of his cover was a string of drop-dead gorgeous girl-friends that he got close to, but never quite managed to walk down the aisle with. Most were aware of his sexual prefer-ences before they hooked up. They were happy to play along. Even though he always made it plain they couldn't be more than friends, that didn't stop more than a few of them from falling head over heels in love and then attempting to seduce him straight.

Adrianna, a stunningly beautiful Victoria's Secret model from Italy, was the latest of his companions to try for the conversion. No matter how much Gray told her this man wasn't for turning, Adrianna simply refused to give up. Her insistence and his refusal were leading to increasingly explosive fights.

"You can sleep here if you like," Sofia said to Gray as he

followed her into her little blue trailer. "I could use the company."

"Oh?" said Gray.

She grabbed two glasses and the rest of the wine from the fridge. Gray was already on the couch. Sofia poured them each a glass of wine and sat down next to him. She wasn't sure why, but she found herself telling him about her near-death experiences first on the canyon road and later on the freeway.

Gray was a great listener. He leaned in, completely intent, deep blue eyes never leaving her face. She kind of understood why women, even when they knew that he batted for the other team, tended to forget after a while. She wasn't sure what the difference was between a great actor and a movie star, but she figured it had something to do with presence. It was like a light they could switch on and off. A great actor walked into a room and people looked, but when a movie star walked in, people stopped talking and stared. Gray was a movie star.

"You've called the cops, right?" Gray asked when she got to the end. She had already planned to tell him the story of her mom's intervention another time.

Sofia shook her head. "No, and I don't plan on calling them either. I'm going to tell Brendan. He'll know whether I should tell them or not."

"But what if it was some crazy stalker?" Gray said, his deep movie star baritone falling away to reveal his higher-pitched real voice. Sometimes Sofia thought that Gray really deserved a lifetime achievement Oscar for his public persona and not his on screen work. Not that he was a screaming queen or anything, but he definitely wasn't the chocolate-smooth, Alpha male 'no female safe' seducer the world thought he was.

"I think it might be connected to this case we're working on," said Sofia.

Now she really had Gray's interest. As much as he had a team of agents, and more crucially, attorneys, to keep his private life just that, he was a major gossip. If you needed to know who in Hollywood was screwing, or screwing over, someone else, Gray was your man.

"What case is this?" Gray asked breathlessly.

"Can't discuss it," Sofia said.

"You're such a tease," said Gray. He put his empty wine glass down on table. "Guess I should head back."

"Will you be okay?" Sofia asked. Adrianna's tantrums seemed to be getting more melodramatic. She'd gone from crying and screaming to throwing plates and threatening self-harm. Sofia worried that Adrianna would eventually take her anger and heartbreak out on Gray.

"She'll probably be asleep," said Gray.

"She did know what the deal was before you started seeing her?" Sofia asked.

"Like that makes a difference," said Gray.

"But she knew you were gay?" pressed Sofia.

"I sure hope so. I mean, I met her when she walked in on me and her brother naked in his apartment in New York," said Gray.

"That's kinda creepy," said Sofia. "Brother and sister."

"Except it's not brother and sister. It's just brother. I have no interest in the sister."

"Shame she doesn't agree," said Sofia.

Gray shrugged. "People want what they can't have. If I was straight and had been trying to get into her pants all this time, she wouldn't have given me the time of day."

Sofia looked at him in the half light as he opened the door. With his chiseled jaw, piercing blue eyes, and broad shoulders, somehow she doubted that. Most women on Earth would have given Gray the time of day, plus a lot more, if he asked.

"Goodnight, Gray."

"Goodnight. Call the police if anything suspicious happens tonight. Then call me."

She listened as he walked out onto the porch and down the stairs. She got up and locked the door behind him. Then she armed her alarm, just in case. Fred was still out there, standing guard, wings tucked in tight against the stiff ocean breeze. She whispered, "Good night, Fred."

36

Before walking into the office the next morning, Sofia took three deep breaths and wondered what Aidan had left on her desk. She opened the door and stepped inside. Aidan was in his usual spot behind his monitors. Brendan was standing over him. They were deep in conversation. It stopped as they looked up and saw Sofia. Brendan put his hand on Aidan's shoulder and whispered something before straightening up and walking back into his office and closing the door.

She walked over to her desk. Her chair didn't have a package of adult diapers sitting on it. Her work space seemed to be completely adult diaper-free. Aidan must have tired of the joke and moved on. He had enough ammunition after last night for a whole new round of jokes, but she guessed he hadn't started that just yet. She booted up her computer, sat down, and checked through her emails. Nothing interesting.

She wondered if Aidan had been telling Brendan about the intervention phone call when she'd come in. Brendan had seemed on edge. He'd barely acknowledged her when she'd walked in. It wasn't like him.

After replying to the most urgent emails, she got up and walked over to the water cooler and filled her bottle. She was dehydrated from the wine she'd drunk the night before with Gray. Aidan got up from his desk and wandered over with his mug. He jammed a coffee capsule in their machine and hit the button to make himself an espresso.

Aidan's not mentioning anything about the phone call was making Sofia uneasy. He usually grabbed any and every opportunity to tease her with both hands.

"Hey," she said, "thanks for clearing up that thing with my family last night."

Aidan shrugged. "No problem."

Huh. This was definitely not the reaction she'd expected.

"I really appreciate it," said Sofia.

"Any time."

"I'm hoping it was a one-off. They worry about me. My mom can be a little overprotective."

When Aidan didn't respond, she decided to change the subject. Maybe Aidan meeting a woman he deemed worthy of a second date was changing him. Maybe his newfound maturity when it came to dating was spilling over, in a positive way, into his work life.

"I'm sorry if it spoiled your date with Sofia." His date having the same name was definitely a little weird. She didn't see the significance that her mom had, but, yeah, it was kind of odd.

Aidan picked up his coffee cup from the machine and waved Sofia's apology away. "Forget about it. That's old news."

"What?" said Sofia, unable to keep the surprise out of her voice. "Already?"

Aidan took a sip of espresso. "Didn't work out. What can I tell you?"

"I thought you really liked her."

"I did, but ..." He trailed off.

"But?" Sofia prompted.

She knew she was moving way out of work colleague territory now, but if she didn't find out the reason for Aidan not wanting to see Other Sofia anymore, it would drive her crazy. She had to know.

"But nothing," Aidan shrugged. "It didn't work out."

Sofia gaped at him. He was holding out on her. Aidan was usually pretty open about sharing the tenuous reasons he had for rejecting any of the dozens of women he'd taken out on a first date only to never see again. He wore his anally-retentive checklist like a badge of honor. Proof that he had high standards and wasn't prepared to settle for just anyone so that he could be in a relationship. It was perfection, whatever that actually was in Aidan's fevered brain (Sofia wasn't convinced that he really knew himself), or nothing.

The water was spilling from her bottle.

"Damn. How come?" She tried to sound casual.

Aidan looked at her. "You'll think it's dumb."

He was right. She probably would. But she still wanted to know. More so now that he'd just said she'd think it was dumb. "Try me."

He slugged down the rest of his espresso and put the cup back down on top of the table with the coffee machine on it. "Okay, but promise you won't use it against me later on. I know you think my lists and spreadsheets are stupid."

"Girl Scout's Honor," said Sofia, putting one hand

behind her back and crossing her fingers, in clear breach of both the spirit and the letter of the Girl Scout's Honor system. But she'd never been a Girl Scout, so it didn't matter.

"Promise?" Aidan asked.

This was going to be good. If even Aidan thought it was dumb, it had to be great. "Sure."

"Okay, she did this weird thing with her fork," said Aidan.

Sofia had to bite the inside of her mouth to keep from laughing. "Weird, how?"

"I told you it was dumb."

"What did she do? Stick it up her nose? What?" Sofia figured that even though Aidan was sensitive about stuff like this, it had to be a pretty serious breach of cutlery etiquette to make him dump a woman who had passed all his other weird tests.

"It's dumb," said Aidan, clearly regretting that he'd said anything and obviously hoping that she would drop it.

Which just was not going to happen as far as Sofia was concerned. Her interest was so piqued that she'd track the Other Sofia down and ask her what she did with a fork if she had to.

"Just tell me," Sofia said, opening a drawer and raking around until she found a plastic fork. She turned the fork around and passed it to him, handle first.

He stared up at the ceiling as if hoping for divine intervention. When that didn't come, Aidan took the fork. He pinched the handle between tips of his right thumb and index finger. He then mimed jabbing at an imaginary plate of food like a swordfighter.

"She ate like this," he said, jabbing some more. "I tried to ignore it. I mean it's not even on my checklist. But by end of the entree it was driving me crazy. Oh, and she'd like jab her fork at me when she was making a point. She could have taken one of my eyes out."

He explained it with such intensity that Sofia didn't laugh. That was the problem with Aidan's crazy rules. He was so definite about them that she could easily be pulled into to thinking they were the product of someone sane.

"Couldn't you have asked her nicely not to jab her fork at you?" Sofia said.

Aidan threw the plastic fork back down on the table. "I could, but I didn't want to appear petty."

Sofia tried to follow the logic, she really did. "You didn't want to appear petty by saying something, so instead, you dumped her?"

"I haven't dumped her yet," said Aidan.

"But you're going to, right? You are going to actually tell her that you don't want to see her again, aren't you?"

Aidan didn't reply. That meant he was going to do that asshole thing men did of not answering the Other Sofia's calls or texts until she either got the message or blew up at him.

"Aidan?"

"We had two dates. That's it."

Sofia could feel her eyeballs about to roll right out of their sockets and onto the floor. "Yeah, but two dates for you is like moving in together for a regular person."

"Wow, did you really accuse me of not being regular, Miss 'Even My Own Family Think I'm So Weird They Staged An Intervention?'"

"Don't try to change the subject," Sofia scolded him. "If you don't learn to accept that people have their flaws as well as their good points, then you're going to end up old and lonely in a nursing home."

At this Aidan let out a sound that was part laugh, part

bark. "Really? The old and lonely in a nursing home meme? That's all you got?"

"It's true."

"Not according to the data," Aidan said.

Sofia folded her arms in front of her. "What data?"

"All the data. You want me to break it down for you?" said Aidan.

"Please do. I hope my tiny female brain will be able to keep up with your brilliant data analysis."

"I'll be sure to speak slowly," said Aidan, matching her sarcastic tone. "As you may know, women in the United States have, on average, a life expectancy that's approximately seven years longer than men born into the same socio-economic group. By the time a man's reached the age of seventy, which I hope to make easily by careful diet, regular exercise, and regular check-ups, there are approximately one point three women for every man. And that's not even going into the whole sexual market value issue, which kicks in way earlier than that."

Aidan stopped. He shot Sofia a smug look.

"What sexual market value issue?" she said, regretting asking the question as soon as it was out of her mouth.

"Women reach their sexual, or if you prefer, their social market value, at the age of twenty-four. Men don't hit their peak until their mid-thirties, and after that, it's a long, slow ride down that curve, while chicks, they hit the freaking wall. It's a goddamn ski slope after twenty-four. By the time I hit the nursing home, I'm going to have my pick. If I go into the home at eighty, I'll still be able to score me a banging sixty-five-year-old."

She just stared at him. This was obviously a matter that he had given some thought to. More than she'd imagined. It also explained his geeky adherence to checklists and brooking no compromise.

"So that's why you're not going to see this woman again? It's got nothing to do with what she does with a fork. It's because you think you'll always be able to do better. That there's a nice piece of candy on the next shelf," said Sofia.

Aidan shook his head. "That's not it."

"Then what is it?" Sofia asked.

"Okay, you want to know the naked, unvarnished truth?" said Aidan, his face growing red. "The fork thing bugged me, but it wasn't a complete deal breaker."

"So what was?"

Aidan stalked back to his desk. His back was to Sofia. "It was her name. It was freaking me out."

Sofia stood where she was, not sure what to make of what Aidan had just said. This was territory she wasn't sure she wanted to get into. It would bring up things she was as eager to avoid talking about as he was.

"Okay," she said finally.

He sat down at his desk. "Hey, so I picked up something from that bug you planted under Moonbow's couch."

"Great," said Sofia, relieved at the change of subject. Work was definitely firmer ground. She walked over and stood behind him.

"Yeah, you might not think so when you hear it," Aidan said, handing her a pair of headphones plugged into his computer.

He full-screened an audio player, and used his mouse to drag the play triangle to two hours and forty-odd minutes into the audio recording. He hit a button to turn up the volume and hit play.

At first Sofia couldn't hear much apart from background noise. Then a cell phone rang and Moonbow answered. His voice was pure Philly rather than the soothing Californian with a hint of surfer voice that he had cultivated as part of his chakra massage healer persona.

"Yeah, that chick who's working with the PI that Melissa's attorney is using showed up here," Moonbow was saying to whoever was on the other end of the line.

The hairs on the back of Sofia's neck stood up. Moonbow had known who she was and who she was working for. Had he known when she'd booked him for a massage, or had he figured it out later? No matter, he'd obviously realized by the time she turned up at his apartment, or shortly thereafter. The idea that she'd walked into his apartment and he'd already known that she was a PI gave her chills.

She reached over, grabbed the mouse from Aidan, and hit pause. She took the headphones off. "Do you know who he's talking to?"

"Not yet, but I'm working on it. Believe me," said Aidan. "Anyway, there's more. Listen."

She put the headphones back on as Aidan restarted the audio. Rogers made a few *umms* and *ahs* before he said, "That doesn't matter to me, okay? I just want this taken care of." There was another pause, presumably while the person on the other end of the line responded, then Rogers said, "Okay, you do that. Send a message. Whatever. But I don't want any more visits. You feel me? Okay, bye."

The call ended. Bobby Rogers put the phone down and moved around his apartment. Sofia took off her headphones. The office felt about ten degrees colder than it had been when she'd arrived.

"You okay?" asked Aidan.

Now he looked worried about her.

37

"Why didn't you call me the first time the guy tried to drive you off Malibu Canyon Road?" Brendan stood behind his desk, glaring at Sofia, knuckles resting on the desk top like he wanted to push it through the floor. Sofia sat opposite him. Aidan paced the room behind her.

"I didn't think it was necessarily deliberate," Sofia replied. "I mean, it's LA. Most people drive like assholes here. Even if you don't want to do it, you end up doing it so you can get to where you were going." It was true. LA was one of the few places where a turn signal was seen as a warning to close the gap so someone couldn't get ahead of you rather than as a common courtesy.

"Look, Sofia, I know this is a male-dominated industry, and you might feel like asking for help will be seen as a weakness, but not calling me or the California Highway Patrol was just plain dumb. You don't have anything to prove to me or anyone else," Brendan said.

"I know, I know, and I was going to call you, but then I got my mom's house, but...." She snuck a glance at Aidan.

She was still amazed that he hadn't said anything about her phone call to his father. "... Well, I got there, and I was okay, and it slipped my mind."

"Someone tries to turn you into lunch meat and it slips your mind?" Brendan bellowed. She had rarely seen him this mad and never this mad at her.

"I'm sorry. I won't let it happen again. If anything like this happens in the future, I'll be sure to let you know immediately." She waited, hoping a sincere apology would do the trick.

Brendan sunk back down into his chair. "This isn't a movie, okay?"

That one stung. Brendan had been one of the few people who hadn't thrown her acting career back in her face or suggested that she didn't take her work at the agency seriously.

"This is real. That's all I'm saying," Brendan continued. "These people aren't messing around." He turned his attention to Aidan. "And as for you, when did you hear that audio?"

Aidan held his hands up. "This morning."

"You didn't think to give Sofia here a heads up as soon as you heard it?" Brendan asked Aidan.

"This all went down yesterday," Aidan said.

Brendan started to get back up, thought about it, and sunk back into his seat. "You didn't know that. For all you knew, they could have had someone waiting to clip her this morning. Someone could have set up in our parking lot. They know she works here."

Aidan went a shade paler. "You're right. I should have called Sofia as soon as I knew."

Clearly, he was hoping that a fast apology would work for him as well as it had for her.

Brendan looked up at the ceiling. "Okay, here's what we're gonna do. I'm going to let Stark and the LA County sheriff know what's happened. If nothing else, that conversation suggests that Melissa wasn't in on any of this and Moonbow knows a lot more than he's been letting on. In the meantime, we're all going to have to be extra careful. You think someone's trailing you, you call it in. Don't take any stupid risks. And, Sofia ..."

"Yes?"

"That car of yours is way too easy to spot. I want you to get a rental. It can go on the company credit card. Once this case is finished, you can go back to driving the Tesla." Brendan didn't ask. He delivered this news as a direct order. It was hard for Sofia to forget that Brendan had not only been a cop but that he'd served his country as a US Marine. She stifled an urge to say "yes, sir!"

What he was saying made sense. But she still didn't want to give up her Roadster, not even for a few days. She loved that car. It was like a part of her. If that car hadn't been the powerful and nimble machine it was the Ford would have creamed her. "Are you sure that's absolutely necessary?"

Brendan's answer came in the shape of a vein-popping glare aimed at her from behind his desk.

38

"Sorry, this is all we have left."

Sofia stared at the brown Ford Kia sitting in the car rental lot. She hadn't seen a brown Kia before. Ever. Certainly not this shade of brown. In fact she had never seen this particular shade of brown on any car before. She suspected that it had been painted this color by mistake and when no one would buy it, it had been unloaded, no doubt at a huge discount, onto the only people who would take it, this car rental company.

"You don't have anything else?" Sofia pleaded. "Even if you just had a return and you haven't cleaned it yet, I can take that, take it down to the car wash myself."

"Sorry, this is it. Everything else is out. First car we have due back is the day after tomorrow." The car rental lady slapped a hand affectionately down on the trunk. "Runs great. Practically no miles on the clock."

I wonder why. Sofia couldn't imagine anyone wanting to be seen in public in this car. Especially not somewhere as image conscious as Los Angeles. If only she had time to find something else. She didn't though. Brendan wanted her and

Aidan to go talk to Nigel's production company partner again this morning.

"Okay, I'll take it," Sofia found herself saying.

"Great," said the car rental lady. "Come on into the office. We'll finish up the paperwork and you can get going."

They started for the office. The car rental lady threw a glance back over her shoulder at the brown monstrosity. "It may grow on you."

Yeah, like hemorrhoids.

FIFTEEN MINUTES LATER, Sofia was back out on PCH in the brown Ford Kia. In one way it was a similar experience to driving her Tesla Roadster. Both cars drew looks. The difference was that the looks the Tesla drew were admiring. People's reactions to the brown Kia were more along the lines of revulsion. Other drivers would change lanes and speed past. Probably wanted to make sure that none of the Kia's ugliness rubbed off on their vehicles. She didn't blame them.

After it had happened a couple times, she started to regard the car a little more sympathetically. It was an ugly duckling that, barring a complete respray, had no chance of becoming a beautiful swan. It was doomed. And it wasn't the poor little car's fault someone had slapped this godawful color on it.

There was at least one upside to having traded her Roadster for the brown Kia. No one in their right mind would want to steal or carjack her for it, which might come in handy given that she was headed for someplace that may have only been thirty-three miles from Malibu, but that might as well have been a different world.

39

Melissa Fairbroad was being held at Lynwood Jail, the main detention center for women in Los Angeles. It housed around two thousand women waiting for release or arraignment, and a few women who had been ordered to serve a jail sentence there. Lynwood was in South Central Los Angeles, a part of the city immortalized in rap songs and movies. Once a predominantly African-American community, its residents were now mostly Latino. With gang activity and violent crime, it was not a place that someone who lived in Malibu would visit without a good reason.

Stark had told Sofia to meet him at the jail's public parking facility on Alameda Street. She parked near an elevator and called him without getting out of her car.

"I'll be there in five," he told her.

She waited in the ugly brown Kia until Stark pulled into a space a few slots down in his Benz. She got out and walked across to meet him. They shook hands.

"Glad you could make it," Stark said.

"I'm still not sure exactly why you wanted me here," said Sofia.

"Let's walk while we talk. I have a busy day. Not enough hours." Stark motioned for her to follow him to the elevator. Sofia fell into step.

"Melissa likes you. I need her to start talking to me about Bobby Rogers," said Stark.

Sofia didn't know if she was more surprised that Melissa Fairbroad had said that she liked her or that she was holding back information from her lawyer that might help her avoid a sentence of life in prison without parole. Probably the former. "She hasn't said anything about him?"

Stark took out a pocket square and used it to cover his hand as he pressed the button to call the elevator. "This place isn't the cleanest."

At least she wouldn't get any jail cooties on the Roadster. The brown Kia was seeming more practical every second.

"Melissa is in love with the man," he said. "That's the only reason I can think of why she won't give him up. Or at least give me something to work with."

That also took Sofia aback. She hadn't put Melissa down as a gooey-hearted, head-over-heels, stand-by-your-man type of gal. Obviously, Moonbow had more than magic hands. Or maybe magic hands were enough.

"Really?" Sofia asked.

Stark shrugged as the elevator doors opened. "Go figure."

Sofia followed him into the elevator and the doors closed. "Does she know that Rogers is a convicted fraudster?"

"Yup. I ran though his record with her. Soup to the nuts. Didn't seem to change her mind. Of course that was yesterday. A night here can bring someone to their senses pretty rapidly, and you being here might help, too. They allow one visitor a day and they only get a half hour. Attorney visits are unrestricted, so if anyone asks, you're my legal assistant."

"Is that legal?" Sofia asked.

"Jesus, you are new to this, aren't you? My office already filled in the paperwork for you, so we're good to go. Just don't go telling them that you're not a legal assistant. This joint doesn't exactly attract the best and the brightest in terms of personnel, know what I mean?"

They walked down a split pea soup-green corridor to a reception area. The officer on duty sat behind a Plexiglas barrier. Stark got out his ID. Sofia followed suit.

"Attorney visit. John Stark and Sofia Salgado to see Melissa Fairbroad. Please and thank you."

The officer behind the screen sighed, put down the doughnut he'd been nibbling, and lifted the phone sitting next to him. "Take a seat."

They sat on a row of plastic chairs bolted to the floor. Always the sign of a classy joint. For a man wearing a three-piece Hugo Boss suit and five hundred dollar Salvatore Ferragamo wingtips, Stark seemed remarkably relaxed in their new surroundings. He seemed perfectly at ease sitting among the great unwashed who were waiting to see a loved one. He leaned over to Sofia. "Brendan told me about your freeway scare. We might want to mention that to Melissa. If this place hasn't scared her to her senses, maybe that will."

"It might scare her enough that she wants to stay," said Sofia.

Stark's name was called. He got to his feet, and Sofia followed him to a blue metal door that had been opened by a guard.

"Believe me," said Stark. "No one's ever been that scared. Plus, if they're ballsy enough to try to run you off the road, then they're plenty ballsy to pay someone to make a hit inside jail. Knowing some of the people who've ended up here, they'd probably get change from two hundred bucks."

They were shown into a small, private side room that smelled of stale sweat and three-day-old cabbage. Melissa was already there, behind a table. She brightened as Stark and Sofia walked in, but she looked like a different woman from the take-no-shit, glamorous Brentwood housewife Sofia had seen at their last meeting.

Appearance-wise she hadn't changed all that much. Her hair didn't have the same sheen, but that could have been down to the lighting. Her make-up didn't seem as fresh. Again, that could have been the lack of natural light and a good night's sleep. What Sofia really noticed were her eyes. The feisty spark was gone, replaced by something altogether sadder, an almost melancholy acceptance of what had happened.

Melissa pushed back her chair and stood up. She walked round to them. Stark gave her a hug. "How you holding up?"

"Okay, I guess. It's ... different." She tried to force a smile, but it didn't stick.

Sofia shook her hand. "Mrs. Fairbroad, I'm Sofia Salgado from—"

Melissa stood up, leaning over the table and clutching Sofia's hand with both of hers. "I remember. It's good to see you. Thank you for making the time to come see me. I don't think I was very polite to you the last time we met. I'm sorry."

Sofia was floored by her reaction. Where had the uber bitch who hated her gone? The one who told her she didn't have any tits, and could barely be bothered to answer Sofia's questions?

Pleasantries exchanged, everyone sat down. Stark put his Italian leather bag on the table and took out some papers. He made a show of shuffling through them. "I've put money into your account here. Two hundred dollars. That should be plenty."

"Thank you." Melissa managed to say the words while looking simultaneously horrified. "That seems rather a lot if I'm only going to be in here for a short time."

Stark's jaw tightened. Sofia could tell he had bad news.

"Bail hearing should be later today, but you should know I'm not optimistic. It might be a good idea if you tempered your expectations, Melissa." He flipped over some of his papers.

"But I've never had anything more than a parking ticket," Melissa protested. "I'm a law-abiding citizen."

Stark looked up from his papers. "I'm going to do my best. I don't want you to get your hopes up. Believe me, it's way worse if you think you'll be granted bail and then you're not. I've seen clients go into a complete tail spin when that happens. I want to avoid that if I can."

"If they're worried about me being a flight risk, I could

surrender my passport. Agree to stay at the house and not leave until this is sorted out. Put on an ankle bracelet like Martha Stewart did." Melissa reached back over the table to grasp Stark's hand. "You can't imagine what it's like in here. The way some of the women guards look at me. It's like I'm fresh meat."

She pretty much was fresh meat. Prime Brentwood grass-fed, twenty-one-day-aged filet mignon. Sofia actually felt a little sorry for her.

"We can certainly offer passport surrender to mitigate the flight risk," said Stark. "But I can't guarantee that will be enough."

"Surely everyone gets granted some kind of bail. It's not like I'm a serial killer," pleaded Melissa.

Stark let go of her hand. "Even if I can persuade them to grant you bail, that may not be the problem."

Sofia already knew where this was going. Stark was trying to break reality to his client gently, but she wasn't sure that was any kinder. It might have been better to treat bad news like this like taking off a Band-Aid. Sometimes it was better to slowly peel it back and prolong the agony. But sometimes it was easier all round to rip it off and get it over with.

"I don't follow you," Melissa said. "They set bail, we lodge the bond, and I can get out of here while Sofia and her colleagues, and you, find out who really killed Nigel."

Her voice was starting to break. She seemed to Sofia to be on the verge of a complete collapse. But she was also, for the first time, acting like an innocent woman, someone sure that more investigation would clear her.

Stark cleared his throat. "It's not quite that simple."

This was horrible. Sofia couldn't take it anymore. She looked at Melissa Fairbroad. "We've been looking into

Nigel's financial affairs. He was broke. Worse than broke. He was in a lot of debt."

Melissa blinked. "What are you talking about? He had three hit shows the last few years. The house. The cars."

Stark held up a hand, cutting Sofia off. "It's true, I'm afraid. The cars are on lease. He had a mortgage and two other loans against the house in Brentwood. The vacation house you had in Maui? He sold that last year."

"That's why he blew up when I wanted to go over there and check on it," Melissa said softly.

"You had no idea?" said Sofia.

Melissa shook her head. "I knew he was stressed. He would see my credit card bill and start screaming about it, so I was cutting back."

"From what we can gather, he did a pretty good job of hiding his difficulties from pretty much everyone," Stark said.

Biting down on her lower lip, Melissa began to cry. "Poor Nigel."

Her response seemed genuine to Sofia. She didn't really care about Sofia's opinion, and she didn't have to prove anything to her attorney. He was going to defend her anyway. Assuming there was enough money to cover his fees, or for as long as what money Melissa had left lasted. From the information that Aidan had gathered, Melissa had a few hundred thousand dollars of her own from an inheritance, but with legal fees and what Maloney Investigations would charge, it would be eaten up pretty quickly. Even though the bond would be a percentage of the overall bail amount, it might still be out of reach.

"I have to stay here?" Melissa sobbed. "Because I can't afford to leave?"

Sofia didn't blame her for being upset. It did look grim.

If it had been a Four Seasons hotel, or even a Ramada Inn, it was still jail. You were still being deprived of your liberty, which was no small matter, especially for someone who'd never experienced what that was like.

Now that the grim reality of what was she facing was staring Melissa straight in the face, Sofia figured this might be the best time to see if Melissa would offer up whatever she knew about Moonbow.

"We've gathered some information that may help your case," Sofia said. "However, we need your full cooperation. The only way we can help you is if you tell us everything that you know."

Sofia reached into her pocket and pulled out a pack of paper tissues. She plucked one out of the pack and handed it over the table to Melissa.

Melissa dabbed at her eyes. Finally, she asked, "What kind of information?"

"About Moonbow, Bobby Rogers. I'm sorry, I don't know what you called him when you were together," said Sofia.

Next to Sofia, Stark was watching for his client's reaction to the mention of her lover's name.

"I called him Bobby. And before you say anything else, I knew who he was." Melissa cleared her throat. "I knew he'd been in prison. He told me everything."

Maybe not everything, thought Sofia.

41

The door opened and a corrections officer escorted Melissa Fairbroad past. Her shoulders were hunched and her gaze was directed at the floor. Stark squeezed her shoulder as she walked past. She looked up long enough for Sofia to shoot her a smile. It was returned, but only just.

Not only was Melissa still in the same waist-high pile of poo that she'd been in before, she now knew that she'd been taken for a ride. As Sofia and Stark had guessed, Melissa knew a lot about Bobby Rogers, but she didn't know it all.

They waited until Melissa was out of sight before going back out into the corridor. Stark walked Sofia all the way back to her car.

"Nice ride," he said as she hit the clicker to open the Kia's doors.

"Boy, you really are an attorney, aren't you? Always diplomatic," Sofia said. "I know it's horrible, but it was all the rental company had."

He took a step back and took in the brown paint job in

all its glory. "I was going to use the word special, but horrible covers it, too."

"So what now?"

Stark shrugged. "I was hoping you guys were going to tell me. The cops have no alibi for Melissa. They have her prints on the murder weapon. They have a life insurance policy taken out before he died. It won't pay out now, but it looks like a clear motive. Even if they pull Bobby Rogers in as an accomplice, I can tell you right now he'll throw Melissa to the wolves to save his own skin."

"It's down to us then," Sofia said.

Stark patted her shoulder. "Yup."

If her job hadn't been real before, it sure as hell was now. She'd wanted a job that counted. Well, now she had one. It wasn't giving her the warm feeling she thought it would. On the contrary, she felt an ulcer starting to form somewhere down in her stomach. A little burning ball of what-the-hell-am-I-doing stress.

42

Stark had been right. Throwing Bobby Rogers into the mix without direct, irrefutable proof of the how and why he was involved in Nigel's murder, or better yet a full confession that exonerated Melissa (which was never going to happen without holding a gun to the guy's head) wouldn't help Melissa. Bobby Rogers would throw her to the wolves without blinking. Even if he went down, he'd be damn sure to take Melissa with him.

More likely he'd try to strike a deal that placed her in deeper trouble than she was now. A man like Bobby would happily perjure himself on the witness stand to save his own skin. All of that meant that if Maloney Investigations didn't turn up something stronger than one half of a telephone conversation that was inadmissible as evidence, Melissa was likely doomed.

Sofia sat across from Brendan and Aidan at a table near the back of the Marmalade Cafe in Cross Creek, Malibu. They had spent most of lunch going round in circles. Brendan flagged down the waiter for the check.

"I want you and Sofia to talk to Tucker Trimble again," he said to Aidan.

"He wasn't very forthcoming the last time we spoke," Sofia said.

"So try again," said Brendan.

She exchanged a look with Aidan. Brendan must have caught it. "What?"

"I think that if anyone's involved, it's Rogers," Sofia said.

"And you may be right," said Brendan.

"So why do you want us to go see Trimble?" Aidan asked.

Brendan took the check from the waiter, and handed over his company credit card. "When you hit a dead end, there's only one thing left to do."

"Talk to someone who probably isn't involved?" said Aidan.

Brendan glared at him. "Why do you always have to be such a smart . . ." He hesitated. "Guy."

"You were going to say smart ass," Aidan said.

Brendan held up his hand. "There you go again. Now, as I was saying, when you hit a dead end, the only thing to do is push on through. In this case, that means go shake some trees. Upset some people. Maybe Trimble isn't involved, but he might still give us something, which is what we need, because right now we got nothing."

AIDAN AND SOFIA stood in the parking lot outside the office. Sofia scanned the lot, still aware that someone had recently tried to run her off the road.

"Let's take your car," she said to Aidan.

"Don't you have a rental?" he asked. She always drove.

"Yes." She didn't want to say any more about the brown Kia than she had to. Aidan hadn't seen it, and if he did it would open up another rich vein of teasing. Plus, brown, adult diapers, he'd make sure it would all hang together, and she'd had to endure enough incontinence gags for one lifetime.

"So why can't we take your car?" Aidan said.

It was like he had a special radar that could pick up any time she felt the slightest bit uncomfortable. "Why can't we take yours this time?"

Aidan cocked his head and stared at her.

"Where is it?" He scanned the parking lot like a vulture looking for a carcass.

"Let's just take yours."

"We're going to be driving up into the canyon. I just got my car cleaned. You have a rental with no deductible. Who cares if it gets dirty?"

Even though getting it dirty would probably be an improvement, Sofia still didn't want to expose it to Aidan's withering assessment. "I never said there's no deductible."

"So is there?" said Aidan.

"That's not the point. I just didn't want you assuming that there wasn't."

"Did you hit your head the other day when that guy tried to run you off the road?" Aidan asked. "You're being even weirder than usual."

"Can we just get going already rather than standing here arguing?"

"Okay, we can take my car," said Aidan. "Jesus, I've never known anyone who worried about looking after a rental."

They walked over to the canary-yellow Porsche. Aidan opened the doors, and Sofia started to get into the front passenger seat.

Aidan had opened the driver's door but hadn't gotten in. He was staring over the roof of his car.

"What's the problem?" said Sofia.

"Is that it?" Aidan pointed over at the brown Kia.

She'd parked it between two large SUVs to try to hide it, but one of the SUVs had just pulled out and left the brown car in plain sight.

"Is what, what?" she said.

"Is that your rental car?" A grin spread across his face. She wanted to punch it right back off.

"Where?"

He jabbed a finger straight at the Kia. He started to walk over to it.

Sofia opened her door and got back out.

"There. The shit-brown Ford," he said.

"No," said Sofia, taking off after him.

Aidan reached the small brown car. He knelt down. "If it's not yours, why is your jacket in the back seat?"

THE DRIVE UP through Topanga Canyon passed in silence. Sofia kept waiting for the jibes about her rental car to start, but Aidan didn't mention it. Instead, he would glance over at her occasionally and smile to himself. She knew better than to ask what he found so hilarious and kept her eyes on the road.

When they arrived at the set, Sofia was directed to park with the rest of the crew vehicles. Aidan got out and walked to where the crew was busy setting up a shot in a patch of woodland. When she turned around, Aidan had disappeared, leaving her to deal with Tucker Trimble on her own. She tried to call Aidan, but reception up here was patchy, and she couldn't get through.

Meanwhile, Tucker started shouting nearby. "Are we going to do this or what? I've been waiting an hour already. I can track, kill, skin, cook, and eat a pig in the time it takes you people to set up a few lights."

Sofia looked around but she still couldn't see Aidan. They had already wasted enough time back at the office arguing over which car to take. She knew what Brendan was saying about shaking some trees but she was pretty sure that Tucker Trimble wasn't going to give them anything new. It was probably best if she just got it over with on her own.

She followed the sound of the Kentucky reality star's tantrum. She found him stripped to the waist, and leaning on an axe, surrounded by a gaggle of crew and production assistants.

"Mr. Trimble, while you wait for this shot to get set up, could I have a moment of your time?" Sofia asked, pushing in between the sound recorder and the boom operator.

Tucker turned to her. He smiled. His tongue flicked out of his mouth as he slowly licked his lips.

"A moment," he said, patting his axe. "I'll give you more than a moment, darlin'. If you don't mind having to share me with my big chopper."

It was amazing. She had actually managed to find the only man in the world capable of sounding like a bigger asshole than Aidan Maloney.

"I just have a few questions," said Sofia. Over the years she'd learned that the only thing you could do with men when they reverted to their twelve-year-old selves was to ignore them. Any response was only read as encouragement.

Tucker Trimble lifted the axe and swung it in a wide arc. The blade embedded itself into a fallen tree trunk. She guessed this was what passed for flirting in the backwoods of Kentucky.

"Take your time, folks," called Trimble to the crew.

He sidled up next to her. "I kinda had a feeling you wouldn't be able to stay away." As he said it, he moved his right arm, wrapping it around her waist. Before she could tell him to move it, she felt his hand sneak down her ass and give it a squeeze.

That was it. She smiled sweetly at him as she grabbed his wrist and bent it backward. The leer on his face was replaced by a grimace as she kept bending. He stepped away, trying to shake her grip. She held the joint lock tight, and kept bending.

"Don't ever touch me," she said. "Remember our last talk?"

Around them, the crew looked at each other. No one wanted to intervene to stop Sofia and help Tucker. She could guess why.

Tucker's face was red. His knees buckled. The more she bent his wrist back, the lower he sank.

"Hey, Sofia, I said talk to the guy. No one said anything about going Gitmo on his ass." Aidan walked over to them.

Sofia slowly eased the pressure on Tucker's wrist and let it go. Rubbing his wrist, he got to his feet. A production assistant rushed over with an ice pack. He took it and held it against his injured wrist.

"You're lucky I didn't break it. I'm guessing an injury to your right hand would pretty much wipe out your sex life," said Sofia.

Aidan leaned over and whispered in her ear. "Good going. Now he's definitely not going to answer any questions."

"I wouldn't be so sure," Sofia replied. She ushered Tucker ahead of her. "Can we talk in your trailer?"

Tucker looked from her to Aidan and back again. "Sure thing, sweet cheeks."

"Don't go calling my colleague here sweet cheeks," Sofia said. "His temper's even worse than mine when you call him names."

Tucker did his best to swagger to his trailer as he pressed the ice pack against his injured wrist. Aidan and Sofia fell in behind him.

TUCKER SUNK into a seat at the far end of his trailer. He massaged his injured wrist and re-applied the ice pack. "So what did you want to ask me?"

Sofia let Aidan take the lead. Aidan introduced himself and apologized to Tucker for his colleague's behavior. Sofia wasn't about to say sorry. She doubted Tucker expected her to.

"So, Tucker," Aidan said, deciding to try a bluff. "Here's the thing. We know you were down at the marina where Nigel kept his boat on the night he was killed."

Sofia kept her eyes on Tucker, waiting for his reaction. His face gave nothing away. It was as calm as a stagnant swamp on a still day.

"Now," Aidan continued, "the only people who know about this are us and the person who told us. We haven't told the cops."

Tucker stood up, squaring his shoulders. "Go tell 'em. I ain't gonna stop you. I got nothing to hide."

"So you admit you were there?" said Aidan.

"Yeah, I was there."

"Why?" said Sofia.

Tucker walked to the far end of the trailer, opened a small fridge and took out a Coors Light.

He popped it open with his left hand and took a sip. "You want one?"

"Bit early for me," said Aidan.

"More of a Miller girl," said Sofia.

"Funny," Tucker said, directing himself to Sofia. "I would have had you down as a Corona girl."

"Why did you go visit Nigel at his boat?" said Sofia, not about to be sidetracked by his suggestion that she'd only drink Mexican beer.

Tucker let out a loud burp. "Why do you think? He was stalling on my new contract."

"You mean he wasn't giving you everything you were asking for?" said Aidan.

Tucker took another slug of beer. "We were in negotiations. I was trying to bring them to a conclusion."

"Someone certainly did that," said Aidan as Tucker sat back down. "You don't get much more wrapped up than shot and thrown overboard."

Aidan's jibe drew a smirk from Tucker. "That's where you'd be wrong. Nigel getting popped has messed things up for me."

A couple of things occurred to Sofia. The first was that if Tucker had forced Nigel out on his own boat and killed him, he probably wouldn't have been nearly as forthcoming as he was being. For a man voluntarily placing himself at a murder scene, he seemed remarkably relaxed. There was something else, too. Almost no one in Hollywood negotiated for themselves. That was what talent agents like Jeffrey were for.

"You don't have an agent to handle things for you?" Sofia said.

Tucker screwed up his face. "Nope. Why am I gonna give someone ten percent for doing what I can do myself? Then you have a manager. That's another ten. Lawyer, that's another five. Then you got Uncle Sam and everyone else wanting their piece. Federal, state, county. Pretty soon you're working for nothing. Gotta save money where you can."

Sofia had to concede that he had a point. If Tucker's approach to business in Hollywood caught on, there would be a lot more bodies washing up on the beach, though the wounds would likely be self-inflicted. "So you went to talk with him on your own? How'd that go?"

Tucker's eyes practically twinkled. "It didn't."

"What?" said Aidan and Sofia simultaneously.

"What do you mean? You just told us you were there so you could speak to him about your new contract," said Aidan.

"I was. But I didn't get to speak with him." Tucker smiled. "Want to know why?"

"You going to tell us or not?" said Aidan.

"My, my, ain't you two tetchy," said Tucker.

Sofia started to get up.

Tucker held up his hands in a gesture of surrender. "Okay, okay, I'll tell you. I didn't get to speak to him because someone else beat me to it."

43

"You didn't tell the cops when they spoke to you?" asked Sofia.

Tucker shook his head. He sat back down, the ice pack pressed against his injured wrist. From time to time, he would take a sip of beer.

"How come?" Aidan said to Tucker.

"Number one, where I come from, folks ain't big into helping the law. It's kind of a point of principle," said Tucker.

"And number two?" Sofia prompted.

"You ever hear the expression 'snitches get stitches?' The guys who were there when I arrived didn't look like they'd take too kindly to my mentioning their presence to the cops. Know what I mean?"

"Guys?" said Aidan.

"Hold up," said Sofia, cutting Aidan off and reading a glare from him for her trouble. "Why are you telling us all this if you're so worried about getting hurt?"

Tucker shook the empty beer can. "I would tell you, but my throat's kind of dry over here."

Aidan got up, walked across to the fridge, got Tucker a fresh one, opened it for him, and passed it over. He must have known that Sofia sure wasn't going to fetch Tucker a beer.

Tucker raised the fresh beer in a toast. "Here's to my wife and girlfriend. May they never meet."

He took a slug and let out another loud burp. At first Sofia had thought that Tucker's whole redneck act was a shtick for the cameras. Now she wasn't so sure.

"So?" said Sofia. "Why the change of heart?"

Tucker raised his beer. "You're not the law. Not technically. And if someone wants to hurt me, it don't matter if I have told anyone or not. But the main reason? I guess that Nigel was a good guy. We might have had our disagreements, but shooting him and throwing him into the ocean? He didn't deserve that. He was a regular guy, a bit fruity, but still regular, not a gangster or a hood. If it hadn't have been for him, I'd still be back in Kentucky with my thumb up my ass. And even though I never really took to that wife of his the times I met her, I don't want to see her go down for something she didn't do either."

Barring the needless imagery of Tucker with his finger up his ass, Sofia supposed that his explanation showed a rough kind of honor. If it was true.

Tucker was still on a roll. "I ain't gonna give this to the law. Not unless I have to. But if I tell you, I won't have to. You can."

Sofia wasn't so sure about that. If they took the information that Tucker had given them to the sheriff's department, they would want to know where it had come from. So would Stark. Not that they needed to tell Tucker that. At least not until he was done talking.

"These guys, you get a good look at them?" Aidan asked,

opening up a Notepad app on his cell and also switching on the voice recorder.

Tucker leaned back. "Sure did. They both looked like guineas to me. Y'know, Italians. Both big guys, like two-forty, two-fifty, but short. First one was maybe five four, the other one was like five seven. But wide, y'know. Muscles on muscles. One guy had dark hair, the other blond. Both dressed for Vegas. Suit, tie, shiny black shoes. Oh, and they were both carrying. Big bulges under their suit jackets."

"No purple robes?" said Sofia.

The question seemed to puzzle Tucker. "Purple? No. My guess? I'd say they were mob guys. At least that's what they looked like. I met a few of them when I was in the joint. They're pretty hard to miss. They don't even try to blend. Guess looking like that with people knowing who and what they are saves them a lot of time."

Judging by the puzzled expression on Aidan's face, Sofia figured he was having the same thought she was. The Mafia? No one had even hinted that Nigel had gotten caught up with the mob. But if Nigel had needed money, maybe he'd ended up dealing with exactly the wrong people. Still, she couldn't imagine how British Nigel could have hooked up with the mob.

But Tucker probably did know mobsters when he saw them. Maybe Bobby Rogers figured in here somewhere.

"Oh, and the one guy had wraparound sunglasses. He had 'em on even though it was already dark, like some kind of asshole."

Blond, muscles on muscles, and wraparound sunglasses. That sounded just like the guy who tried to drive Sofia off the road.

44

They drove back down through Topanga Canyon Boulevard. Neither of them spoke until Sofia turned the brown Kia back onto PCH.

"You hungry?" Aidan asked.

"I could eat," said Sofia.

"Cholada?"

"Sure."

Cholada Thai Beach Cuisine was a beach hut restaurant right on PCH. It didn't look like much from the outside. It didn't look like much inside either, but the food was terrific, and by Malibu standards, it was great value for money.

Sofia turned into the parking lot.

"Can you not park near the door?" said Aidan. "In fact, why don't you pull all the way in back?"

Sofia didn't need the prod. She didn't want to be seen in the brown rental any more than Aidan did.

She parked as far back as she could. They got out, walked up the steps and inside. It was quiet. They took a table in the far corner so they could talk without anyone being able to eavesdrop.

"You think he's telling the truth?" Sofia asked Aidan once the young Thai waitress had taken their order and returned with drinks.

Aidan was looking at the cars whizzing past on PCH and the ocean beyond, Nigel's all but final resting place. "I'm not sure I buy the sudden change of heart. If he really wanted to, he could have told the cops without anyone knowing. He didn't have to tell us."

"He could have killed Nigel and then invented this story."

"But he's not in the frame," said Aidan, pulling out his chopsticks from their paper wrapping. "Melissa is. Telling us that he was there complicates matters for Trimble. If he was involved, then surely he'd be better not telling us anything. But he didn't."

"Except we said we have someone who places him at the scene," said Sofia. "This could be his way of explaining that away before the questions get really awkward."

"Too much of a jump. If he was worried, he'd wait for the cops to come calling. Not start coughing his guts up to a couple of PIs. No, something tells me that he's telling the truth. Only problem is we still don't who the guys are or why they were there." Aidan broke off as the waitress came over with their appetizers—an order of *kanom jeep*, delicious steamed wontons filled with pork and chestnuts, and an order of Thai vegetable spring rolls.

Sofia jabbed at a wonton with the business end of her chopstick and took a bite. She had to juggle it around her mouth to cool it down. Across the table, Aidan seemed to enjoy her discomfort.

"Bit off more than you could chew?" he asked.

"Maybe we both have." She took a sip of water. "So, what next? We go to the cops?"

Aidan stared out of the window. "It's flimsy. Plus we're working for Melissa and her attorney, so the cops are going to be predisposed to dismiss anything we bring them unless we can stand it up. Tucker telling us that he saw some guys with Nigel who may or may not have been mafia because they were wearing shiny suits isn't much. We should run it past the old man, but I'd say that's going to be a hard sell."

Sofia knew he was right. The cops had the murder weapon with Melissa's prints on it and it had been found on the boat next to pools of Nigel's blood. It would take a lot to shift the cops and the DA away from Melissa as the killer. What Tucker had told them was a start. But that's all it was. At least he hadn't seen Melissa in the marina. He had seen two unidentified men. Men who may or may not have been the ones who tried to run Sofia's car off the road. They needed something more concrete.

What that concrete thing was suddenly struck Sofia.

"The guy who tried to force me off the freeway. I'm pretty sure his car was totaled. The crash was all over the news. My stepdad knew about it by the time I got to my mom's. Someone had to have taken his name. The cops, a paramedic, an insurance company. I mean, even if he isn't one of them men who went out with Nigel that night, we're fairly sure he's connected to this somehow. Otherwise, why was he targeting me?" Sofia said, jabbing her chopstick in the air for emphasis.

Aidan stared at her. She remembered what he'd said about Second Date Sofia jabbing her fork in his face and laid down her chopsticks on the side of her plate.

"Just a theory," she added.

Aidan still hadn't said anything.

Aidan waved over the waitress. "Hey, could we get the rest of our order to go?"

As the waitress headed for the kitchen, he got up and pushed back his chair, grabbing a spring roll as he started for the door. He glanced over his shoulder at Sofia. "Don't just sit there. To the shit-mobile, Batgirl!"

"**O**kay, well thanks, buddy." Aidan killed the call and tossed his cell phone down onto his desk. With a sigh, he pushed his chair back and stood up.

Sofia was still on the phone with a hospital administrator who was freaking out that the Sofia Salgado speaking to her was the Sofia Salgado who'd played in *Half Pint Detective.*

"You're kidding me, right?" the administrator said.

"Nope," said Sofia. "One and the same. Now did you have anyone admitted after a motor vehicle accident on the 210 yesterday? We're working on behalf of a family member who's trying to trace him to make sure he's okay."

"Is this one of these radio prank calls?" the administrator asked.

"No, ma'am," said Sofia. "It's not a prank."

"You're sure?" the administrator said.

"I give you my word."

"Because I can't release that kind of information to just anyone," the lady on the other end of the line told her.

Sofia was hoping that her former star status would elevate her from "just anyone" status to someone the administrator would be prepared to confide in. "I absolutely understand that, but it would be a big help if you took a look for me."

"Well, Sofia . . . you don't mind me calling you Sofia, do you?" the lady said.

This was good. Chatty and familiar always worked when it came to prying information from people. Sofia guessed that this was the upside of her previous career. People automatically assumed they knew her. Most of the time this made life awkward and uncomfortable, but maybe this was one of the exceptions.

"Not in the slightest," said Sofia.

"Thanks, Sofia," said the administrator. "Can I ask you something else, too?"

"Sure. Go right ahead."

"Did you and Frankie Davis, y'know?" asked the administrator.

Frankie had been another cast member. He'd played the part of the Half Pint detective's annoying younger brother. Kind of a fictional Aidan Maloney. Even though he was a year younger than she was and had become more and more obnoxious as his Hollywood career had progressed, as soon as Sofia hit sixteen, there had been tabloid speculation that they were an item. Because Frankie was a bit of a teen heartthrob, the network had done nothing to quash the rumor, much to Sofia's chagrin.

Even now Sofia would still get asked about it by people who'd watched the show. Still, it beat being asked about why she'd given up acting, or being photographed peeing outside a rehab clinic.

"No, we never did whatever it is you're thinking. Ever,"

said Sofia. "Now, do you have any record of someone from that accident being admitted?"

"You're sure?" said the lady.

"I think I would have remembered," said Sofia.

"Huh," said the lady, obviously deflated. "I'm looking at my system and I don't see anyone admitted after a crash on the 2."

"Okay, well, thanks for your time." Sofia hung up before the lady could trawl for any more celebrity gossip. Picking up a pen, she struck through the sixth hospital on her list. She'd already covered all the emergency rooms within a ten-mile radius of the Flintridge La Canada area.

She threw her pen down onto the desk. Aidan walked over and stood next to her. "No luck?"

Picking up her call sheet, she held it up for Aidan to take a look. "A big fat zero. You?"

"Worse than zero," said Aidan. "Just spoke to a buddy of mine at CHP. The driver of the SUV somehow managed to flee the scene. They think he might have been picked up by someone else."

CHP was the California Highway Patrol. "Did they get a name from the vehicle?"

Aidan smiled. "Rental under a false name. He picked it up in Santa Monica about three days ago. CHP already checked it out. The name on his ID belongs to a guy who died in Philly about twenty years ago. To be fair to the guy, he did take out the full insurance package."

"Philly?" Sofia said. "Hometown and former stomping ground of Bobby Rogers."

"Yeah, that's what I thought. But we still don't have a name," said Aidan.

"What about former associates? Guys he was in jail with? That kind of thing."

"The old man has a couple of calls in," said Aidan with a nod toward Brendan's office door. "But we can't count on anything showing up."

So there was someone out there who wanted to harm Sofia, and no one knew who he was. Now he was really pissed and had a good reason to finish the job. Not that she could mention her concerns to Aidan or Brendan. They would put on her a flight out of town. If that happened, she might as well go back to playing a detective on TV. If Moon-butt and his buddies from Philly wanted to make it personal, then they'd better realize it was going to be a two-way street. She wasn't going to sit and wait for them to take another shot at her, or for Melissa to rot away in jail while they got away with murder.

She grabbed her bag from under her desk and started for the door.

"Where you going?" said Aidan.

"I'm gonna go pay Bobby Rogers another visit," she told him.

46

Aidan caught up as she was getting into the Kia. He opened the passenger side door and got in next to her. Before she could start the car, he reached over and grabbed the keys out of the ignition.

"Hold on there. Before you go racing off to vanquish evil, do you have an actual plan or did you just have too much coffee earlier?" he asked.

"Of course I have a plan."

"Okay," said Aidan. "That's great. What is it?"

"May I have the keys?" she said, reaching out a hand.

Aidan held them up just out of reach like she was five years old. "Soon as you tell me what you're planning on doing."

"My keys, please."

"You don't have a plan, do you?" said Aidan.

"It's a work in progress," Sofia told him.

His fingers closed around the keys. All the anger she'd felt toward the dumb jerk who'd tried to kill her transferred to the dumb jerk sitting next to her in the passenger seat. What was it with men? Aidan wouldn't have dared pulled crap like this if she'd been a guy. He'd have gotten his lights punched out.

"Now," said Sofia. "Give me the keys, or I'll…"

"Or you'll what?" smirked Aidan.

She reached over, grabbed his wrist, and twisted it until he yelped in pain. The keys fell out of his nerveless fingers and into his lap. She scooped them up, jammed them in the ignition, and turned it on.

"What the hell did you do that for? Have you lost your freakin' mind?" He massaged his wrist and glared at her.

"Let me see," she said. "Yes, yes I have. Someone trying to kill me tends to make me grouchy. But of course you'd be totally okay with it if it was you. You'd sit in your office and make some phone calls and see what turned up. That's what you'd do, right?"

She stopped, running out of steam. Aidan stared at her like she was some kind of alien being. She hadn't really hurt him, just got her keys back.

"Because guys never act on the spur of the moment, do they? And when a woman does it, she has to be saved from herself by some macho white knight who takes the keys to the piece of shit rental she's only driving because of a dickwad like Bobby Rogers and his buddies." Sofia had found a second wind. "So, yes, I don't have a plan, but I will have one by the time I find him. Now, if that's not okay with you, then get the hell out of the shit-mobile and let Batgirl go to work."

Aidan grinned. "If it's all the same to you, I kind of want to see this go down."

47

Fifty-two minutes later, Sofia pulled into a visitor's spot at Dolphin Bay apartments. She and Aidan got out.

"Sure you still want to do this?" Aidan asked.

She'd calmed down on the drive over, and now she wasn't so sure. But she wasn't about to get back in the car and drive all the way back to Malibu with him laughing at her.

She started toward the apartment complex where Bobby Rogers lived. Aidan fell in behind her, a roll of quarters in his pocket weighing down his sports coat so that it didn't ride up and reveal the shoulder holster with the .357 Magnum he was wearing.

Reaching the building, they took a short flight of steps down into the parking structure. A brand new white 3-series BMW was parked in the spot designated for Bobby's apartment. Aidan took a quick walk around the car.

"Who knew unblocking chakras paid so well?" said Aidan.

"I think he earned that with his lustrous jewel polishing."

Sofia knocked at the apartment door and stepped off to one side so she was out of view of the peephole. If one or more of Bobby's buddies were inside, they might not bother opening the door before they took a shot at her.

Aidan stood on the other side of the door. His hand reached into his jacket as he waited for Bobby to answer.

"I have a plan," she whispered. "Remember the *Half Pint Detective* where she had to trick that guy to rescue the Saint Bernard puppy?"

Having tagged along with his dad to the set often, Aidan had a fairly good knowledge of the show. He gave her a thumbs-up.

She knocked again and stepped back. "Bobby, it's Sofia Salgado. I need to speak with you."

A few moments later, there was the sound of a bolt being thrown back, and the door opened. Bobby Rogers stood in the doorway dressed in jeans, low top Converse sneakers and a purple polo short. As Sofia stepped in front of the door, she saw a couple of suitcases lying in the hallway behind him, but she didn't see any angry mobsters.

"Going on a trip?" she asked.

"What do you want?" he said.

Aidan stepped out from the other side of the door, gun in hand. He kept it down by his side. "Let's discuss what we came for inside. Before someone sees you talking to us."

If Bobby was impressed by the gun, he didn't show it. He eyed Aidan. "Sorry, buddy, I don't do men."

"Me neither," said Aidan, shouldering his way past Bobby and into the apartment. As Bobby moved to grab

Aidan by the shoulder, Sofia walked in and closed the door behind them.

Aidan and Bobby were eye to eye.

"I didn't invite you in," Bobby said.

"Sure you did," Aidan replied. "You heard him, didn't you?"

"You'd be amazed at the things we can hear," Sofia said to Bobby with a smile.

Aidan took a step back. "Yeah, you have some interesting friends, Bobby. You've made some interesting phone calls to them."

For the first time since he'd opened the door, Sofia saw a flicker of discomfort cross Bobby Roger's face.

"That's kind of why we wanted to talk to you. You mind if we sit down? It's kind of rude to leave guests standing in the hallway," Sofia said.

Aidan half-walked, half-muscled Bobby into the living room. Apart from the furniture, all his Austin Powers accessories had been packed away, presumably in the boxes stacked in the middle of the room. Aidan pushed Bobby down onto the couch. "Take a load off."

Bobby glared at Aidan but didn't make a move. "Tell me what you want to tell me and get out. I have some place to be."

"How long this takes is kind of up to you, Bobby," Aidan said. "You tell us where we can find the people you asked to run Sofia here off the road and we'll leave."

Sofia walked around the small apartment, checking every room to make sure that it was empty.

"I ain't got no idea what you're talking about," said Bobby.

Aidan loomed over Bobby. He raised his hand like he was about to hit him. To his credit, Bobby didn't flinch. Sofia guessed that guys in the pen who flinched didn't last too long.

"We heard you talking to them, Bobby," Sofia said.

Aidan reached down and put a hand under the chaise lounge. He came up with the tiny listening device Sofia had planted. He threw it over to Bobby. Bobby caught it one-handed. He turned it over in his hand.

"So what's to stop me going to the cops and telling them you planted this in my apartment? This shit's illegal, unless the government's doing it." Bobby pronounced government like gub'mint.

Sofia shrugged. "Nothing at all."

"Go right ahead. You can use my phone," Aidan added.

Bobby looked at both of them. The look on his face told Sofia that Bobby wasn't quite following why they were so relaxed.

"You have no idea, do you, Bobby?" Sofia asked.

"Not a clue," said Aidan.

Sofia dug her cell phone out of her pocket. She hit the green phone icon, pulled up the contacts list and scrolled down the names. "Hey, Aidan, John Agnew's the lead on the Fairbroad homicide, right?"

"Yup," said Aidan.

Sofia tapped her cell phone screen.

"Here it is. Knew I had it," she said, holding the phone out to Bobby. "This is his direct line. If he's not there, it'll probably redirect to his cell or you can leave a message and he'll call you straight back."

Bobby looked at Sofia's cell phone like it was a hand grenade with a loose pin. "What kind of bullshit are you trying to pull?"

"No bullshit," Aidan said.

Bobby eyed him. "Anything you might have recorded can't be used against me. It's not evidence."

"We know that," said Sofia.

"So what's all this?" Bobby asked again.

"It's really simple, Bobby. Melissa Fairbroad is sitting in jail looking at a murder charge when we both know that she didn't do it," Sofia said.

Bobby didn't say anything.

"It doesn't bother you that she's looking at life without parole?" Aidan said.

"It's nothing to do with me," said Bobby.

Aidan laughed. "That's funny, man. You even managed to say that with a straight face. Look, here's the deal, your buddies who tried to hurt Sofia are the same people who took Nigel out on that boat, shot him, and dumped him over the side. We have a witness who puts your Philly pals on the boat that night. My old man, who knows everyone you need to know in law enforcement in LA, is about to sit down with them right now and play the tape of what we recorded here last night. And give them the name of that witness."

The color drained from Bobby Roger's face. An illegally obtained recording was one thing, but an eyewitness who'd talked to a respected retired homicide detective was something else. The cops could do a lot with that.

Aidan continued, "Now, one thing we couldn't figure out was how Melissa's prints were on that gun. She doesn't even have a memory of picking up a gun. So it had to have been someone close to her who helped put them there. Say for instance she's asleep, and you put it in her hand for a split second and press down. Was that how you did it, Bobby?"

Bobby didn't flinch. "No one's going to believe that. She would have woken up."

"Maybe, maybe not," said Aidan.

"Okay," said Sofia. "Even if the cops can't prove that, we all know that you asked your old buddies from Philly to get rid of Nigel. With our recording to start them off, they're sure to link them up to the guys our witness saw. And when they do, your call to them makes it conspiracy, which is as bad as if you'd pulled the trigger yourself."

"What we're saying is that you ain't walking away from this," Aidan said. "That's just not going to happen. If the cops don't get you, do you think your buddies are going to take the rap on their own while you fly off into the sunset? These kind of people have a reach as long as their memory."

"I don't know what you're talking about," said Bobby. This time he sounded less certain, less sure of himself.

"He doesn't know what we're talking about," Sofia said to Aidan.

"Yeah," said Aidan. "That's pretty much what I'd say if I were him."

"You wanna go get some coffee?" Sofia said, both of them acting as if Bobby wasn't even in the room.

"I could use coffee," Aidan said. He patted Bobby on the shoulder. "You take care now, Bobby."

Bobby didn't move but his head must have been spinning. Sofia and Aidan headed back to the hallway, leaving Bobby in the living room. Sofia glanced across at Aidan as he opened the door. He gave her a thumbs-up.

"You plant it?" Sofia when they were out of earshot in the hall.

Aidan smiled. "Same place as before."

48

As they reached the elevator, Aidan reached into his jacket, pulled out a pair of earbuds, and plugged them into the headphone socket of his phone. He took one earbud and popped it in his ear. He offered the other one to Sofia. She took it and placed it in her ear.

Via the second listening device that Aidan had planted when he was removing the first one, they could hear everything happening inside the apartment. They pushed through a door into a stairwell and leaned against the wall.

It was just like the episode of *Half Pint Detective* with the puppy. The exact same scam. Aidan had played his part in the scene perfectly. If he'd wanted to, he could have been an actor.

In the earbud, she heard Bobby pacing up and down, muttering under his breath. A few moments later, he made the call that they'd hoped he would.

When the person on the other end of the line picked up, they heard Bobby say "Yeah, it's me. They know... What do you mean who? Who do you think? ... That's what I'm telling you. They know. Their boss is talking to the cops right now, and I ain't hanging around to see if they believe him or not. You do what you gotta do, but I'm outta here."

Aidan shook his head as they listened to the last part.

"Bad move telling them that," Aidan said, keeping his voice down in the echo chamber of the stairwell.

Aidan reached over and plucked the earbud from Sofia's ear. They walked down the stairs together. At the bottom, they pushed through the door and into the underground parking garage. They ducked into an alcove next to the entrance to the stairwell. From here they had a clear view of the elevator, and of the spot where Bobby's white BMW was sitting. He'd backed into the spot so that the car was facing nose out, ready for a quick exit.

The plan was for Sofia to act as lookout, while Aidan planted a small tracking device inside the alloy wheel rim of the BMW. That way they wouldn't have to worry about Bobby Rogers spotting them while they tailed him in the Shit-Mobile. Chances are he would head for LAX, but wherever he went, Aidan would call it in to Brendan. It would easy enough for Brendan to make a call and have him detained.

But they couldn't plant the tracking device until the garage was empty. A Honda sedan with tinted windows had just rolled in. Sofia watched as the Honda cruised slowly down the line of spaces. She nudged Aidan but he was already watching it.

A resident driving into the garage would have headed straight for their slot. They were all pre-assigned. There was a visitors' parking section where drivers could grab the first available spot, but that was at the end of the parking garage and was clearly signed. This car was acting weird.

The Honda kept cruising slowly down the line of resident spaces. The car slowed almost to a complete stop, rear brake lights flaring red, as they reached the white BMW. The Honda driver backed into an empty parking slot about three cars down from Bobby's.

The Honda's engine switched off. None of the doors opened. No one left the vehicle. Seconds passed. Then a minute. Out of the corner of her eye, Sofia saw Aidan pocket the black tracking device and reach into his jacket for his gun. Aidan was obviously thinking the same thing she was. That they weren't the only ones waiting to see if Bobby Rogers was about to skip town.

Sofia nudged Aidan in the ribs.

"Should we call the cops?" she whispered as softly as she could.

Aidan shook his head. He dug out his cell phone and pulled up a notepad application. Setting his phone on silent, he tapped out a reply and held the screen up for Sofia to read the message.

"Too loud. Text Brendan with an update," the message read. "He'll call them. Better to look stupid than dead."

Sofia pulled out her own cell, checked that it was also set to silent, and tapped out a quick text to Brendan. She angled the screen so Aidan could read it. He nodded. She hit send.

No one had moved from the Honda. It was starting to look more than a little suspicious. Even if someone was gathering up bags from the back seat, they would have been able to do it by now. It just looked like they were waiting. Or maybe it was a young couple making out. Yeah, that didn't seem likely.

Sofia started as the elevator next to them shuddered into life and began to ascend. Next to her, Aidan tensed. He spent so much of his life in smart ass mode, or hunched over his computer, that it was easy to forget that he had been a cop.

The Honda was still parked. The doors still closed. The occupant or occupants were still inside. Sofia tried to crane her neck a little farther. Aidan reached out, put his hand on her shoulder and pulled her back in as the elevator descended. He shook his head, indicating with his hand that she was to stay down.

Sofia held her breath as the elevator slowly descended. Nothing and no one inside the garage moved. There was a chime as the elevator reached the garage, and the doors began to open.

49

Bobby Rogers stepped out of the elevator. He was pulling the two suitcases that had been sitting in the hallway of his apartment. He took a quick look around and stopped, no doubt checking that the coast was clear.

The Honda still hadn't moved from its spot near Bobby's car. If there was someone inside the Honda waiting for Bobby, all they had to do was wait for him to pop the trunk of his car and start loading his luggage. They wouldn't even have to step out of their car to have a clear shot. All it would take was lowering their window.

If Bobby was killed, Melissa's best chance of beating a first-degree murder rap would die with him. Sofia couldn't stand by and watch it happen. No matter how much of an asshole the guy was.

As Bobby wheeled his cases forward a few steps and the elevator doors closed, Sofia stepped out of the alcove. Aidan went to grab her, but she ducked out of his reach.

"Not going to say good-bye?" she said to Bobby.

Her voice bounced off the walls. Bobby startled. He slowly turned round to face her. He was smiling.

"What? You gonna arrest me?" Bobby said.

Sofia looked over Bobby's shoulder to the Honda. It must have been sitting there for over five minutes by this point. What could anyone inside be doing? Apart from waiting for Bobby.

"Don't have that power," Sofia said.

"Well then," said Bobby. "Adios."

Aidan had stayed where he was in the narrow alcove. Sofia couldn't tell if Bobby had seen him or not.

"Before you go," Sofia said. "That Honda down there. The one that's three spaces down from your car? Does that belong to one of your neighbors?"

Bobby's gaze slowly tracked down the line of cars to the Honda. The color drained from his face.

"It pulled into that spot five minutes ago, and no one's gotten out of it yet," Sofia continued.

Bobby was staring at the Honda as if it had some sort of malevolent power. His hands lifted from the handle of the suitcases he'd been wheeling.

The Honda's engine roared into life. It edged forward. Rather than turning left and heading back toward the garage entrance, the driver turned right. The nose of the Honda aimed at them.

Bobby Rogers took a backward step. One of the suitcases fell forward. He didn't reach down to pick it up. Instead, he seemed to freeze, not sure whether to turn and run or stand his ground as the Honda crawled toward them.

Through the front windshield of the Honda, Sofia saw two men in the front seats. They were big guys, wide with muscle, and wearing suits. One of them, the one sitting in the passenger seat, had his left arm strapped across his chest in a sling and wore wraparound sunglasses. Sofia was pretty sure he was the guy whose car had been totaled on the freeway as he'd tried to run her off the road. At least he'd hurt his arm in the crash.

The Honda passenger's right arm came up as the Honda picked up speed. In his hand was a black handgun. The Honda shifted direction, crossing the center line and making straight for them.

Sofia moved first, grabbing Bobby's sleeve and pulling him back. He turned around, and together, they ran for the elevator. All Sofia heard was the roar of the Honda's engine as it bore down on them.

With her hand still grasping Bobby's sleeve, she pulled him to the side, between the two cars parked closest to the elevator. He lost his footing and stumbled, balance thrown off by the sudden change of direction.

The Honda was almost on top of them. The gap between the cars was less than three feet. But they weren't going to make it.

Sofia glanced over her shoulder at the squeal of brakes. The Honda slowed and turned. The front passenger window was gliding down. The guy with his arm in the sling raised a gun with his uninjured hand, his index finger moving down onto the trigger.

There was the deafening sound of a single gunshot. Sofia's ears popped. She dove toward the gap between the cars, pulling Bobby with her. Her ears rang. Out of the corner of her eye, she saw a muzzle flash as Aidan stepped from his hiding place. His gun punched out, he fired a second shot at the Honda. The round clipped the edge of the windshield, shattering it into a spider web pattern.

The gunman in the passenger seat swung his arm round and squeezed off a shot at Aidan. Sofia scuttled forward on her hands and knees toward the gap between the cars. Bobby was ahead of her, crawling for cover.

The taillight of one of the parked cars shattered as a bullet slammed into it. A car alarm wailed.

Bobby made it between the cars first. He turned around and reached a hand out to Sofia. She grasped his hand, and he pulled her to him. Her knees scraped painfully against the concrete. Behind them, Aidan fired again. She couldn't see him, but at least it meant he was still standing.

She pushed herself into a crouching position. She hunkered down next to a car with Bobby. He lifted his head to take a peek. She grabbed his shoulder and pulled him down as a bullet flew over their heads through the windows of the car. It pinged against the concrete wall behind them.

She swallowed hard, trying to clear the buzzing in her ears. Somewhere off in the distance she thought she heard sirens.

At least she hoped she did.

She looked back at Aidan. He wasn't where he had been standing. She looked around frantically. The Honda driver put the car into reverse and backed up at speed.

Sofia still couldn't see Aidan. Maybe he'd been hit and had crawled back into the alcove. Her heart leapt into her mouth at the thought of him bleeding out alone on the concrete floor. She had to get to him, to make sure he was okay.

The Honda turned around and sped off, tires squealing as it accelerated toward the exit. Sofia ran from the gap between the cars toward where she had last seen Aidan, staying low.

The sound of police sirens grew louder.

She reached the alcove. Aidan was sitting down, his back to the wall, his gun still in his hand.

"Are you okay?" she asked, out of breath. When he didn't answer, she grabbed his shoulders and started running her hands up and down his body, looking for a wound.

Aidan caught her wrist. His hands shook, probably from the adrenalin, but other than that he looked fine. "I'm fine. Thankfully that guy was about as crappy a shot as he was a driver. He's zero for two. Where's Bobby?"

"Back there," Sofia told him.

"You sure about that?" Aidan asked.

She looked around to see Bobby back by the elevator lifting his suitcases. He grabbed the handles and wheeled them toward his car. Sofia took off running after him.

He glanced round, saw her coming up fast behind him, and quickened his pace. But with two heavy cases, even on wheels, he couldn't move fast enough. She caught up as he closed in on his car.

A sheriff's department police car raced down into the parking garage. Bobby popped the trunk and started lifting the first overstuffed case into the back. Sofia clamped a hand down on his shoulder. He turned to look at her, an apologetic grin on his face.

"We just saved your ass," Sofia said. "Time you did the right thing."

Aidan caught up with them and pointed at the police cars blocking the exit.

"Not like you have any other choice," Aidan said.

50

Like any good criminal, the first thing Bobby Rogers did when he was arrested was request an attorney. According to Brendan's sources within law enforcement two days of bargaining between Bobby's attorney, the LA sheriff's department and the district attorney's office had followed. Once a deal was reached, Bobby talked. The only problem they faced at that point was getting him to stop talking.

He gave the cops and the DA everything, and then some. Luckily for Melissa what he had to give them cleared her of any wrongdoing. It also, somehow, managed to cast Bobby in a not altogether unflattering light.

The story that Bobby told the cops and the district attorney was a simple one. It was one that had left pretty much everyone, Sofia included, feeling both satisfied and stupid at the same time.

Yes, he admitted, he'd had an affair with Melissa after he'd met her at the spa. As Sofia had suspected, he'd had liaisons with more than one married client, though the one with Melissa had been a little more serious than the others. But none of that was how Nigel ended up shot and floating face down in the ocean. In fact, Nigel had never suspected his wife was having an affair.

Or maybe he had, but if he had, he hadn't mentioned it to anyone, never mind confronting either Melissa or Bobby. Before his death, it turned out that Nigel had other, more pressing, matters on his mind. Like how he was going to avoid complete financial ruin.

As Aidan had discovered, Nigel had big financial problems. Financial problems that Nigel thought he could solve with a short-term injection of cash. Except he had already tapped out all his credit cards, taken out several loans with the Brentwood house as security, as well as taking out a second mortgage on a vacation property they had in Lake Tahoe, and borrowing money from any family and friends who'd lend it.

He had gone to the regular channels such as his bank, but they'd taken one look and politely declined the opportunity to lend him any more money. Then he had bumped into Moonbow. Nigel had been so consumed by his own financial worries that he hadn't been troubled by the fact that his wife's chakra therapist was hanging out at their home. Or maybe he didn't care as long as Melissa was happy and didn't ask him any awkward questions about why he'd cut up her store cards the previous week, and why their mail was suddenly being redirected to his office.

Moonbow and Nigel had begun talking in the kitchen. Nigel hadn't exactly spilled his guts. Not even close. But Melissa's pillow talk had ensured that Moonbow had an idea that her husband had financial worries, even if she hadn't recognized them. And while Moonbow may have been good at reading auras, Bobby Rogers, with all his experience in cons and fraud, was an expert in reading people.

It had taken another couple of 'accidental' encounters where Moonbow happened to run into Nigel before Nigel had really begun to open up. He needed money. Fast. Moonbow had told Nigel that he might know people who could help him out. Nigel was eager to hear more. That was when Moonbow had told him to forget that he'd ever said anything. It was a bad idea. They could help Nigel, but they weren't like a bank. You'd be paying a lot more. They'd didn't talk about interest rates so much as 'the vig'.

Despite Moonbow's backtracking, Nigel was already on the hook. All he needed was a short-term cash injection. Once he had cash flow, everything else would work itself out. He had two shows about to be recommissioned. All he needed to do was keep his head above water for another month or two. When the deals cleared, he'd be able to start paying everyone back. Like a drowning man, Nigel Fairbroad had grabbed for a rope, not realizing that on the other end was an anchor and the end he'd wrapped both hands around was now glued to his skin.

In the end, Nigel had talked Moonbow into hooking him up. Moonbow had made the introductions, and claimed a finder's fee from his buddies, though it was probably closer to a 'mark's fee.' As Bobby had explained it, he had expected Nigel to take the money and pay it back, along with a hefty chunk of interest. He certainly hadn't anticipated that anyone could be as naive as taking mob money, which was what it was, if there was any chance they couldn't make a repayment.

Nigel had stumbled into a world he not only had never encountered before, but one he didn't understand. To him the mob was an abstract concept. He was using to dealing with companies and organizations who destroyed your credit record, or at worst, repossessed things and sued you if you didn't pay them what you owed. He didn't grasp that the people he'd taken a bunch of money from had more permanent methods of debt collection.

Again, according to Bobby Rogers, by the time he'd realized that Nigel wasn't going to be able to make payments, it was already too late. His new deals had fallen through. He didn't have a way of paying the mob their money. Bobby had (according to him) done his best to mediate. But finally, Nigel had been given an ultimatum. Payment was demanded and two guys from Philly were dispatched to Los Angeles to collect. When Nigel didn't have the money, they killed him.

That only left the question of how Melissa had been framed for it. Here Bobby had been less forthcoming, at least until he had his plea bargain and an offer of a new identity in place. As Sofia and Aidan had suspected, he'd helped to frame Melissa, though he claimed his own life was under threat if he hadn't.

It helped that the FBI were also running a much wider investigation into the Philly mob. In fact, that probably saved Bobby Roger's ass when the FBI got wind of the Philly connection to the LA homicide investigation. Shortly after giving his statement, Bobby Rogers was disappeared and the LA district attorney's office made a call to John Stark. They would drop the charges against Melissa with immediate effect if she didn't make too much of a fuss.

A deal was reached.

The only loose end was the two guys from Philly who had tried to kill Sofia not once but twice. They had slipped the cops somewhere near Venice Beach, a short distance from Marina Del Rey, and gone to ground. No one had seen or heard from them since. It was assumed they had either headed back to their home turf or made for the Mexican border.

51

Two weeks later

A CATERING COMPANY truck was parked outside Melissa Fair-broad's Brentwood home as Sofia drove her red Tesla Roadster down the long sweeping driveway. She was so glad to have her own car back. Sofia parked and got out as white-aproned staff busied themselves carrying supplies from the truck into the kitchen.

After some legal wrangling, Nigel Fairbroad's life insurance policy had been scheduled for payout, and Melissa was planning a less-than-understated party to celebrate her financial redemption. If it seemed kind of tasteless, that was probably because it was. But, as Sofia reminded herself, this was LA where taste was in the eye of the beholder.

Sofia was here on Brendan's orders. Since her release, Melissa had decided that Sofia was pretty much the best thing ever. And because Stark threw so much business the way of Maloney Investigations, and Melissa's case had been a marquee victory for Stark, Brendan had asked Sofia to indulge Melissa's desire to be pals.

"She'll get tired of you in a while," Brendan had reassured Sofia. "Broads like her always do."

"Voice of experience?" Sofia had asked.

"Don't be a smarty pants," he'd told her. Smarty pants was about as close as Brendan got to using bad language. "Just play nice."

"Just play nice," Sofia muttered to herself as Melissa came rushing out of the front door toward her. Her hair and makeup were perfect, and she was dressed in a designer small black dress with red Louboutin stiletto heels. The heels must have been five inches tall, and they made Melissa taller than Sofia, so that she could look down on her. No surprises there.

Melissa gave her a hug, complete with double air kiss. "Mwah! Mwah! How are you, my darling?"

"Great," Sofia told her, which had been pretty much true until she'd had to come here. "How's the party planning going?"

Melissa rolled her eyes. "Staff are a nightmare. Thankfully I have Leo helping me out."

"Leo?" Sofia asked. She guessed it hadn't taken long for Melissa to not only find a replacement for her deceased husband, but for Bobby as well.

"You may have met him," said Melissa. "He's been incredibly supportive through this whole thing. I don't know how I would have coped without him being there for me." Melissa hesitated and suddenly looked anxious. "You've been great, too. A real tower of strength."

"Happy to have been able to help." Sofia wished she could tell Melissa that the only reason she was here was because Brendan wanted to maintain a good relationship between Maloney Investigations and Stark's law firm. But she couldn't. Not even hint at it.

Melissa craned her neck over Sofia's shoulder. "Speak of the devil. There's Leo now."

Sofia turned around to see the young blond man who'd manned the reception at the Brentwood Organic Spa pulling up in a blue Mustang. Melissa ran over to greet him. Sofia had assumed when she'd met him that he was gay, but judging by the passionate kiss he exchanged with Melissa, maybe Sofia needed to go get her gaydar recalibrated. Or maybe Leo followed the money instead of his inclinations.

Melissa made the introductions. If Leo recognized Sofia, he didn't let on.

"Darling, I'm so glad you're here," Melissa said to Leo. "If you could keep an eye on the catering people, that would be wonderful."

Leo gave Melissa a plastic smile. "Absolutely."

"Okay," said Melissa, kissing him on the cheek. "Sofia and I need to go get the costumes for later, but we shouldn't be long. I'm on my cell if you need me."

As she started to turn away, Sofia asked, "Costumes?"

This was the first she'd heard that Melissa was throwing a costume party.

"Yes," said Melissa. "I decided to do a prison theme. You know, convicts and guards."

Wow. There was bad taste and then there was this. A few weeks ago Melissa had been looking at wearing an orange jumpsuit for the rest of her life. She had actually seen what conditions were like for women in jail. Women who may not have been angels, but who still had to endure all kinds of indignities, as well as being separated from their families, and often their children. And now Melissa thought their suffering made for a good Brentwood party theme. Sofia made a promise to herself that she wasn't going to dress up to match the theme of the party, no matter what Brendan might say.

"I thought about doing the whole orange thing," Melissa garbled on. "But I thought that might be a little tacky, so instead I went with the classic black and white stripes." She turned back to Leo. "Though stripes can be kind of fattening. What do you think, sweetie?"

Leo gave Melissa another of his fake smiles. He certainly wasn't the actor that Moonbow had been. "It's not possible for you to look fat."

"Isn't he a sweetheart?" Melissa asked.

It took Sofia a few seconds to register that the question had been addressed to her. "Totally."

"We have to dash," Melissa said, and Leo nodded and wandered into the house.

Sofia fell in next to her as Melissa headed for the house's triple garage. Melissa dug a door opener out of her handbag and hit the button.

"We can take the Range Rover," Melissa announced. "We'll need the room."

How many costumes were they picking up? An entire prison's worth? Sofia didn't want to know.

The garage door glided open. As they stepped into the gloom of the garage, Sofia caught a glimpse of Nigel's Mercedes sitting next to the Range Rover. She felt a pang of grief at the sight. Even though she'd only met him once, it was odd to think that he'd never drive it again. Or any other car. That he was completely gone. She wondered how Melissa could be so blasé. Even if she hadn't had any feelings for Nigel at the end, she must have loved him at some point.

Maybe this was just her way of coping. Sofia had seen something like it before with the recently bereaved. A manic need to stay busy and somehow stave off their emotions. Maybe this was what the party was. A way of pretending that none of what had happened was real. Or, it could be that deep down Melissa was really shallow. Sofia bet on that last one.

Melissa opened the driver's door and got in. Sofia got into the front passenger seat next to her. The Ranger Rover eased out of the garage and down the driveway. Melissa waved cheerfully at Leo. He gave her an unconvincing smile back. Any director Sofia had ever worked with would have made him do another take on that smile.

They reached the gates at the bottom of the driveway. Melissa reached up to the sun visor, and pressed a button on the clicker that controlled the gates. The electronic gates swung slowly open and the Range Rover nosed its way through and out onto the street.

Melissa picked her handbag off her lap and handed it off to Sofia while she drove one-handed. "Could you be a dear and put that on the backseat?"

"Sure," said Sofia, taking the bag from her.

Sofia shuffled around in the large, leather-upholstered seat and turned to the back of the car. A hand appeared from the backseat foot well and grabbed her wrist. Sofia screamed and tried to yank her hand back, but she was caught in a tight grip.

A man with a gun sat up in the back seat. He pressed the

gun barrel into Sofia's cheek. She gasped and then tried to sit very still.

Melissa screamed and almost lost control of the Range Rover.

"Keep us on the road," the man instructed Melissa. "One wrong move and I blow her head off. You got me?"

52

Sofia had come pretty close to losing control of her bladder for the second time in only a few weeks. The cold metal of the gun pressed painfully against her cheek didn't help.

Next to her, Melissa straightened the Range Rover and slowed down. With the tinted windows, no one could look inside the SUV and see what was happening. They were on their own and at the mercy of the gunman. At least they had solved the mystery of where the two Philly mob fugitives were. They could now account for at least one of them.

Sofia had studied mugshots released by the LA County sheriff and LAPD. She had a good memory for faces, and she was pretty sure that the man holding her at gunpoint was Vincent 'Little Vinny' Chitti. He was a mob enforcer, and he was suspected of having killed before. Sofia pushed his rap sheet out of her mind and tried not to panic.

"Okay," Little Vinny told Melissa. "Pull over on this corner."

Thankfully, Melissa did as she was told because Sofia

was pretty sure Little Vinny would have shot her to make a point. In fact, apart from her initial scream, which Sofia wasn't really in a position to comment on, because she had had the exact same reaction, Melissa had stayed pretty calm, all things considered. A man dashed from behind a hedge. Little Vinny reached over, the gun dropping from Sofia's face for a second, and opened the passenger door.

Little Vinny's partner in thuggery, Michael 'Big Mike' Barbina, clambered in the back. He, too, looked just like his police mug shot, except tanner and bigger. He was the guy who had shot at Sofia and Aidan in the parking garage, and the one who had tried to run her off the road. Sadly, his left arm seemed to be all healed.

He grabbed the back of the front seats and pulled himself forward. "Thanks for the ride, ladies. Much appreciated. You can keep driving, toots."

"Where are we going?" Melissa asked.

"Good question," said Big Mike. "You see, even though your departed husband, God rest his soul, is no longer with us, the money he took and didn't pay back is still an outstanding debt. So you're going to drive us to your bank and arrange a wire transfer."

"You're crazy," said Melissa. "They'll ask questions."

Little Vinny pushed the gun back into Sofia's face. Even though the element of surprise was gone, she still didn't feel any better about a loaded handgun being held to her head. Especially because Vinny seemed the jumpy type, and not the brightest. He seemed as likely to pull the trigger by accident as by design.

"Then you'd better think of a good story," countered Big Mike.

Sofia had already realized that Melissa stood some

chance. They had a use for her. Without her, they couldn't get their hands on the money they were owed. Until that was in their hands, they wouldn't kill her.

Sofia was a different matter. Not only was she dead weight, she had foiled them not once, but twice. First on the freeway going to her mom's house and then when they arrived to kill Bobby Rogers. If she didn't do something about it, she couldn't see herself getting out of this situation alive. No matter how scared she felt, she had to start thinking and fast.

"I can help her with that," she piped up. "Coming up with a story I mean."

"Oh yeah?" Big Mike didn't seem all that convinced by her offer of help.

"Sure," said Sofia. "I used to be an actress. Part of that is being able to improvise."

Melissa glanced across at her. She looked skeptical. "I think I'll be fine on my own."

Sofia's elbow shot out to nudge Melissa. She leaned across and whispered. "I'm dead meat if I don't get in the bank with you."

Little Vinny reached past Big Mike, through the gap in the seats, and jabbed Sofia in the ribs with his gun. "No whispering. You have something to say, you say it to us, 'kay?"

"Sorry," said Sofia. "But you're going to need me inside. I was a professional actress. I can convince people to do anything."

Big Mike made a barking laugh that made him sound like an over-excited seal. "Oh, yeah?"

"She's right," said Melissa. "And I'm not doing it unless she comes in with me."

The gun swiveled from Sofia to Melissa.

"You think we're asking you, toots?" said Little Vinny. "We ain't."

Sofia may not have liked Melissa, but she didn't deny that the lady had a steely inner core. As she pulled the Range Rover into the bank's parking lot, she stared down the gun and the man holding it. "It's both of us or you can whistle for your money."

"Okay, okay," said Big Mike. "But any funny stuff and you both die."

"Understood," said Melissa.

"There won't be any funny stuff," Sofia lied.

Melissa pulled into a parking spot two lanes back from the bank's main entrance and switched off the engine. Twisting around in her seat, Sofia saw Little Vinny nudge Big Mike.

"Can I ask her now?" Little Vinny asked Big Mike.

Big Mike looked aggravated. "You have to?"

"Well, yeah." Little Vinny pulled the gun away from Sofia and tucked it back into a shoulder holster. He fished in his inside jacket pocket and pulled out a small black notebook.

"Go on then," said Big Mike.

Little Vinny thrust the notebook at Sofia. "Could I get your autograph?"

Sofia stared at him. She had been asked for her autograph in strange places and strange circumstances, but this had to be the weirdest. Even by LA standards, this was completely over the top, and that was really saying something.

"A minute ago you were going to shoot me and now you want my autograph?" she said as Little Vinny held the notebook out to her and dug back into his pocket for a pen.

He looked a little sheepish. "If you wouldn't mind. I'd really appreciate it."

She took the notebook and the pen, flipped to a blank page and signed her name with a flourish. She handed the notebook back. She kept the pen. Maybe she could stab him with it later. What would Violet do? *Aim for his carotid artery.*

Little Vinny took the notebook, opened it to the page she'd just signed, and smiled. "That's terrific. Thank you so much." He turned to Big Mike. "Last thing she signed. This could be worth big money."

Sofia felt cold all over, and she gulped. Even Melissa jumped.

Big Mike glared at his partner.

"He's kidding! Aren't you?" he asked Vinny, giving him a sharp-elbowed dig in the ribs.

"Oh yeah," said Little Vinny. "After a while you kind of get a dark sense of humor doing this job."

"No kidding," said Sofia, not believing a word of it. At least she knew for sure now that this was her one shot at saving her life.

Melissa cleared her throat. "Do you guys want your money or do you want to sit here chatting? I have a party to organize. God only knows what the caterers will do if I leave them to their own devices for too long." She glanced at Sofia. "Leo looks pretty but he'd not exactly an organizational wizard, know what I mean?"

Sofia had to hand it to Melissa. She really wasn't a fan of small talk, not even when she was being kidnapped at gun point. The woman had shit to get done, and she wasn't going to let a little snag like an unexpected abduction by two mob killers ruin her soiree. That was focus for you.

"Okay, go ahead, but remember, you try to alert anyone, and we'll shoot you both," said Big Mike. "*Capiche?*"

The way he asked them in Italian if they understood, Sofia had the impression he'd been dying to use that word. Probably made him feel more like a mobster. All four of them got out of the car at the same time. Melissa and Sofia walked toward the bank entrance with the two guys a few steps behind. Sofia felt their escorts watching her every move.

As they got closer to the entrance, Big Mike fell in step with Melissa. "I'll have to give you the details of the transfer." He eyed Sofia. "Toots, you stay with Vinny."

Sofia did an inner eye roll. She was going to 'toots' someone where the sun didn't shine as soon as they got inside the bank. As dumb and as violent as they were, she didn't think these two thugs would risk shooting her in the middle of a busy bank in Brentwood. They would want to be in and out as quickly as possible and with the minimum fuss. They'd try to avoid anything that would draw attention to themselves. Or at least she hoped so. Even if they shot her, the bank was still her best hope of survival.

Melissa walked into the main bank foyer with Big Mike by her side. Sofia followed, Little Vinny glued to her side. As Melissa headed over to the line with Big Mike, Little Vinny motioned for Sofia to take a seat.

"I prefer standing," she told him.

His eyes narrowed. "Si' down."

"You're not the boss of me," she said, raising her voice.

He tried to grab her elbow, but she pulled away.

"Take your paws off me," she said even louder.

Her behavior was getting the desired effect. Customers and bank employees looked over at her. She hadn't been lying about being prepared to improvise. Acting had also given her one other ability that was coming in handy. As long as she was playing a character rather than just being herself, she really didn't care what people thought. The character she had chosen to play on the brief walk from the Range Rover was Complete Pain in the Ass.

"Keep your voice down," Little Vinny hissed.

Big Mike looked ready to spontaneously combust as he waited in line with Melissa. He kept shooting looks at Little Vinny.

"Sorry," Sofia said to Vinny. "I'd really rather not sit down though."

"Okay, don't sit down," he said.

She counted that as a point for her side. She needed to get everyone's attention, but not make him so mad that he shot her. It was going to be a delicate balance.

"Hey, can I ask you a question?" she said, raising her voice again and drawing more attention. She heard an elderly couple talking at a nearby desk, the woman insisting that "the girl over there is an actress" while her husband looked baffled. Sofia turned her attention back to her guard. "Why do they call Little Vinny? Is it because...?"

She wiggled her pinkie finger while staring at his crotch.

"I said, keep your voice down," Little Vinny whispered.

"Sore point, huh?" Lowering her voice fractionally before raising it even louder again she added, "You know you can get these like pump things to make it bigger. Or maybe you could tie a weight to it or something. Y'know stretch it out. Although if it's like really little. I mean how little are we talking here?"

Little Vinny looked like he was about to explode. He leaned toward her. "That's not why they call me Little Vinny. It's because I'm short."

Sofia held up her hands. "Sorry! Didn't mean to touch a nerve. Yeah, I'm sure that's the reason they gave you that nickname." She had gotten so loud that by now pretty much everyone in the bank was staring at her and Little Vinny. Good.

Less than ten yards away, an elderly woman nudged her husband. "It's her. I'm telling you. She was in *The Enquirer*." The woman leaned in a little closer to her husband. "Drug problems," she whispered, taking out her cell phone and taking a picture while her husband looked embarrassed. "She's the one who peed right in the street in the middle of the day."

It seemed that Sofia wasn't the only person who had overheard the gossipy woman. Little Vinny's face lit up. "Oh yeah, I saw that video."

Melissa was at the counter with Big Mike and was busy filling in what Sofia guessed was the wire transfer authorization. She seemed to be trying to draw it out as long as possible. Sofia didn't blame her. Nigel's life insurance money wouldn't cover a woman like Melissa for long. She needed enough money to grab the next wealthy guy who passed her way.

It was time for Sofia to make her move. She planned on wrapping her arms and legs around the nearest desk and demanding to speak to a manager. That ought to get enough attention to drive Little Vinny and Big Mike out of the bank.

As if he read her mind, Little Vinny tightened his grip around her elbow. "We should get you back to the clinic," he said to Sofia, raising his voice to match hers.

Oh crap.

Little Vinny smiled at the woman who had taken the picture and was busy taking even more. He raised his voice so that everyone in the bank could hear him. "We need to get you back to the rehab clinic. Where you're being held under *court order*."

Double crap. So much for her plan to stay in the bank.

Now Little Vinny was pretty much free to drag her out of the bank kicking and screaming. Everyone would just assume he was from the rehab facility and taking her back into treatment.

Even if she tried to explain, people probably wouldn't believe her. Whatever she said would be interpreted as a drug-crazed celeb trying to avoid going cold turkey. Staying in the bank and waiting for help to arrive wasn't an option anymore.

She had to get away from Little Vinny and Big Mike. She could make a run for it. But not on her own. There was no way she was going to leave Melissa to the tender mercies of Big Mike. He'd kill her as soon as he got the money.

A side effect of Little Vinny's loud public announcement was that more and more customers and staff were looking over at her. The whispers were growing louder. A teenage girl who'd come in with her mom took a sneaky picture. Her mom dug her in the ribs. "Chelsea!"

Sofia smiled at Chelsea. Maybe there was still a way to turn this to her advantage.

"Don't worry," she called over to the teenager. "Takes as many pictures as you want. Just make sure you get Vincent Chitti here in them, too."

The teenager took more pictures and Sofia posed for her. Her mom managed a tight smile.

Little Vinny turned quickly so that his back was to the teenager and her mom.

"Come on," Sofia said. "Don't be shy."

"You're going to be heading back to the clinic in the trunk of a car if you don't shut your yap," he growled.

Sofia lowered her voice. "You know those pictures are going to be all over social media in about two minutes, right?"

"We'll be out of here in two minutes." Little Vinny said.

"They'll still know your name," she said.

Little Vinny looked like he didn't know what to do with that information. He grabbed her elbow and hustled her over to Big Mike and Melissa.

Little Vinny leaned in to Big Mike. "Get this broad to hurry it up. We got people taking pictures over here."

"And filming us," Sofia added.

"Damn," Melissa said, striking through a section on the form. She looked apologetically at Big Mike. "You'd think I'd remember my own address, right?"

Big Mike glared at Melissa. The stress was clearly getting to him. The longer he and Vinny were out in public, the higher the risk. "You got two minutes to finish up."

"You forgot to say *capiche*," Sofia added unhelpfully. "Oh, and I could really use my next shot of methadone."

Big Mike looked at her like she was crazy. "Vinny, take her out to the car."

"It's okay. I'm fine right where I am," Sofia said.

"Let's go," said Little Vinny, stepping behind her and wrapping his arms around her waist.

Melissa dropped her pen back down on the counter. "Hey, leave her alone."

Sofia realized that it was pretty much now or never. If Vinny dragged her back out to the car, that would probably be the last anyone would see of her. She didn't think they were planning on taking her for a scenic drive out to wine country. Unless it involved a shovel and garbage bags.

As Melissa took two steps toward Vinny, Sofia simultaneously bent at the waist, moved her butt out to the side, and dropped down. She brought her left elbow back hard, smashing it into Vinny's face as he leaned over, trying to maintain her in the bear hug. After her left elbow connected, she moved it forward and threw it back again as hard as she could. This time it smashed into his cheekbone. The impact jolted up to her shoulder. He yelped.

Taking a step back, Sofia wriggled free. Big Mike went to grab her as Little Vinny clutched his face. Rather than retreating, she took a step forward, and brought her knee up as hard as she could into Big Mike's groin.

She reached out, grabbed Melissa by the wrist, and ran for the door as the people in the bank either stood there dumbfounded or fumbled for their cell phones so they could film what was destined to be a YouTube classic. Judging from the blinking red light on her cell phone, the teenage girl was already filming.

The bank's security guard started toward her, but Big Mike knocked him on his ass and grabbed the gun out of his holster as he fell.

Chelsea screamed.

Sofia ran back to the counter and climbed on top, dragging Melissa along. Leave it Melissa to bank someplace that didn't have bulletproof glass anywhere.

Glancing over her shoulder, Sofia saw Big Mike and Little Vinny stumbling after them. Big Mike was limping, and Little Vinny was clutching a hand to his face.

"Take off your heels," Sofia said.

Big Mike had recovered and was charging toward them like a bear. He clearly didn't care one bit that he was in a bank.

Melissa was struggling with the strap of one of her shoes. Sofia knew that they didn't have a second to spare. She reached down and yanked the shoe from Melissa's foot.

"Are you crazy?" Melissa shouted. "We're never going to outrun them."

Sofia wrenched the shoe from Melissa's foot and grasped it in her hand as the two men bore down on her.

"Who said anything about outrunning them?" she said, stepping between Melissa and Big Mike, who was heading toward them.

Sofia's hand tightened around the toe of Melissa's Louboutin. She drew her arm back. Big Mike was still coming at her, full tilt. Sofia waited. Like throwing a punch, timing was everything.

Big Mike was almost on top of her, Sofia pivoted hard, throwing her hips round, and whipping her arm forward in a big, looping haymaker. The spiked end of the Louboutin heel smashed straight into Big Mike's left eye. The impact sent a shockwave down Sofia's arm.

Big Mike screamed in pain. Sofia pulled her arm back, wrenching the shoe from his face. Big Mike's arms flailed out toward her. She stepped back. Big Mike's arms windmilled helplessly in the air.

Behind Big Mike, Sofia saw Little Vinny reach into his jacket, going for his gun.

Sofia took aim. Pulling her arm back, Sofia pitched the shoe as hard as she could straight at Little Vinny.

Time slowed. The Louboutin arced heel over toe through the air. Little Vinny's hand came out of his jacket. The red-soled shoe spun through the air as he raised his gun. A look of shock registered on Little Vinny's face as the Louboutin spun toward him. His mouth opened. His hand fell to the trigger.

Sofia was rooted to the spot. All she saw was the barrel of the gun pointing at her. The Loubotin traveled the final yard through the air, its aim true. Sofia heard the familiar click of a paparazzi's camera as it captured the scene. When had they arrived?

Sofia heard the gunshot. She saw the muzzle flash. She closed her eyes.

53

Before the gunshot had died to an echo, she heard a scream of pain. Her senses completely overloaded, Sofia couldn't tell whether it was her screaming or someone else.

She could still feel her feet on the floor. She was fairly certain she was still upright. Slowly, she opened her eyes.

She looked down to see Big Mike, one hand clutching his eye, the other rubbing his leg as he yelped in pain. "My leg. Holy Mary Mother of God. You asshole, Vinny. You shot me in the freakin' leg."

Behind Big Mike, Little Vinny wasn't faring much better. He was lying flat on his back, his arms and legs spread out, still slightly stunned from the shoe. Sofia quickly reached down and pried the gun from his hand.

Someone else yelled from behind her. "Police! Put the gun down!"

Still bending down, she swiveled her neck to see two cops, guns drawn, standing in the doorway. Slowly, she put the gun down on the ground, and kicked it away from Little

Vinny's reach. More cops came in behind the ones in the door. It was a river of blue uniforms.

Sofia followed the officer's instructions, raising her hands, and lacing her fingers behind her head before she slowly knelt down. Cops swarmed in from all directions, cuffing the two mobsters and Melissa, who yelled at them in protest. "I was just kidnapped, you assholes. I'm the victim."

A burly cop hauled Sofia back onto her feet. She held out her hands to be cuffed, and the entire bank erupted into applause. She had to admit it had been one hell of a performance. She resisted the overpowering urge to bow, and kept a straight face.

When she looked around, she was relieved to finally see a friendly face. Brendan was pushing his way through the police perimeter toward her with Aidan a few steps behind.

"How did you get here so fast?" Sofia asked Brendan.

Brendan nodded to Aidan. "He monitors you on twitter. We called the cavalry when we heard."

"You're the number one topic trending on twitter right now," Aidan added unhelpfully.

Sofia looked around at the carnage. The two prostrate mobsters who everyone thought were rehab nurses. The blood-soaked Louboutin heel. The crowd of paparazzi who had gathered in the bank to capture every single frame of the drama. Melissa in her bare feet.

"That's number one topic in the country," Aidan grinned. "Not overseas."

Sofia looked to the heavens. "Great. That's just great."

"You always say it's a waste of time," Aidan said. "But twitter just saved your life."

54

T hree days later
Nirvana Cove, Malibu

FRED THE SEAGULL SQUAWKED LOUDLY, flapping his wings and taking off from the porch of Sofia's trailer, hotly pursued by Violet and Van. Fred had caught on to the kids right away.

"Come back," shouted Van.

"Yeah, come back, you stupid bird," Violet shrieked as Fred gained height. "We haven't finished playing with you yet!"

Fred circled high above them, caught a thermal, and turned for the hills above the cove. Fred was no fool, and he wasn't coming back.

"After breakfast, why don't we go down to the beach?" she asked her niece and nephew.

"Yeah!" said Violet, punching the air.

"You have to finish breakfast first," said Emily as she

hustled through from Sofia's kitchen with a pitcher of fresh orange juice and put it down on the small round table.

Emily was followed by their mom, Janet, carrying a plate piled high with bacon. She put the plate down, and the kids immediately descended on it. A couple of seagulls swooped down to take a look, saw Van and Violet, and took off again. They probably figured they might be the next course if they stuck around. They were probably right.

Ray and Tim were walking up from the beach. Tim was carrying a sand wedge and a couple of hollow plastic practice golf balls. Ray was checking something on his phone.

"Hey, Sofia, you see this?" Ray said, palming his cell off to her.

The headline on the news site screamed in all caps "SALGADO COMES OUT SWINGING ON SUNSET" She got as far as reading "Troubled star, Sofia Salgado" before she handed it back to Ray.

"Thought you should know," he said sheepishly.

Her mom snatched the cell phone from Ray and read what was on the screen. "I hope this has at least brought you to your senses. You could have been killed."

Sofia folded her arms. She'd been waiting for this conversation since the cops had showed up at the bank, and she'd realized she wasn't going to die. "Mom, I saved an innocent woman from being killed. Not on screen, in some movie, but for real."

"And we're very proud of you, darling. Aren't we, Tim?"

"We sure are. That was a hell of a throw," Tim said, miming Sofia's shoe launch.

That footage had also gone viral and launched a thousand Internet memes and an online discussion that she could play the lead in a remake of the nineties movie, *A*

League Of Their Own. Nobody was talking about the peeing incident anymore.

"Thank you, Tim," said Sofia.

Her mom was staring at her. "You're still serious about this detective business, aren't you?"

To be honest, Sofia hadn't even considered giving up and going back to acting. It might have sounded cheesy, but she felt like she had achieved more in the months she'd worked for Maloney Investigations than in her years as an actress. It was a real job in the real world.

Okay, there weren't trailers and craft services and people kissing your ass all the time. Those luxury items had been replaced by sitting on stake-outs desperate to pee, sack lunches eaten in cars, and people shooting at her or trying to run her off the road. But she knew which job she wanted to do. She didn't expect people to understand. She didn't blame them for thinking she was crazy. But it was her life to live the way she wanted.

Everyone was looking at her now. Her mom, her sister, Ray, Tim, even the two kids.

"Sofia," said her mom, "are you still serious about it?"

"Yeah, I guess I am," Sofia answered.

"You go girl!" shouted Violet, thrusting a fist in the air and holding it there. "Black power!"

Emily put an arm around her daughter. "Honey, what have I said about not shouting that in public?"

No one else seemed to match Sofia's niece's enthusiasm. But no one tried to argue with her, either. That was progress.

If only the same could be said for Jeffrey who was rushing down the path toward the little blue trailer, waving a piece of paper in the air like a crazed politician.

"Do I have a deal for you," he shouted, completely ignoring the fact that she was enjoying brunch with her family. "Six episodes. One million per episode. And back end. Gross points not net. Plus an overall holding deal at Fox."

Sofia looked down at her niece. "Violet?"

"Yeah?" said Violet, the picture of innocence.

"You know that new move you came up with?"

"The flying death slam?" asked Violet.

"You see that man there?" Sofia said, pointing at Jeffery. "He's a talent agent. You know, kind of like Simon Cowell, but without the charm. But if you show him what you got, then maybe he can get you your own TV show."

"You could call your show *Violet's Death Match*," Van chipped in.

"Awesome!" Violet launched herself off the porch and ran full pelt toward Jeffery.

Everyone on the porch watched as Violet closed in on Jeffery and karate kicked him in the knee. He went down with a cry of pain. Violet threw herself on top of him and launched a furious flurry of blows. Jeffery rolled into a ball. Emily and Ray took off after Violet and finally dragged their daughter off him.

"I'm sorry," said Emily. "Really sorry."

Jeffery slowly got to his feet and dusted himself off.

"It's a no, then?" he asked Sofia, who had watched the mayhem without leaving the porch.

Fred the seagull, spotting his opportunity, swooped back in low. Sofia picked up a tiny piece of bacon and tossed it to Fred. He caught it midair and swallowed it.

Sofia looked out to the blue carpet of ocean and smiled. "It's a no."

"B" IS FOR BAD GIRLS

Sofia Salgado, is back on the case that turns into her mother's worst nightmare when she ends up undercover in one of Malibu's many rehab clinics.

If she doesn't solve the mystery in time, she and all the bad girls she meets inside, including rock star Brandi Basher and reality TV train wreck Monaco Jane might just end up going to the big rehab center in the sky.

Read the first three chapters below.

CHAPTER 1

Sofia Salgado had paint in her hair. After a broken toaster had spewed smoke and soot all over her ceiling, she'd decided to repaint it herself. She'd budgeted a couple of hours for the task, but so far all she'd accomplished was putting newspapers on the countertops and stove, covering the edges with blue tape, and somehow managing to drip yellow paint on her head.

She looked around at the messy mobile home she'd bought with the money she'd made starring in a TV show called *Half Pint Detective*. Even in its current state, she loved everything about the place. It had a full kitchen, a cute breakfast nook, a living room, two bedrooms, and two bathrooms. It reminded her more of a ship than a regular house —lots of wooden built-ins, smaller than average appliances, and a view of the Pacific Ocean from her living room.

The mobile home sat off the beach in Malibu, California, in a trailer park called Nirvana Cove. The park was originally built for people with ordinary incomes, or folks who wanted a cheap weekend or summer getaway, but had become crazy expensive in the past thirty years. Now some of the trailers sold for over a million dollars. She'd paid the money because it was only a short walk from the ocean, and nobody bothered her here in her own little slice of Paradise.

Still, right now, a hotel would be nice. One someone else had already painted. Something clean and tidy. With room service.

"Hello!" Emily called, from outside the front window.

"Crap!" Sofia muttered, under her breath. She looked guiltily at the yellow smiley-faced clock on the kitchen wall. Mr. Smiley said Emily was two hours early. Her sister was usually late, and Sofia had counted on it this morning. She hadn't even showered, and wore beat-up clothes under her white painter's jumpsuit.

Emily wore a red sundress and was, as always, perfectly turned out. When they were kids everyone said Emily looked like a little lady, Sofia like she'd fallen out of a tree, then rolled down a hill and into a duck pond.

Emily waved through the window at Sofia. Sofia waved back.

"Anyone home?" a little girl's voice asked, right before something that sounded like a sledgehammer pounded on Sofia's metal front door. It quaked, as if ready to come off its hinges.

Sofia sprinted to rescue it, tripped on the half-full tray she'd left in the middle of the kitchen, and splashed out yellow paint. Good thing she'd put down those newspapers. Too bad about her shoe.

"Now, Violet." Emily sounded manically cheery. "Leave that."

Sofia flung open her front door. Her seven-year-old niece held a wooden leg that Sofia could have sworn was usually attached to the table on her front porch. She caught Violet's arm mid-swing and twisted it out of her hand. The bistro table stood at an accusing angle on its three good legs. The marble top looked ready to slide off.

Sofia summoned up her former child-star training and gave the whole family a bright smile. "It's great to see you!"

She was being so perky her face hurt. But she meant it. It was always great to see Emily and her kids. She took off her paint-covered shoes and dropped the table leg on the chair seat. She'd have to fix it after the kids left. No point in putting it back on only to have them take it off again. Luckily, it was an IKEA table—easy to take apart and put back together.

Violet gave a shrug in the direction of the listing table with its three legs. "It was loose."

Her brother, six-year-old Van, hastily stuffed something into his pocket. It looked like a screwdriver, but it couldn't be. His parents kept all of the tools in their house locked up tight.

"We really appreciate you taking the kids!" Emily beamed up at her husband, Ray. He had on black board shorts and a white T-shirt. They looked as if they were about to head out on their honeymoon, happy and guilty at the same time. "I know we're early. Is that OK?"

"Of course," Sofia lied. If they'd come on time, the ceiling would have been done and everything put away. At least, that had been the plan.

"You can always call us if it gets bad," Ray said. "We can come right back."

"It's only for the weekend!" Sofia said. "The kids and I will have some great adventures together. I thought today we'd go—"

Sofia's phone played the first few bars from the theme of the old TV show *Dragnet*. Everyone looked at it.

"Sorry, that's the agency," she said, pulling the phone out of the pocket of her paint-splattered overalls.

CHAPTER 2

The agency was Maloney Investigations. Detective work involved a lot of drudgery sometimes, but she loved it, except when they called her on weekends. Her boss, Brendan Maloney, had been kind enough to take her on as a trainee private investigator when she'd decided to quit acting and get a real job. She'd met him on the set when he worked as a consultant to her TV show, and he'd taken her under his wing. She sometimes wondered if she'd be a zookeeper now if he'd been consulting on that.

"I'll just be a minute," Sofia said to the two kids.

She wanted to go inside and take the call in privacy, but she didn't dare turn her back on Violet and Van. They'd dismantle her home in five minutes if she let down her guard. "Sofia here."

"I know you were supposed to be off this weekend, but something's come up. You're needed in the office for a meeting." Aidan Maloney, son of the agency's owner, and Sofia's sometime friend, sometime arch-nemesis. "Urgent business. Only you will do."

"I'll call you back in exactly one minute," Sofia told him.

She smiled at her sister. "Or maybe three minutes. But soon."

She disconnected and looked at her sister and brother-in-law. They'd been planning this trip for months. Usually Sofia and Emily's mother and stepfather watched the kids, but they were out of town on a cruise. If Sofia didn't come through, Emily and Ray would have to cancel their plans.

"Is everything OK?" Emily bit her lower lip, and Ray squeezed her against his side. They were so darn cute together.

"It's just a meeting." Sofia took a deep breath of bracing sea air. She could do this. "I can still take the kids. Don't worry."

Ray jumped forward as if he'd been hit by a cattle prod. "Great!" he almost shouted. In less than a second, he had dumped two backpacks on the front porch and slapped a set of car keys into Sofia's hand. "As long as you're sure."

Sofia was feeling a little dazed. "Yup."

Ray hugged Violet and frisked Van, producing a screwdriver the child had hidden in his front pocket. That explained the table leg.

"Is this yours?" he asked Sofia.

She shook her head. Her stepfather had bought her a toolset when she'd moved into the trailer. All her tools had pink handles, even the drill. Van's screwdriver was black.

"I found it in the parking lot," Van said. "Just sitting there."

Sofia tried to imagine who would have left a brand new Craftsman screwdriver in the parking lot. Nobody in Nirvana Cove would ever work on their car in the lot. The other residents would probably barbecue them if they did.

"I'll put the screwdriver back there," said Ray, "when we come to get you on Sunday night."

Emily pulled each kid into a long hug and kissed the top of their heads. Violet squirmed away, but Van stood still and rolled his eyes, like only a six-year-old boy could.

"Remember, you can't let Van have any tools." Emily shook the screwdriver at him. "And they both had baths this morning and breakfast, so you don't need to worry about that. Bedtime is nine, since it's a weekend. I packed some books in their backpacks with the clothes."

Sofia looked at the backpacks. Violet's was pink and, rather incongruously, had a princess on the front. Van's was orange and looked like a giant Lego brick.

"We'll be fine," Sofia said. "I bought a new Lego airport set for Van, and I got a bootleg copy of *The Ultimate Fighting Challenge* 2010 for Violet. It's from back before they added those safety rules."

"Cool!" the kids chorused in unison.

"You bet!" She was Cool Auntie Sofia, after all. She had a reputation to maintain.

Emily's brow creased in worry. "I know you'll be fine, but—"

"Time to go, honey." Ray kissed Violet's cheek and patted Van's head. "Sofia's a brave little soldier. She'll get through. We've got places to go, things to do."

Emily gave Ray a smile Sofia could only describe as lascivious. She was kinda shocked her sister had done that next to the kids, even if they were facing away from her.

"One more thing," Emily said. "Absolutely no sugar. It makes them totally hyper. You remember when we watched that movie *Gremlins* and they fed the creatures after midnight? It's like that, only worse."

Holy crap, thought Sofia. More hyper? Only the Tasmanian Devil was more hyper than those two. "No sugar. I promise."

Ray took Emily's hand, and they practically sprinted back up the path toward the parking lot. They didn't get enough time alone together, those two.

"Want me to show you my new move?" Violet asked. "I'm calling it the Nutcracker!"

Van shifted away from her and held both hands in front of his crotch. Sofia had a pretty good idea what the move might entail.

"Maybe later," she said. "I picked up some fresh cherries from a road stand yesterday. How about you guys have a snack while I clean up the painting stuff?"

Sofia's pseudo-pet, a seagull named Fred, came in for a landing on her porch. He wanted his breakfast. Sofia usually left bread or lunchmeat out for him, and he stopped by whenever he saw her outside. He banked hard to the right when he spotted the kids, flapped his wings a couple of times and headed back to the beach. Fred had dealt with Van and Violet before.

Sofia grabbed each kid in a hug. Sure, they were active, but she adored them. Nothing wrong with knowing who you were and what you wanted. Half of Los Angeles would give their eyeteeth for that kind of certainty. She picked up their backpacks, noting that Van's seemed ominously heavy, and led them into the house.

On cue, her phone rang. *Dragnet* again. Aidan again.

"I said I'd call right back," she snapped.

"I didn't get that message." It was Brendan, Aidan's father and Sofia's boss. "Did I catch you at a bad time?"

Sofia looked at the open paint can in the kitchen, and the two kids staring up at her. "Not a bad time. Just gimme one second, Brendan."

She plonked the cherries on the coffee table and muted

the phone. "Please stay on the couch. Eat the cherries. Don't swallow the pits."

The kids nodded obediently, which made her suspicious. She went back to the phone. "Here I am."

"I know you were supposed to have this weekend off, and I apologize," Brendan sounded genuinely remorseful, "but a case has come up that I think you'd be perfect for."

Please don't let it be a honey-trap. Please don't let it be a honey-trap.

The last honey trap had gone horribly wrong. She'd dressed in her best business slutty to see if she could pick up a client's husband because his wife had hired them to see if he was being unfaithful. The guy hadn't been interested, and he'd ended up dead not long after. *Please not a honey-trap.* "What kind of case?"

She pounded the top back onto the paint can with one of her pink screwdrivers. She looked around for a place to hide it from Van, but didn't see one. Her brother-in-law had a giant toolbox with a lock. She needed to get a smaller version of that. She put the screwdriver back into the pink toolbox and slid the whole thing into the oven. Van probably wouldn't look in there for it.

"The client is in the entertainment industry, and I thought you might be able to put her at ease," Brendan said. "You're good that way."

Not a honey-trap! Just a simple meeting. How bad could that be? "Happy to help."

"Her brother was the singer Craig Williams."

"I see." Sofia took everything out of Van's backpack. Socks, superhero underwear, pajamas with pictures of tools on them —the only tools he was allowed to have—T-shirt, pants, and books. Nothing that could be used to take apart the television.

"As you probably know, Craig Williams was found dead in his apartment with a needle in his vein."

Sofia stuffed Van's clothes in the backpack. "Wasn't he a heroin addict?"

"Yes, he was."

Nobody had been surprised by his death, and police had ruled it an accidental overdose. But Brendan knew all that, so there must be something more than met the eye. "But it wasn't an accidental overdose?"

"It's open right now. What I'd like is for you to come in for the meeting with Mr. Williams's sister. We'll see where it goes from there."

She wanted to say, 'not this weekend,' but she knew one of the reasons Brendan had brought her into the agency was because of her industry connections and understanding of how 'the town,' as people in the entertainment industry referred to it, worked. "I have Emily's kids this weekend. She and Ray needed a break."

"Bring them along," said Brendan. "Aidan can watch them while we have our meeting."

The thought of saddling Aidan with Violet and Van made the whole thing worthwhile. "I'll be there in a half hour." The sound of glass smashing came to her from the living room. "I gotta go."

"A cherry pit went through the window," Van said. "Sorry, Aunt Sofia."

"We were having a spit fight," Violet said, pulling a pit from her mouth, and holding it up for Sofia to inspect. "With the right technique, you can really get a lot of velocity on these little suckers. You want me to show you?"

Sofia didn't have time to cross-examine them, but she didn't see how they could have broken the window with a cherry pit. She peeled off her overalls. "Maybe later. Hey, who wants to go to a real live detective agency?"

"Me!" shouted Violet.

"Me, too!" shouted Van.

She left the paint in the tray. She'd heard you were supposed to let it dry, then peel it off and throw it away. She balled up the wet newspapers and tossed them in a giant black trash bag. The rest of the newspapers she left alone. Maybe she could get Violet and Van to help her paint the ceiling later.

She stomped on a cardboard box to flatten it, then had Violet and Van hold it while she stuck it over the broken window with the blue masking tape she'd been using for the painting. She'd get the glass fixed later, maybe after the kids fell asleep. Assuming they ever slept. They had a nine o'clock bedtime, but she just knew they'd pop up like jack-in-the-boxes after she'd tucked them in.

A few minutes later, Sofia had changed into some decent clothes and maneuvered the kids to the parking lot without breaking anything else. She lugged her heavy pink toolbox because she'd decided that the oven wasn't secure enough, and the only safe place she could think of was the trunk of her car. After the window, she was taking no chances. She'd even double-checked that she'd set the alarm on the trailer. Without a window there, it would be easy to break in.

"I see two Ferraris and a Lambo!" Van's eyes were big and round.

"A Lambo?" Sofia asked.

"A Lam-borgh-ini," Van spoke slowly, as if he were talking to someone who was deaf, not too bright, or possibly both.

One of the park's idiosyncrasies was that residents couldn't drive to their homes but instead had to walk or take golf buggies to them, leaving the parking lot littered with expensive cars.

"Can I drive that?" Violet pointed to a blue buggy with a fish painted on the side and a surf board bungeed to the top.

"Maybe we can ride in one later," Sofia said. "But I have to drive it. California state law."

She didn't know the law on driving golf buggies on private property, but she didn't want to give Violet control of a moving battering ram.

Van had already reached Sofia's car, a red Tesla Roadster. Sofia looked at it longingly, all plugged into its charger and ready to go. She loved that car. But it had only two seats, so it was going to have to stay where it was. She opened the trunk and put in the toolbox, safe from Van's prying hands. The smell of leather drifted out.

"How are we going to fit?" Violet asked, eyeing the Roadster.

"I could ride on the roof," Van volunteered.

"Me too!" screamed Violet.

"We're taking your mom's car." Sofia pointed to her sister's forest-green minivan. She hoped Ray had given her the right set of keys on the porch. He had to have because he was tooling up the coast in his lime-colored Mustang with his beautiful wife. They probably had the top down and the breeze in their hair. They'd earned it.

She beeped the minivan open. A streak of fresh bird poop ran down the windshield. She couldn't help wondering if Fred was taking revenge. He could be jealous when it came to having Sofia's full attention, and she didn't put anything past him.

She hustled the kids into their car seats and buckled them in. So far, so good.

Her phone rang again. *Dragnet.* She really had to find another ringtone.

"Sorry, Brendan," she said. "I'm on my way."

"It's Aidan. I thought I'd fill you in on some details before you got here."

Sofia ducked her head to look inside the minivan. Violet and Van were sitting quietly in their seats. Violet gave her a dimply smile, which made Sofia worry.

"This is a good time," she lied.

"Three weeks ago Craig Williams was found dead in his apartment of an apparent overdose. There was a needle in his arm, heroin in his bloodstream. It looked pretty open and shut. It was all over the news. You probably heard about it."

"I did." She hadn't envied Craig the pressures he must have faced as a superstar. "Brendan already told me."

"Did he tell you that Craig had recently completed drug rehab and been declared clean? He passed a drug test when he left the center. It looked as if he might have beaten his addiction."

"Sometimes it goes like that." She'd lost a good friend, a teenaged actress on *Half Pint Detective*, to drugs. Everyone had thought Zoe was doing better, until her body turned up in a 7-Eleven bathroom. After that, the air had gone out of the show. Sofia had grieved, and it had shown on screen. She still thought about Zoe sometimes. By now she would have been twenty-seven, except that she would never be twenty-seven.

Sofia glanced into the minivan. Still nothing suspicious. Which was suspicious.

"His sister, Jenna Williams, is our client," Aidan said. "She's the only family member he was in contact with, and she thinks his death wasn't an accident."

This sounded like a terrible case to take on. Brendan was usually more careful about picking his clients. "What if it was?"

"Then we'll have to—"

"If you hold my foot, I can take off the rear-view mirror," piped a little voice from inside the minivan.

"Don't touch the mirror!" She yanked open Van's door and grabbed his wrist. Her phone clattered to the asphalt. She didn't let go of Van as she bent to pick up her phone.

"—so you can see why there's doubt," Aidan was saying.

"Sure," Sofia said into the phone. "I'll see you in a minute."

She ran around to the driver's side and slipped behind the wheel. The minivan smelled like Hawaiian Punch. Violet and Van flashed innocent-little-angel smiles.

"Back in your seats!" Sofia sounded more like a prison warden than a cool aunt. And they were only ten minutes into the visit. She aimed for jaunty and fun. "We're going to the detective agency!"

Violet folded her hands in her lap. She looked suspiciously demure. Sofia looked around the car and couldn't see anything wrong. "Does the car always smell like this?"

"Smell like what?" asked Van.

Sofia ransacked the whole van and found a red neon stain under the driver's seat. It was long dry, so at least it had happened before she'd come on duty. She sniffed the stain, hoping it wasn't blood or something worse. Nope, Hawaiian Punch. She ought to get the car detailed for Emily. That would be a nice gesture. Emily didn't have time to do stuff like that, what with the kids and her work in Ray's plumbing business.

Sofia climbed into the driver's seat and buckled up. "Onward ho!"

"Mom says we shouldn't use that word," Van piped up.

"What word?" said Sofia, confused.

"Hoe," said Van.

"It means prostitute," Violet added.

"That wasn't the word I was using," Sofia countered.

Violet eyed her from the back seat. "Sounded like it to me."

"No, 'onward ho' means..." Sofia couldn't actually think what it literally meant. "It means let's go do this."

"Like we're going on an adventure," Violet shouted.

"Precisely." Sofia pulled out of the parking space and headed in to work.

"With pirate prostitutes," Violet whispered to her brother.

"Cool," said Van, apparently satisfied with this new definition.

CHAPTER 3

Sofia's right eyelid twitched like a Mexican jumping bean. She couldn't remember the drive ever taking so long before. Traffic was light, but it still felt like she was crawling along in a giant rubber boat. She missed her Roadster. She'd be there already if she'd been able to take it. And she'd never really appreciated how quiet her own car was.

"Van's hand is on my side of the seat!" Violet said. "I can hit anything on my side."

"Don't hit your brother." Sofia had turned into her own mother in exactly fifteen minutes. "Van, keep on your own side."

"I dropped something," he said.

"What did you drop?" He wasn't supposed to have anything. She'd checked.

"Nothing," he said.

Her phone rang before she could pursue that further.

"It's me," her sister said. "I wanted to check in that everything was fine."

She sounded calmer than she had since Violet had turned two and morphed into an ultimate fighting machine. Had she and Ray pulled over for a quickie by the side of the road?

"Say hi to your mom, kids!" Sofia called.

"Hi, Mom," they chorused.

"Sofia is taking us to the detective agency," Violet yelled. "They have guns there."

"Sofia?" Emily didn't sound calm any more.

"We're going in for a meeting. There won't be any guns." She'd have to text ahead to make sure. "You know Brendan is a stickler about gun safety. The weapons are kept in a safe. It's always locked."

Sofia's head hurt. She hadn't had her morning coffee yet, and breakfast had been a handful of cherries.

"We can come back," Emily said. "It's not a problem."

"I got this." Sofia decided then and there that she wasn't going to mention the broken window. She'd have to get it fixed before they got back.

Emily rang off.

Sofia now had four things on her weekend list:

1.Have fun with the kids without anyone ending up in the emergency room.

2.Convince Brendan to give her the rest of the weekend off like he'd promised.

3.Get the window fixed before Emily got back and asked about it. She had enough on her plate as it was, and it had been an accident. Kind of.

4.Get the car detailed before she passed out from Hawaiian Punch fumes.

She pulled into the agency's parking lot, where she saw Aidan's canary-yellow Porsche and Brendan's black Crown Vic. She parked the minivan in a corner, well away from them both. She didn't want to hear any crap from Aidan about driving a minivan now.

It was Saturday and, other than their cars, the lot was empty. It didn't look like Jenna Williams had arrived yet. That would give Sofia a chance to touch base with Aidan and find out why there was any doubt about Craig's death.

She turned off the car and looked at the kids. "OK, guys, so this is my work. You need to be on your best behavior in there. No taking things apart." She looked at Van, who nodded.

"And no attacking anyone." She looked at Violet.

Violet seemed to mull over Sofia's request as if it were one of life's big questions. "Only in self-defense. Everyone needs to defend themselves if they're attacked. And to defend others."

"OK," Sofia said. That would have to do.

She herded them out of the car and through the door into the office. She glanced around for hazards. The room was pretty bare—a ficus tree near the window that constantly shed yellow leaves on the floor, two desks with computers and messy piles of paper, two more or less ergonomic chairs, the gun safe, which she could see was locked, and a coffee machine in the kitchenette.

"Thanks for coming in!" Brendan came out of his office. "Hey, Violet and Van!"

"Hello, Mr. Maloney," they said in unison, still on their best behavior. Sofia hoped it would last.

"Hi, kids," said Aidan. He had come out of his dad's office behind him. He was the spitting image of his Irish father—blue eyes, dark hair, and a rugged face that wouldn't have looked out of place on the big screen. He was, in short, too handsome for his own good.

"Hello, Mr. Maloney Junior," the kids answered.

Aidan tightened his jaw, and Sofia bit back a grin. Aidan hadn't known she called him that.

Brendan walked over to the gun safe and pulled on the lock to make sure it was closed, then gave each kid a hug. They beamed at him. Kids always loved Brendan.

He pulled out the printer tray and fished out some paper. "I'd like you guys to draw me a picture of Aidan, like a police sketch artist would. If you do a good job, I'll buy your best drawing for a dollar. One from each of you."

The kids snatched the paper and ran over to Sofia's desk. They each took a pen from the cup on her desk and bent over their work.

Sofia made a beeline for the coffee machine. "You're a genius, Brendan."

"I had some practice." He gestured toward Aidan. "Hard to believe, but he was a hellion."

"It's not that hard to believe." Sofia took a long sip of coffee. She burned her tongue, but she didn't care. Her headache eased, and she felt better. If she could get some food into her, that would be heaven.

"You have paint in your hair." Aidan pointed to the top of her head. "Lemon yellow?"

"Buttercream." She reached up and tried to scratch it out with a fingernail.

"When you do that with your hair, you look like a monkey picking out lice," Aidan offered helpfully.

Brendan had a strict policy against swearing, and she was pretty sure flipping the bird fell into that category, so she settled for a glare.

"I'm sure Aidan filled you in on the details," Brendan

said. "I'd like you to be your usual compassionate self. Help Miss Williams feel more comfortable. Put her at her ease."

"I'd like to go over the details again," Sofia said. "To be thorough."

"Why do you have a picture of a naked lady in your email?" asked Van. He'd moved his drawing over to Aidan's desk, and pointed his pen at the screen.

Aidan hurried over and shut off his monitor. "Probably a sunbather."

"My mom says those pictures objectify women," Violet said. "Have you ever killed anyone?"

"I've thought about it," Aidan said.

"The best defense is a good offense," Violet yelled. Then she launched herself across the room and head-butted Aidan in the groin. He folded up like a ladder and pitched onto the floor.

Van crossed his legs. "That's the Nutcracker right there."

Brendan laughed so hard Sofia thought he might have a heart attack. She went over and held a hand down for Aidan. He took it and let her pull him to his feet before collapsing into his chair. He was ashen and muttering all kinds of words that broke the anti-profanity rule.

"Are you OK, Mr. Maloney Junior?" Violet asked.

"I'm. Fine," Aidan said, through gritted teeth.

"I didn't want to hurt you, but you said you were thinking about killing someone, so I had to take action." Violet sounded earnest.

"We use our words." Sofia winced because, again, she sounded like her mother. "We don't hit people unless we have to, and we usually don't have to."

"You definitely didn't have to," said Aidan. "I was just kidding."

Brendan wiped tears from the corners of his eyes. "If you can't block a kindergartener, son, your nuts deserve to be cracked."

"I'm in second grade," Violet said.

Aidan took a couple of deep breaths. Sofia actually felt sorry for him.

"Excuse me?" A thin blond woman stood in the doorway, hand raised as if to knock. She looked as if she hadn't had a good night's sleep in weeks. Her dark circles had dark circles. She was dressed in People for Peace jeans, with a long-sleeved black T-shirt and carried an oversized black leather bag. "I'm looking for Maloney Investigations."

"Miss Williams!" Brendan crossed the room and took her hand in a hearty shake. "I'm Brendan Maloney. This is Sofia Salgado, and my son, Aidan. Plus Sofia's niece and nephew, Violet and Van. As you probably saw, we use Violet as our training officer."

Jenna Williams smiled at Violet, who stood next to Aidan's desk in a karate pose, with a cherubic smile. "She seems pretty experienced."

"I took karate lessons for two months." Violet brushed her curly blond hair back. "So I am very experienced."

Brendan took Jenna's elbow and ushered her into his office. "Sofia, you're with me. Aidan, you're in charge of the training officers."

Aidan looked like he'd bitten into a lemon, and Sofia had to admit she kinda liked it.

"Don't give them any sugar." She gave Aidan a meaningful look.

He grinned at her. "Why would I do a thing like that?"

She regretted saying it. He liked to do things to drive her crazy, and here she was giving him ammunition.

"Be good," she told the kids. "Mr. Maloney Junior needs to recover from that Nutcracker."

READ THE REST OF "B" IS FOR BAD GIRLS

MORE MALIBU MYSTERY BOOKS

"C" IS FOR COOCHY COO

Former child star Sofia Salgado is finding her feet as a trainee investigator at Malibu detective agency, Maloney Investigations, when a new case throws her, and everyone else at the agency, for a loop.

Maloney Investigations are drafted in to help thirteen-year-old Daniel find his birth father. There's only one snag. According to Daniel's mom, former Los Angeles party girl, Candy, there's more than one candidate. A lot more!

"D" IS FOR DRUNK

Roll up your pant legs and bare your feet, there are barrels of grapes to crush in this hilarious fourth installment of the Malibu mystery series.

Maloney Investigation's new client? An eccentric vineyard owner convinced his even more eccentric neighbor is siphoning off his precious water.

But of course it's not as simple as that. Or as dignified.

"E" IS FOR EXPOSED

Sofia Salgado's latest case at Maloney Investigations has some pretty tempting ingredients: blackmail, male strippers, and whipped cream.

When a friend of Sofia's mom finds herself the victim of blackmail, stuffy Aidan has to go undercover as an exotic dancer, much to Sofia's delight.

Can Aidan make it in the cut-throat world of male stripping? Can Sofia stop her mom from getting too involved? Does whipped cream have more or fewer calories when it's licked from a man's naked torso?

"F" IS FOR FRED (Coming in 2018)

"G" IS FOR GROOVY (Coming in 2018)

ALSO BY REBECCA CANTRELL

The World Beneath

The Tesla Legacy

The Chemistry of Death

A Trace of Smoke

A Night of Long Knives

A Game of Lies

A City of Broken Glass

The Blood Gospel (with James Rollins)

Innocent Blood (with James Rollins)

Blood Infernal (with James Rollins)

iDrakula

iFrankenstein

ALSO BY SEAN BLACK

The Ryan Lock Series in Order

Lockdown (US/Canada)

Lockdown (UK/ Commonwealth)

Deadlock (US/Canada)

Deadlock (UK/Commonwealth)

Lock & Load (Short)

Gridlock (US/Canada)

Gridlock (UK/Commonwealth)

The Devil's Bounty (US/Canada)

The Devil's Bounty (UK/Commonwealth)

The Innocent

Fire Point

Budapest/48 (Short)

The Edge of Alone

4 Action-Packed Ryan Lock Thrillers: Lockdown; Deadlock; Gridlock (Ryan Lock Series Boxset Book 1) - (US & Canada only)

3 Action-Packed Ryan Lock Thrillers: The Devil's Bounty; The Innocent; Fire Point (Ryan Lock Series Boxset Book 2)

The Byron Tibor Series

Post

Blood Country

Winter's Rage (Pre-order)

MALIBU MYSTERY NEWS

Want news about the latest Malibu Mystery books plus exclusive free content?

Then sign up here to join our mailing list.

Your email will be kept confidential. You will not be spammed (we hate spam emails!). You can unsubscribe at any time.

You can also follow us on Facebook here:

https://www.facebook.com/malibumysteries/

You can contact either of us via the website www.malibumysteries.com

Thanks for reading!

Rebecca & Sean